THE
COUNTESS OF MONTE-CRISTO

ALEXANDRE DUMAS

THE COUNTESS OF MONTE-CRISTO

VOLUME TWO

Fredonia Books
Amsterdam, The Netherlands

The Countess of Monte-Cristo
Volume Two

by
Alexandre Dumas

ISBN 1-58963-214-1

Reprinted from the 1902 edition

Fredonia Books
Amsterdam, The Netherlands
http://www.fredoniabooks.com

CONTENTS

PART II

CONTENTS

THE
COUNTESS OF MONTE-CRISTO

PART II

CHAPTER I

DOUBLE RUIN

IT is time that we return to other persons in our story, whom we have neglected too long.

The malady which had gnawed at the Count de Puysaie's heart a long time had made rapid progress since the flight of his wife, and since Nini Moustache had deserted him.

Nothing remained to buoy him up but the tender yet painful attachment of Cyprienne and the deceptive friendship of Colonel Fritz.

That friendship was distrustful and cautious, such as it only could be with accomplices in crime.

Sooner or later a day comes when accomplices generally have a falling out and hate each other. A shrewd observer would soon have noticed that this was already the case between the count and the colonel.

One morning, as the former had locked himself up in his study, and was thinking over his troubles, a servant begged for admittance to deliver a package, which had just been sent in, and was marked urgent.

The count opened the door, and the servant handed him a large package and a letter.

The count took the package, and with a careless air threw it on the nearest table.

The letter would undoubtedly have followed the package if the count's eyes had not unconsciously glanced at the address.

He trembled, and hurriedly broke the seal.

He had recognized Nini Moustache's handwriting.

The letter comprised four finely-written sheets.

Nini Moustache wrote:

"MONSIEUR LE COMTE—I know how painful my separation from you must have been, yet am not vain about it. If it were in my power to console you I swear to you that I would not hesitate a moment, even though it were to cost me my life.

"Since a short while I have reflected, and I feel that many things about which I have laughed till now are, nevertheless, the most painful and serious in life.

"As I have firmly resolved never to see you again, I write in order to exclaim from the depths of my solitude and sadness:

" 'I have done great harm to you, Loredan! Forgive me.'

"Forgive me, for I was led astray, and am not bad. While I prepared sorrows for you, I suffered myself, and to-day an unconsolable heart comes to confess its torture to an unconsoled man.

"Ah, my friend, why did we ever become acquainted?

"Why did fate make me the instrument of your misfortune? Why did you prefer me, the unworthy, to the saint who would have made your life happy, your mind calm, and your heart as noble as she is herself?

"Our story is a very sad one, Loredan, although it is not new.

"We are both dead to love, but have not even the consolations of recollection; for in all the days when we swore we loved each other, there is probably not one in which we really and truly loved.

"Your love for me was never free from contempt, mine to you was never free from shame.

"If you had loved me after the fashion of the others, something like loving a handsome dog or a handsome horse, from caprice or vanity, I would no doubt have remained what I was when you first made my acquaintance.

"I would perhaps have ruined you then too, but at least we would not have tortured each other.

"Unfortunately you loved me sincerely and truly, and at the same time, frightened and humbled, I measured the impassable abyss which separated us.

"I felt a new being awake in me, and just in proportion as I became better through you, the certainty that you would lose me became greater.

"On the day, therefore, that I love you as you deserve, I separate from you.

"Yes, Loredan, to-day, when I know that you will never see me again, when I do not fear a weakness from your side or mine, I can say it—I love you.

"I love you for the sake of the grief which you made me feel, a noble grief, which in my own eyes gives me back my honor.

"I love you, because in making the sacrifice which separates us, I feel myself to be a better woman, and almost worthy of you.

"And now listen to me, my friend.

"You will never hear of me again. Think of me as a dear departed one who still thinks of you, and loves you from the depth of her grave.

"Look upon this letter, which I send you, as a holy will, and swear to me to follow the instructions contained in it.

"Your generosity made me rich. This wealth burns my hands. Besides, dead people do not need any diamonds, do they?

"I therefore return to you everything you sent me, and beg you on my knees to take it back again.

"In making you my heir, and returning what I owe to your generosity, I have a favor to ask of you, a favor which would be doubly dear to me if done by you.

"I have a sister, a poor girl, who occupies that half of my heart which does not belong to you.

"Loredan, I leave my sister to you.

"Make her pure and good, and love her as she will love you, for she will only have you to be thankful to for everything, and I do not desire her to know even of my existence.

"She is still a child. Vice has not, even from a distance, stained her pure soul.

"Until to-day she passed her childhood with a good woman, named Madame Gosse, who lives in the Rue Rambuteau.

"My sister's name is Lila.

"Oh, you will love her, Loredan, will you not? You will love her in memory of her who will bless your name even in death.

"I have taken everything from you, my friend, except your honor. To-day, however, I have the consciousness of restoring your lost happiness to you, by sending you this angel.

"Perhaps you will find out some time—but no, it is better if you do not find out. Oh, my friend, if you only knew how happy I am at this moment, what new confidence fills my heart, and how strong and submissive I feel! Oh, how good it is to do one's duty.   CELINE."

Three times the count read this letter.

No egotistical thought marred his joy.

He resolved at once to fulfil Celine's last wish. Yes, Lila would find a home with him. He already thought he pressed her to his heart and heard her call him father.

What joy the future had in store for him now!

While he was thus walking up and down the room in joyous excitement, Colonel Fritz entered.

Loredan clasped his hand as if he desired to crush it.

He was happy; he felt no more hate.

He then exclaimed, after he had pulled the bell, to the servant who entered, and without answering his friend's questions:

"My coach! Quick! At once!"

In the hallway he met Cyprienne and clasped her in his arms with a tenderness she had not believed him capable of.

He pressed his lips to her cheeks and softly murmured:

"You will not be jealous, Cyprienne, if I give you a sister, will you?"

"A sister?" asked Cyprienne in surprise.

"Yes," replied the count, mysteriously: "do not say anything to anybody yet. Her name is Lila—a sweet name, eh?"

The servant announced that the carriage was ready. The count laughingly slipped from Cyprienne's grasp. "Do not detain me!" he said. "I hurry to fetch her." With these words he hurried away.

Cyprienne, as we know, knew her mother's secrets, and the announcement of Lila's forthcoming arrival and the count's joy must have appeared like a miracle to her—a miracle for which she had her unknown protectors alone to thank.

CHAPTER II

THE SECRETS OF THE GOSSES

PECULIAR, unheard-of things which bothered the gossipy neighbors had occurred in the house in the Rue Rambuteau.

Among these things was, in the first place, the simultaneous disappearance of Pippiona and Ursula, and secondly the extraordinary change in the relations between Monsieur and Madame Bebelle.

The "dear little husband" had become transformed into a monster over night, and if the "worshipped Bebelle" still remained the "worshipped Bebelle," there was nevertheless a touch of bitterness in the tone with which Monsieur Gosse pronounced the words now.

He had changed in other ways too.

Formerly he came and went with the regularity of an automaton, but now nothing more of this regularity was to be seen.

Sometimes he not only came home two hours late, but very drunk besides.

Sometimes his office remained closed the whole day.

There was no doubt about it, the dear little fellow was on the road to ruin.

Besides all this, Monsieur Gosse had been seen in suspicious places, on the corner of a dark street, in the rear of a cafe, in a rapidly moving cab, and always in conversation with a mysterious individual.

This man was none other than the gentleman whom the friendly neighbors had given the worshipped Bebelle for an unknown protector.

Namely, the gentleman in the brown coat.

On the other hand, the gentleman never showed himself in the Rue Rambuteau any more, and seemed to have broken off his *liaison* with Madame Gosse.

Nevertheless the latter had plenty of visitors.

Among them was the handsome workman Joseph, who lived on the fifth story.

He had been seen to slip into Madame Gosse's apartments when the latter's husband was not at home.

Besides Joseph two ladies had been noticed among the visitors; they were both dressed in black and heavily veiled.

One of the two ladies was about forty years of age, but still very handsome.

The other one was surpassingly beautiful, and still in the first flush of youth.

At first the two ladies had come separately and afterward together.

On the latter day the handsome Joseph had gone to Madame Gosse's apartments too.

These two ladies who aroused the curiosity of the neighbors in the Rue Rambuteau were none other than the Countess de Puysaie and Nini Moustache, or Celine, as she called herself now. These two Magdalens had understood each other at the first glance, and with outstretched arms had exclaimed to one another: "My sister!"

Both the countess and Nini Moustache owed their rescue to the institution of the Countess of Monte-Cristo, the Institution of the Sisters of Refuge.

CHAPTER III

BEBELLE'S SECRET

THEY both came to Madame Gosse's house on the same mission—to make good the wrong they had done the Count de Puysaie, by giving him a support to lean on and raise himself up by.

They thought they had found this support in Lila.

From Celine's letter to the count, we have seen that she had not refrained from telling a pious lie, which was asked of her, to induce the count to receive Lila in his house.

To make this fable plausible they needed Madame Gosse's assistance.

This worthy woman, as we know, really had had a sister of Celine's in her care, and it was not likely that the count, if he sought for further information, would especially inquire as to the age of his charge. Besides, Nini Moustache was still young enough to have a sister eight years old.

Madame Gosse was, as our readers know, not over scrupulously conscientious, nevertheless her last affair with Legigant had made her a little suspicious.

She began to see the danger of such things and did

not care to lose everything she possessed in a hazardous attempt to make more.

Therefore, although she knew Hortense to be Lila's mother, although Nini Moustache gave her undeniable proof of being Ursula's sister, she nevertheless opposed the combination, with which they were both satisfied, to the extent of her powers.

Hortense and Celine had made repeated but vain attempts to induce her to reconsider her determination.

To the one she had answered, "If the sister is satisfied;" to the other, "If the mother is of the same opinion."

To-day mother and sister paid a visit together, but the midwife still answered:

"No; it is impossible."

This was the day on which the gossips had seen the two veiled ladies go up together.

On the strength of the formal promise Madame Gosse had given each of them. they had not hesitated any longer to carry out their plan.

Nini's letter to the Count de Puysaie was written and sent off. The count might be expected every minute, to get Lila; and now, when they were near the goal, the obstinacy of this woman threatened to foil everything.

Prayers, entreaties—all were in vain—even the twenty new thousand-franc notes, which Nini Moustache had placed on the table, proved fruitless.

"I cannot! I cannot! I have already done too much! I would compromise myself!"

The door opened softly, and a firm, manly voice said:

"Madame Gosse is right."

And encouraged by this unexpected assistance Bebelle cried, with renewed energy:

"I cannot!"

Hortense and Celine turned hurriedly around toward the new-comer, who smilingly winked at them.

They were both acquainted with the secrets of the Countess of Monte-Cristo, and comprehended that everything was successful.

"Madame Gosse is right," repeated Joseph; "she does not want to get entangled in the meshes of the law."

"Yes, that is true," murmured Celine, who did not know what Joseph was driving at, yet instinctively felt that she must say as he did.

This immediate acquiescence made Madame Gosse suspicious.

"Madame Gosse," began Joseph again—"Madame Gosse is perfectly right if she refuses to sanction a lie which hurts her feelings, and I do not think, ladies, that it is your intention to lead her conscience astray. Madame Gosse is free, absolutely free, and I am positive that none of you wishes to have her enter this intrigue against her will."

"That's a fact," said Nini Moustache.

The Countess of Puysaie nodded assent.

"What trick do they want to play me?" thought the worshipped Bebelle.

"Only—" continued Joseph.

"Ah, now it is coming," said the midwife to herself.

"Only it is in our interest, in the future, to break off all relations with Madame Gosse."

Celine began to understand, Madame Gosse also.

"Two children," continued Joseph, "have been intrusted to Madame Gosse—one of them, Lila, has been given back to its mother; the other one, the sister of this lady, still remains under Madame Gosse's protection. You can give Ursula back to her sister, and we will not ask you any more to be our accomplice.''

''But you know—'' said Madame Gosse.

''I know nothing,'' interrupted Joseph. ''I only know that a young girl named Ursula was intrusted to your care; that her natural protector, her sister, sits here, and that she demands her back again.''

''But did you not tell me yourself that she was in your power?''

''That,'' said Joseph, smiling, ''is a secret which all three of us know, and which none of us will betray, except probably yourself. The police will believe you if they so desire, but I fear they will not believe you. Do you know, Madame Gosse, what the officials will see in this thing? Shall I tell it to you? Nothing else but unlawful detention of two minors, of which one is still a child—I say *two*, for the robbers abducted Pippiona at the same time.''

Madame Gosse looked at the speaker in amazement.

''You want to ask me, I suppose, where are the proofs?'' continued Joseph. ''There are more than sufficient. First, we have the testimony of Louis Jacquemin, who was hired for this business, but who refused to have anything to do with it at the last moment. What Jacquemin don't know Cinella will tell, for he loved Pippiona. He is looking for her now.''

Joseph paused again; but, as Madame Gosse still remained silent, he continued:

''Cinella saw you sitting quietly in the coach for ten

minutes, and all the tenants in the house have testified that during the night of the double abduction you were not at home.''

''What shall I do?'' murmured Madame Gosse.

''I do not know,'' replied Joseph. ''Ask your conscience.''

This was a day of great surprises for the inhabitants of the Rue Rambuteau.

A magnificent carriage, with a coat of arms on the panel, drove up in front of Madame Gosse's house, and Count Loredan de Puysaie, leaning on the shoulder of a lackey, entered the house door, and inquired for Madame Gosse.

Ten neighbors at once offered to lead him there, and the sound of their voices filled the house.

Joseph hurried to the window, and, bending out, he saw the equipage. He then hurried back to the countess and shoved her into a neighboring room.

''Quick, quick!'' he said; ''it is your husband.''

Madame Gosse wrung her hands in agony, and incessantly cried:

''What shall I do? What shall I do?''

CHAPTER IV

THE FOSTER-DAUGHTER

IT WAS high time. Hardly had the bedroom door closed behind the Countess of Puysaie, than the deafening chatter of the neighbors was heard on the stairs.

"Madame Gosse! Madame Gosse!" they exclaimed, "a gentleman wishes to speak to you!"

Joseph went and opened the door.

Nini Moustache stood in the darkest corner of the room.

The count did not perceive either of them.

He went straight to the midwife.

"Are you Madame Gosse?" he asked.

The good woman, in her embarrassment, could only answer with a deep bow.

"Were you not," continued the count, "intrusted with the care of a child named Lila?"

"Yes," stammered Madame Gosse.

"Where is she?" asked the count; "lead me to her."

The midwife did not know herself. She stood there, motionless, with gaping mouth.

Loredan thought the woman did not trust him.

"Calm yourself," he said, "you can speak without fear; and, to prove to you that I am well acquainted with all the circumstances surrounding this child, I merely mention that Lila is the sister of Celine Durand! Am I not right? Well, then, I am intimately acquainted with Celine; she has willed her sister to me, and if I ask the latter from you to-day, it is because I wish to make her rich, because I wish to make her my daughter.''

Madame Gosse still remained silent.

She only cast imploring glances at Nini Moustache and Joseph, as if to say to them:

''Please, please! get me out of this embarrassment! Say what you wish; I will confirm it!''

The count noticed these looks, and turning around saw Nini Moustache standing in front of him.

''You here!'' he exclaimed, in astonishment.

''Yes, Loredan,'' said Celine, ''it is I—I who swore never to see you again, yet who feels herself happy at being able to say good-by forever to you personally.''

''Why good-by?'' murmured the count.

He saw such firm resolve in Celine's eyes that he did not repeat the question.

''You are right,'' he added; ''it is better thus.''

''Yes,'' said Celine, ''it is better thus, my friend. We have both been very weak and very cowardly. Let us atone for our cowardice and our weakness with one day's courage.''

She approached close to him, and laid her hand on his shoulder.

''You have accepted my will, Loredan,'' she continued, ''and I thank you for it from the bottom of my heart. To-day, you give me the last joy which I am still able to feel. Lila—''

''Lila!'' cried the count. ''Ah, Celine, have no fear.

I shall love that girl as if she were my own child, because she will be the last souvenir I have of you."

"Thank you," said Nini Moustache. "The moment has now come when we must part forever. Lila is in Passy, in a boarding school, the address of which is here."

She pulled a card out of her pocket, and continued:

"Madame Gosse will accompany you. Lila knows nothing of her family; say nothing to her, but if you think an untruth—"

"I will tell her I am her father," replied Loredan, "and I swear to you I will be so in reality."

"I know it, Loredan, I know it. Time is pressing, though, and I would like to know already that Lila is in your arms. Go quickly, my friend, go quickly, and—good-by!"

"Good-by!" said the count, stretching out his arms toward her, as if desirous of clasping her to his bosom forever.

How gladly Nini would have liked to have thrown herself on that bosom, within which beat a heart that loved her so much! How gladly she would have liked to lean her forehead on her lover's shoulder and shed the tears which welled up from her heart!

Her eyes, however, fell on the door behind which Hortense was concealed, and, triumphing over her weakness, she exclaimed, for the third time:

"Good-by!"

Loredan saw that all was over, and, taking Madame Gosse by the hand, he said:

"Come quickly! Come quickly!"

As soon as he was gone, the countess, pale as a spectre, appeared on the threshold of the bedroom.

Nini Moustache wrung her hands and burst into tears.

Hortense went toward her and kissed her on the forehead.

"Thanks, my sister," she said.

All the tenants in the house were at the windows to see Madame Gosse get into the Count de Puysaie's carriage.

With a footman in front and a *piqueur* at the back, the carriage rolled off.

The ride through the market-place was a perfect triumph.

The street boys ran ahead, and announced the wonderful news.

"Who wants to see Madame Gosse ride with a prince?" they cried.

The vegetable sellers left their stalls, the porters put down their bundles, and the idlers grouped about the saloon doors.

Madame Gosse was a well-known personality.

One is not a midwife twenty-five years for nothing.

The people would gladly have liked to shout as she passed by: "Long live Madame Gosse!"

No one paid any attention when Joseph and the two veiled ladies left the house.

Yet they lost a good deal. The second exit would have surprised those who had taken the trouble to see it, even more than the first.

Madame Gosse in an aristocratic turnout was certainly something remarkable; a slim silversmith, though, dressed as a cavalier, and leading two handsome, elegantly dressed ladies on his arm, was something unheard of.

Of course the three took a modest hack, and the crowd only runs after carriages.

On the sidewalk in the Point Saint Eustache stood a man reading the last lines of a letter.

"What an idea," he said, shrugging his shoulders; "the count should get Lila himself and take her to his home! What folly! This Aurelie is just like the others, she promises more than she can keep."

At this moment the carriage came rolling up amid the clamor of the crowd.

Legigant, for it was he, raised his eyes and recognized Madame Gosse, who was sitting next to the Count of Puysaie.

"Already!" he exclaimed. "That woman is really satanic, and just the accomplice I want."

CHAPTER V

MONSIEUR GOSSE'S SECRET

L EGIGANT followed the coach with his eyes a few minutes longer. He then pulled out the letter again which he had put in his pocket, and read it once more carefully.

The letter contained a few closely written lines.

They read:

"Remember our agreement; do your work. I have already begun mine. The consent of the Countess de P. will arrive to-morrow. The Count de P. will go to Madame G.'s house to-day to bring Lila to his home."

There was no signature to the letter. On the edge of the note was, in an elegant coat of arms, the device:

"*Fac et Spera.*"—"Do and Hope."

"Do and Hope!" That was at once a command and a promise. And at the thought of all that lay in that word "Hope," Legigant felt his nerves vibrate and his blood boil.

Yes, he had to acknowledge it; he was conquered by Aurelie.

He loved her.

It was the love of the tiger for his tamer who whipped him, and whom he always felt like tearing to pieces with his claws and sharp teeth while he continually licked his hands.

For one moment only he had felt able to resist.

He had said to himself:

"She prides herself on having conquered me? Her power is deceiving; she wants to play with me, but I will do it with her."

But already on the first day she proved her power by an undeniable fact, and Legigant was forced to acknowledge the truth of the same.

This power made him afraid, for he felt it press upon him as heavily as upon the others.

He could not banish from his memory the terrible impression she had made upon him, when she rose before his eyes like a phantom, and approached him with outstretched hands and threatening look.

And in his tortured brain he mingled the names: Aurelie, Helene. Yes, in loving Aurelie, he loved Helene too—Helene, his victim, whom he could never forget, and his love became all the stronger in consequence of his remorse.

To be loved by Aurelie—what misery and what joy! It seemed to him that he would clasp, in her, Helene to his arms. At this thought his hair stood on end, and yet he only lived now to realize that idea.

"*Fac et Spera.*"

But suppose Aurelie betrayed him!

Suppose she had lied; suppose her whole manœuvre had no other purpose than to get a dangerous rival out of the way, or make him neutral; suppose on the day of her triumph she said to him:

"I do not know you!"

As Legigant thought this, he clinched his fist; but soon his love thoughts returned, and he laughed at his fears.

"She is a lioness," said Legigant to himself, "and I am a lion. She knew my strength, as I did hers; she loves and fears me as I love and fear her. What she orders I will do."

And his lips mechanically repeated the three Latin words which Aurelie had chosen for her motto:

"*Fac et Spera.*"

On the corner of the Porte Saint Eustache stood the shop of a public writer.

This dirty shop bore the legend:

"Gosse, Public Writer."

Here the love-letters of scullion-maids and the anonymous notes of rejected lovers to jealous husbands were manufactured.

From morning to night Monsieur Gosse's elegant hand glided over the paper.

Who never saw Monsieur Gosse in his office—that was the euphemistic name he gave to his shop—never knew Monsieur Gosse.

This is the case with all great men. They have a public and a private physiognomy.

Just as timid and submissive as Monsieur Gosse was at home, he was dignified and resolute in the exercise of his business. No one understood better than he how to write a congratulatory letter to a grandfather on his birthday, or a begging letter to a protector.

According to his opinion, everything depended on the style.

The form of a letter was the principal thing.

He also knew what was best for his customers better than they did themselves.

His intelligence and happy facility of expression—he had been educated in one of the best Latin schools in Paris—had almost made him an authority in his neighborhood.

It was to this celebrated shop that Legigant now went.

When he saw the great crowd which hung about the door waiting for admittance, he could not help giving vent to his disappointment. Nevertheless he decided to take his turn too.

The crowd pushed on, one after the other.

Finally, after waiting several hours, Legigant presented himself at the sliding window.

"Well, is it all right?" he asked.

Monsieur Gosse—this was an extraordinary occurrence—immediately arose, dismissed those who still remained with a wave of his hand, and left his shop to close the shutters.

CHAPTER VI

THE GREEN PORTFOLIO

WHILE Monsieur Gosse was doing this, Legigant went inside and seated himself in the public writer's green chair. He waited.

When the last shutter was up, Legigant pointed to a wooden chair and briefly said:

"Sit down there."

Monsieur Gosse seated himself with the alacrity of a boy who is to receive a scolding and knows that he deserves it.

"You have not done anything yet, Monsieur Gosse," said Legigant sternly, "although I told you that you were in a difficult position."

"My wife always takes the keys along," remarked the public writer, timidly.

"The affair does not concern me personally," continued Legigant, "although I do not wish to imply that I have not my little interest in it. My principal motive, though, is the friendship I have for you and the thought of the danger which threatens you."

"I know it—I know it," sighed Gosse, hypocritically.

The two upright men were trying to outlie each other.

They both knew it, but paid no attention to it.

They were both business men.

"You know now the source of your wealth," said Legigant.

"My wealth! You mean to say my wife's wealth."

"That's all the same; you are responsible for your wife's actions."

"The unfortunate woman," exclaimed Monsieur Gosse, "and I knew nothing about it!"

"I have opened your eyes, though. You see yourself, now, implicated in an affair which will end in the courts. It is a case of unfaithfulness, in which you are charged with being an accomplice."

"I!"

"Your wife, but I have already proved to you—"

"Yes, yes," interrupted Gosse, "I am responsible for my wife's actions. But what harm can that do me?"

"Not much, of course. Accomplices in such cases generally get off with a light punishment. Very often they are merely publicly insulted."

Gosse said nothing, but only snapped his fingers as if to say:

"I don't care anything for that!"

"I would not have come on that account," continued Legigant; "but to-day the matter is more serious."

"Really?" said Gosse, ironically.

"Yes, certainly," continued Legigant, in a tone of sincerity. "It is now not only a question of breaking one's marriage vows, but also the substitution of a child—a crime which the penal code punishes severely, my dear Monsieur Gosse."

"But I do not know anything about all that!" exclaimed

the little man. "I am as innocent as a new-born babe, and the judges will see that."

"The judges will only see one thing, my dear friend—that you have derived a benefit from the plot, though not directly implicated in it. If I should advise you, do not let them spy into your private affairs. Those people always think the worst. Besides, it is in your own interests to keep your affairs apart from those of your wife."

"I've got you there!" thought the distrustful Gosse. "You think yourself very shrewd, my dear friend, but I know very well that you will not betray me."

Legigant in the meanwhile thought to himself:

"He does not look frightened. I think much cannot be done with him by threats."

He then added aloud:

"Would two or three thousand francs embarrass you in the pursuit of your duty, Monsieur Gosse?"

The public writer was hardly able to repress an exclamation of delight.

Three thousand francs! How many pints of wine could he not drink for this sum!

He restrained his enthusiasm, and indifferently replied: "That depends."

"Well, let's say five thousand, but that's all," said Legigant.

"Five thousand francs!" exclaimed the former pupil of the Latin school. "*Mi Hercle!* what am I to do for that?"

"Nothing but your duty," replied Legigant; "you shall defend society and the family to the extent of your powers; prevent a strange child from usurping one of the greatest names in France, and a fortune which does not belong to it—in a word, you should deliver the papers to me which your wife so carefully preserves, and which prove Lila's illegitimate birth.''

Gosse broke into a loud laugh.

''You clever little fellow! What are you talking of society and the family?'' he exclaimed. ''Confess that if you offer me five thousand francs for Bebelle's green portfolio you have been offered ten thousand for it.''

''Business is business,'' replied Legigant. ''You can give me the name of the real father, together with the necessary proofs, and I know the supposed father, who is unknown both to you and your wife.''

''That's right—speak out! Five thousand francs is a small sum, still we can do something for it. You will do the business with me alone, without letting Bebelle know anything about it, won't you?''

''Certainly.''

''And I have nothing to fear?''

''If you wish, the papers can be sent anonymously.''

''Good! I am satisfied with that.''

''You will send me the green portfolio then?''

''To-day, if necessary. I am not such a fool as I look. I knew two days ago what you were after, and have taken the green portfolio away from the old woman already. Give me the five thousand francs and you can have the green portfolio now.''

With these words Gosse quickly opened the drawer and showed Legigant the portfolio lying therein.

Legigant took a package of banknotes from his pocket and counted out five.

The exchange followed.

A match cracked, and soon after a wax candle lighted

up the dark shop. Gosse wished to convince himself of the genuineness of the banknotes, and Legigant of the contents of the portfolio.

Affecting confidence!

The notes were genuine, and the portfolio contained two letters from Colonel Fritz, which left no doubt about his *liaison* with Hortense.

"Now," said Legigant, "do me one more favor. Take the pen and write."

Gosse seized his pen, and Legigant dictated.

"Count—One of your most faithful friends desires to deliver to you the proofs of the dastardly betrayal of which you have been the victim. The inclosed letters will enlighten you as to the degree of respect you have to show to your table companion and the most repugnant of all traitors."

Gosse was about to date the note, but Legigant restrained him.

"No date," he said.

"Then the letter is finished!" exclaimed Gosse. "My Bebelle will be terribly angry when she finds out that her green portfolio is gone; but I don't care a snap."

CHAPTER VII

LILA

WHILE Legigant and the public writer were concluding their bargain in the tavern which Gosse knew, and where the wine was so good, the carriage of the Count de Puysaie rolled along at a sharp trot toward Paris.

Madame Gosse no longer sat in the magnificent coach, but followed behind in a poverty-stricken hack.

In her place, the passers-by admired a beautiful child—Lila!

She sat next to Loredan, who devoured her with his eyes. She had already learned to lay her little arms about his neck and pronounce the two divine words:

"My father!"

And he, delighted with the heavenly music of her voice, never tired of kissing the small, round hands and the rosy cheeks.

"My daughter! My daughter!"

Yes, Celine was right. This little darling would console and cheer Loredan.

How could he be sad and low-spirited now, when he was to have continually before him this living image of youth, joy, and hope?

The carriage rolled on and on. The bright blue sky was reflected in the waves of the Seine, and the people on the streets seemed to smile at this picture of fatherly joy. How gladly he would have wished to call out to them:

"Look at my daughter! How handsome she is!"

Lila was in an ecstasy of joy and delight. Until now she had never known anything of her family, and the only happy weeks she had passed were those she had spent with the Countess of Monte-Cristo.

Her little heart had loved but three beings until then—Mamma Helene, Uncle Joseph, and Cyprienne.

The latter had only been an ephemeral appearance in the dreams of the child.

The Countess of Monte-Cristo had said to her that day:

"You must love Cyprienne very much."

And since that morning Lila had not let a day pass without thinking of the beautiful and gentle girl whom she had kissed on the threshold of the hothouse.

Poor little Lila! Such recollections were rare in her deserted childhood.

When she thought of the past, she saw in a vision again the little farmhouse where she had been brought up by a hired nurse. Until her fourth year she had remained at the farmhouse.

She had pretty dresses and embroidered chemises, and was called mademoiselle.

Yet, in spite of that, she knew she was unhappier than her coarsely dressed playmates, and had often noticed that the eyes of her foster-mother looked commiseratingly upon her, as she murmured:

"Poor little thing!"

A veiled lady visited her a couple of times.

This lady had taken her on her lap and kissed and caressed her.

When the lady had gone away her foster-mother invariably said to her:

"Lila, that was your mother!"

She retained a dim recollection of her mother.

Her father she never knew.

A father, according to her childish idea, was a mighty, divine being, a kind of guardian angel, who is never seen, yet who watches.

And now, just when she least thought of it, this father, this guardian angel, revealed himself to her.

He came like the princes in the fairy tales, in a beautiful two-horse carriage, and would, no doubt, bring her to a fabulous palace, where she would discover all those again whom she loved.

Her poor little heart beat with stormy hope. Perhaps she would find there too the black dressed lady with the long locks—her mother.

The carriage had turned into the Place de la Concorde.

Until now, Loredan and Lila had exchanged but two words:

"My daughter!" "My father!"

When the heavy doors of the mansion in the Rue des Varennes swung open a different state of affairs than usual was revealed.

The count sprang from the carriage to the porch with a light, springy step.

He had got back his youth again, together with his happiness.

Loredan called out to the servants who stood in the doorway:

"Tell my daughter that I bring a sister to her."

They did not have to go far.

Cyprienne was waiting for her father's return.

She, too, had pondered the whole day over the word her father had whispered in her ear as he went away:

"Lila."

Far from being jealous, she thanked God for this miracle which brought back peace to the house.

How had this miracle come about?

Could the count know the secret of Lila's birth?

Cyprienne did not know, and did not care. Her duty was clear and distinct. She should love this orphan as she would be loved by an elder sister, a mother.

More she did not know and did not wish to know.

While the Count de Puysaie gave his orders, he hurried up the stairs at the same time, and the astonished lackeys followed him with their eyes, while they said to one another:

"How young he has become all of a sudden; this morning he looked so old!"

Lila ran after him like a fawn. The magic palace was to open!

What she found was better and handsomer than anything a magic palace could offer her.

Cyprienne smilingly extended her arms to her, the same Cyprienne of whom the Countess of Monte-Cristo had said to Lila:

"You must love her very much."

The veiled lady with the long locks, however, was not there.

Lila looked about the entire room for her. Her big uneasy eyes filled with tears, and she murmured:

"And mamma?"

The Count de Puysaie held down his head and did not know what to reply.

Cyprienne passionately clasped the little one in her arms, kissed her rosy cheeks and softly asked:

"Lila, shall I be your little mother?"

Lila threw her arms about Cyprienne's neck, and smiling through her tears, pressed her lightly to her bosom, exclaiming:

"Yes, yes; be my mother!"

The count observed this delightful spectacle—a virgin mother embracing her child.

He did not know what courage Cyprienne showed by pressing the only cause of her unhappiness to her bosom.

Cyprienne smilingly turned to the count, and said:

"Papa, we are agreed. You give Lila to me, and she is mine."

"Yes, she is yours," he replied, "but," he jokingly added, "you will lend her to me sometimes, won't you?"

Cyprienne smiled, and said with trembling voice:

"I am not egotistical. Lila will belong to both of us."

"Yes, to both of us!" exclaimed the count, "and you are both mine. Oh, Cyprienne, Lila, dear children, come to my arms, and feel my rejuvenated heart beat against yours. This is the first happy day I have had in ten years."

Thus the three stood together, and formed the prettiest sight that could delight a human heart, when suddenly the arms which had clung to each other until then became loosened.

The common enemy, Colonel Fritz, entered.

Loredan received the colonel coldly, and taking the little one by the hand, he introduced her with the words: "My daughter Lila."

At this name the colonel became pale, but quickly collecting himself, he bent over the little one, and wanted to embrace her.

Loredan, who had no suspicion of what was passing in the soul of his comrade, looked at him with a smile.

Lila fled into Cyprienne's arms, and murmured:

"Oh, little mother, do not let him kiss me! I am afraid of him!"

CHAPTER VIII

LEGIGANT GAINS A POINT

AT LILA'S words, "I am afraid of him!" the colonel turned livid with rage.

Lila was his daughter, and even a monster would be shocked if he heard his child say:

"I am afraid of him."

When Loredan had introduced the little one with the words: "Lila, my daughter!" he had believed that everything was discovered.

Loredan, however, did not know anything; his smile and his proffered hand betrayed this.

The colonel bowed, and said:

"I see I am in the way, and will, therefore, come some other time."

With these words he walked toward the door.

Loredan did not ask him to stay, and he really went.

As soon as he was out of the house he allowed his pent-up rage full play.

He had loved Hortense passionately, he loved her still, but he had sacrificed her to his low interests.

He pitied her, too, and his whole hate was directed against Loredan.

This rival—for he looked upon the count as such—took his daughter from him too.

Lila called him "father," and of him, the colonel, she said:

"I am afraid of him."

Fritz clinched his teeth together, and hissed:

"He must die!"

In this way he walked onward, without looking to the right or left, and before he knew it, he found himself in the Rue Faubourg Montmartre, in front of Legigant's house.

He paused, and slowly retraced his steps toward the boulevard.

The first fit of rage was over, and he reflected.

Lila's reception in the Puysaie mansion could not be an accident, but was no doubt an intrigue of Legigant's.

For who but Legigant had any interest in the Puysaie house?

But why had he not informed his most intimate accomplice of this new scheme?

The colonel suspected treachery, and knowing that cold blood was necessary, he tried to regain his composure.

He entered a café, sat at the window, and slowly drank a glass of iced lemonade.

He then went back to the Rue Faubourg Montmartre.

He was ready.

He slowly ascended the stairs, asked in his usual tone if Monsieur Legigant was in, and upon the affirmative reply of the clerk, he entered the private office.

Legigant sat at his desk writing, and hardly turned his head around.

"Ah! is it you, colonel?"

"Yes," replied Fritz briefly.

He then took a seat on a chair.

"Is there anything new?" asked Legigant.

"Yes, several curious things," replied Fritz.

"Really!" observed Legigant.

A short pause ensued, which was broken by Legigant.

"Relate what you know," he said; "I am listening."

"Lila," said Fritz, slowly and clearly, "Lila is in the Puysaie mansion."

Legigant turned around, and looked fixedly at the colonel.

"I know it," said Legigant.

The duel began.

"Then it's your work," said Fritz.

"Yes, it's my work."

These two answers followed each other like cannon shots.

"Then you have known it a long time," said Fritz, bitterly, "and did not inform me of it."

"It was impossible," replied Legigant, simply.

He knew people. He knew that it would be dangerous to weaken a particle when opposed to persons like the colonel.

Therefore after he had said, "It was impossible," he was silent, without making any further explanation.

"Why was it impossible?" asked the colonel.

"Because Lila's introduction in the Puysaie mansion was absolutely necessary for the success of our plan, and you would have opposed it."

"I certainly would."

"There you see."

"Friend Legigant," said Fritz, in a burst of anger, "I warn you that I will not permit any one to make a fool of me!"

"Who wants to make a fool of you? I think you are out of your senses."

"But what right have you to dispose of my daughter without my permission?"

"Because your daughter is the person upon whose head we wish to unite the fortunes of the house of Puysaie and the house of Matifay; because we are now on the eve of the great game, and because we must prepare our play in advance like shrewd people, so as not to lose like blockheads."

He paused a moment, and as the colonel did not reply, he continued:

"Have you not thought of all this yourself? Have you not said to yourself, that on the day the trial, which is to establish Lila's identity as the daughter of the count, begins, any proof is good—a moral as well as a legal one? Don't you see that Lila's introduction in the house by Loredan is, in a measure, a confession of his paternity?"

As the colonel still remained silent, Legigant added:

"In any case, you know it is to our interest that Loredan does not contradict the statements that we shall see fit to make."

Fritz cast down his eyes, and was compelled to admit the plausibility of Legigant's reasoning.

"Yes," he said, as he raised his head again, "that may all be true, and the thing has been shrewdly conducted, yet the interests of my daughter Lila are so closely related to my own that I do not see why I should not have something to say about it. I want my daughter to love me, and it fills me with rage to see her in the arms of the man who steals her caresses from me. Ah, I hated him before, I hated him for the happiness he robbed me of; but to-day, when he takes Lila from me, I hate him still more."

Legigant smiled.

"Who knows but it may be a part of my plan to have you hate him? You do not bother about it, though that was the portion of the plan intrusted to you. You conducted yourself very foolishly, my friend. Toinon would have done it better."

Legigant looked sharply at the colonel. The latter kept silent, and Legigant continued:

"Outside of the affair with Nini Moustache, which you conducted pretty well, you have only made blunders, my son. The countess ran away on the eve of the consummation of our plan, without your knowing anything about it, and without your being able to find out any trace of her. You are so jealous about Lila, yet if it were not for me, you would not know even to-day where she is. You see, therefore, my dear colonel, that if I interfere in your affairs, it is because they are so mixed up that it is absolutely necessary for me to do so."

"Yes," replied the colonel briefly. "You are my master, and I acknowledge it. Yes, you discovered Lila after I tried in vain to do so. Yet I repeat to you, that one question outweighs all others with me in this matter—the sentimental question, as you call it. I do not want my daughter to say to me on the day I make her rich: 'I do not know you.' I do not want her on that day to pity the lot of those whom I have sacrificed to her. You know that I am ambitious, for I have become your accomplice, but I must remind you that I am a father.''

Legigant wished to interrupt the colonel, but the latter paid no heed to him, and continued:

''Oh, let me speak, Legigant! Since I have known you, I have allowed you to get the upper hand often enough. Permit me this time to tell you what I think and what I wish. Until to-day I have always obeyed you. You have not a single passion, so far as I know, that is to say, not a single weakness, and you will remain invulnerable until the day this power seizes you. That day will come, though!''

Legigant murmured as he thought of Aurelie:

''Yes, that day will probably come!''

''That day will come,'' continued the colonel; ''and if it does not come for you alone, it will surely come for one of your faithful allies, probably for myself. Do not force me to the worst, for otherwise I would blow both you and myself in the air.''

Legigant looked at the speaker without moving a muscle, and the latter continued:

''Listen to me:

''When I saw you for the first time I had sunk very low, and really admired you. If I have become your ally, it was voluntarily. I was young and impulsive; you needed me as well as I needed you.

''Mutual need brings forth mutual alliances, and I became your friend and accomplice.

''I became more than that—I was your tool.

''One day you said to me: 'The Countess of Puysaie must become your friend.' She did so.

"This *liaison* with an aristocratic family flattered me, and yet—and yet I felt I was doing wrong.

"As soon as passion mingles with anything, all is over with it. I am not a schemer, and a woman who weeps, suffers and implores moves me.

"You are of steel; you do not understand that.

"Is it a genuine feeling or merely a recollection of the stage which goes from my head to my heart? I do not know. Are these thoughts and feelings mine, or are they phrases learned by heart? What difference does it make?

"I only know one thing, namely, that I have suffered.

"The confidence of the poor woman I betrayed caused me pain. I am not used to playing third parts. The lying denunciation you made me send to the count pained me also. It was repugnant to me to profess friendship for a man dishonored and whom I hated.

"Yet I never told you a word of all these tortures.

"Have patience a little while longer. You permitted me to declaim a little while ago. That will be the first and last time that I will really play a farce to you. You shall see me as I believe I am. Hold the reins firmly, Legigant. On the day you let go of them, all will be up with you."

Did Colonel Fritz really mean what he said?

After a short pause the colonel continued:

"You forced me to commit dastardly things, and I did not rebel. You threw me into the arms of another, Nini Moustache, and I loved her, and did not complain. You forced me to torture Hortense, which I did at the cost of my own heart, and I said nothing. At present I have only one corner in my soul that you have not disturbed —Lila—and I warn you to keep from doing so. In case it comes to the worst, I shall blow both you and myself in the air, as I told you before.''

This confession of weakness was in truth a triumph for Legigant.

Yet this triumph made him pensive, and he could not help saying to himself:

"If Aurelie should betray me! Lila's introduction into the count's house, an introduction which is not MY work, only proves one thing—the distinctly pronounced enmity of the colonel. I have lost my most faithful tool to-day. The triumph belongs to Aurelie.''

CHAPTER IX

THE ROSE GARDEN

THE place is charming. What name it bears on the plan of the suburbs of Paris I do not know. Clement had found one for it, however, which was as balsamic as the name itself. He had baptized it the "Rose Garden."

The house was small, and was covered with vines and flowers like a nest; the garden was shady and sweet-smelling; the inmates were cheerful and gentle as singing birds.

In this peaceful retreat, far from the madding crowd, lived Madame Rozel and Ursula.

Never had the latter felt herself so happy since she had left the convent. In this selected spot nothing was missing, not even news of Cyprienne.

The magic which had formerly puzzled the "Blue" now did the same for the "White," for she found every morning, without being able to find out how it happened, a letter from Cyprienne lying upon her table.

Another laconic letter—this one was from an unknown hand—had asked her to place her replies on the same spot, and they would be delivered to Cyprienne by the same messenger.

Ursula was brave, and this magic did not frighten her at all, for she quickly guessed who the fairy was.

How fervently, though, did she pray every evening for Madame Lamouroux!

Who else could it be but the silent benefactress of all the poor?

Was not Madame Rozel the right hand of the humane widow?—Madame Rozel, who had been given to Ursula as a protectress and companion in exile.

Madame Rozel was still quite young, and was agreeable, cheerful and bright, and from morning to night her rippling laugh was heard in the house.

There was one day in this house, where every day was a festival, which they awaited with impatience.

That day was Sunday.

On that morning the house looked as quiet and retired as usual, but I would like to wager that there was less sleeping done behind the green shutters than on week days, and that two merry eyes already watched the sandy road at eight o'clock.

At nine o'clock no one could be seen on the road, but through the branches came the refrain of a cheerful spring song.

"Ah!" exclaimed Madame Rozel, as she opened the window, "that is the 'Marseillaise' of love."

The voice sounded nearer. A few minutes later the singer himself appeared.

Madame Rozel opened the gate and received Clement with mock reverence.

Clement was not alone, though. Louis Jacquemin timidly followed behind him.

These weekly promenades to the Rose Garden were

the latter's reward for the week; for he was now always the first to work and the last one to leave the shop.

He kept away entirely from the saloons, where he was wont to spend his nights and days.

There was a purpose in his life now. After six days' hard work, he knew a seventh, full of peace and joy, awaited him.

Any one that had known Louis Jacquemin before would hardly have recognized him now, in his clean short coat, well-combed hair, and fearless look.

His eyes, which had formerly looked watery and glassy, now sparkled with youthful brilliancy; his limbs had recovered their former buoyancy and vigor, and he had learned to smile again.

And who had worked this miracle?

Ursula's gentle glance.

He loved her as tenderly as he had formerly loved Celine.

He had at length come to know that love was not only a pleasure but also a duty.

Astonished at feeling his heart beat as it had never beat before, he had said to himself:

"Yes, it is Ursula who has saved me!"

Could he hope that she would love him some time?

He did not know; he did not even think of it. He was satisfied that she allowed herself to be loved.

"I am becoming intimate with her," he said; "I am getting to be worthier of her."

And this conviction gave him strength and courage.

Clement had told him Ursula's story, but had purposely hidden from him her relationship to Celine.

Louis, therefore, only knew that Ursula was poor as

he was himself; that she lived, like him, from the work of her hands; and that one day she would wish to enjoy her share of the world's joys, and would then need a hearth and a heart she could trust.

How fervently he wished that she would select *him* as the man!

Yet when Sunday came, and Louis ascended the steps leading to the Rose Garden, his hopes seemed to him to be childish follies.

He measured with a single glance the abyss which still separated him from this pure young girl, and exaggerating his own unworthiness, he murmured:

"Nevermore!"

Nevermore! Always! Perhaps!

These are the three words of lovers, infinite as love itself.

When Jacquemin was far from Ursula, he thought: "Perhaps!"

In her presence he bitterly exclaimed:

"Nevermore! Nevermore!"

Ah! would the day ever come when he could murmur:

"Always?"

Ursula did not look upon Louis Jacquemin with an indifferent gaze.

She was a brave and noble girl—a sort of Sister of Charity.

She knew everything about Louis Jacquemin—his disappointed love and his sufferings—and before she herself knew it, the wish awoke within her to console that tortured heart, to dry those tears, and to reassure that failing courage.

I would not care to maintain that she loved Louis already. Yet, if it was not love, it was pity—and that is often the mother of love.

The timidity of the young man and his low spirits were just the things to win the heart of the sensitive Ursula.

Ursula was the incarnation of common-sense and shrewdness. She knew that the time when princes married shepherd girls was over. She had, therefore, never dreamed of a hero, but only of an upright man who loved her sincerely.

One Sunday morning, Madame Rozel and Ursula were promenading in their garden, awaiting the customary visit from Clement and Jacquemin.

Madame Rozel, who was generally so gay and lively, looked serious and mysterious.

Two or three times she had seized Ursula's arm as if she wished to tell her something, only to let it fall again as quickly.

Finally, however, she gathered her courage together, and seized the bull by the horns.

"What do you think of your friend Jacquemin, little one?" she asked.

Ursula blushed to the roots of her hair.

"Don't you think he's a nice fellow?" continued Madame Rozel. "Of course he is not always gay and lively; the poor fellow has so many troubles that he cannot be as merry and cheerful as Monsieur Clement, for instance."

As soon as the conversation embraced Clement, Ursula felt more at ease. She immediately assented to Madame Rozel's eulogy, and did not fail to praise Clement's good qualities as they deserved.

"Then you do not think my choice a bad one?" asked Madame Rozel.

"What? What do you mean, madame?"

"Yes, yes, my dear Ursula, I have decided to get married, and my choice fell upon Monsieur Clement. He is so good, so agreeable, and has such a good heart! The thing is settled, and in a few months Madame Rozel will call herself Madame Clement. As soon as he comes to-day I will tell him."

"And he will be very happy to hear it, madame."

"I hope so," replied Madame Rozel, with a smile; "but you, too, my dear child, are big and grown up, and it is about time that you thought of founding a home for yourself."

"I?" exclaimed Ursula, sighing.

"What a pity," continued Madame Rozel. "What a pity it is that Jacquemin loves another! He is so good and gentle."

She felt Ursula's arm twitch.

"What ails you, dear child?"

"Nothing, madame—nothing."

"I thought you were trembling."

A pause ensued.

Ursula walked with downcast eyes, and Madame Rozel looked stealthily at her, and bit her lips.

"Were you not going to relate something about Jacquemin, madame?" asked Ursula, finally.

"Yes," replied Madame Rozel, "I said he was in love; I ought rather to have said he has loved, and unhappily, too. Perhaps he has consoled himself again; for his own sake, I hope so. He suffered a great deal, and such a

past in an adorer is always a source of uneasiness to
a young girl.''

Ursula felt her heart swell.

''On the contrary,'' she eagerly cried.

She paused and blushed.

Madame Rozel clasped her in her arms and kissed her
upon the forehead.

''You are an angel,'' she said. ''Do not hide anything
from me. Am I not your friend?''

''Yes, certainly.''

''Well, will you not have pity for that poor heart, my
daughter?'' asked Madame Rozel. ''What I said before
was merely a joke. Jacquemin loves you; he loves you
sincerely. I would not say so if I were not convinced of
it. He has suffered though, and on account of an unfortunate, who, when you come to know her, will be dear to you
nevertheless. It is almost your duty to cure these wounds.
I have not said anything to you yet, as I did not wish to
interfere with your conscience: but now, when I see that
you love our poor Louis, I can tell you all. You love
him, do you not?''

''I think so,'' said Ursula, blushing.

Then, as if ashamed of her bashfulness, she raised her
head, and looking at Madame Rozel with her big black
eyes, which were as pure as her soul, she added:

''Yes, I love him. This morning I was still unaware
of it. You have revealed it to me. God forgive me, but
when you spoke to me before of the other one I was jealous. Were I alone I might perhaps still hesitate, but if
you and Monsieur Clement tell me to love him, I shall
follow your advice!''

Suddenly the noise of carriage wheels was heard.

"My child," said Madame Rozel to Ursula, "the fate of the two beings who love you will be decided this morning—the fate of your sister and your future husband."

Ursula looked at Madame Rozel in surprise, and the latter continued:

"You will see to-day, for the first time, a great sinner. Wait here."

Madame Rozel kissed the young girl and hurried away.

Behind the thick bushes could be heard Clement's voice.

Ursula covered her eyes with her hands and murmured:

"O Lord, my God, how I do love him!"

CHAPTER X

THE ELDER SISTER

THE noise of a footstep was heard on the terrace.

Ursula raised up her head and saw Louis Jacquemin in front of her.

He was as pale and uneasy as she herself.

He walked two steps toward her and then timidly stood still.

In a voice trembling with excitement, he said:

"I love you, Ursula. Will you try to love me?"

She advanced two steps now and took the proffered hand.

·I look upon you as an honest man, Louis," she replied, "and I love you."

Oh, how beautiful it was that morning in the Rose Garden!

Intoxicated with his happiness, he sank down upon a wooden bench which stood near by.

Ursula sat close to him, as if to say:

"I know that you have suffered. Your sorrow does not belong to you alone. I wish to share it."

"I have suffered much," said Louis, as if in answer to her thought.

"I know it," she said.

"You knew it, and you loved me?"

"I love you since I know it."

This simple yet sublime expression brought tears to Jacquemin's eyes.

"Forgive me! Forgive me!" he murmured. "It is remorse which brings these tears. I have been weak and wicked—forgive me!"

"I do not forgive you, Louis. I have nothing to forgive you for, and I love you all the more for those tears."

Oh, how beautiful it was that morning in the Rose Garden! Along the flowery lanes Madame Rozel and Clement promenaded arm in arm.

There were no tears there; Clement felt more like singing.

"It is settled now," said Rosa, who figured now under the name of Madame Rozel; "we are engaged."

"Yes, as much engaged as any couple can be."

"In that case I owe you a confession, Clement," said Madame Rozel, casting down her eyes.

"What? A secret?" cried Clement, uneasily.

"I have been in love once before," said Madame Rozel, with a deep sigh.

"Really!" exclaimed Clement.

"Yes; but I do not love the man any more, at least not the same way I did then."

"And what is his name?" asked Clement.

"Joseph!" replied Rosa.

Clement burst into a loud laugh.

"That's a good joke!" he exclaimed. "You are trying to make a fool of me. You can love Joseph as much as you want to, but no one else, and I can assure you I will not get jealous."

Rosa began to laugh, too. Her mind was easier now that she had made the confession.

She had regarded it as her duty to tell it to Clement before she took him for a husband.

She had loved Joseph when they were both children, and before circumstances had placed an impassable gulf between them.

Now she placed her hand in Clement's, but felt herself obliged to say to him:

"I have loved Joseph!"

He looked upon the confession as a joke. So much the better.

Oh, how beautiful it was that morning in the Rose Garden!

Jacquemin and Ursula had taken seats in the arbor, and were telling each other confidential stories.

Louis concealed nothing, and did not wish to conceal anything.

He told the story of the watchmaker and his daughter Celine, the visit of the tempter and the fall of the dearly beloved girl.

In this way Ursula heard, without suspecting it, out of the mouth of her intended, the story of her own family.

Jacquemin then touched upon the story of his own escapades.

From time to time he paused and murmured in a tone of despair:

"Ah, when you know all you will not love me any more; I am an honest man, though, and must tell you everything."

"You have suffered too much not to be good," replied Ursula. "I love you."

He told the story of the abduction, and the ride in the early morning.

Ursula shuddered as she learned for the first time in what danger she had been, and how close she had stood to the brink of destruction.

She looked at Louis, and observed such sincere remorse in his eyes that she said to him again:

"I love you."

Oh, how beautiful it was that morning in the Rose Garden!

For some moments this affecting scene had been witnessed from behind a bush by a veiled lady dressed in black.

Her bosom heaved as if it cost her an effort not to burst out into loud sobs.

She softly murmured, as if speaking to an invisible being:

"You have kept all your promises. Thanks, you saint, you angel! Thanks, Helene!"

Louis raised his eyes, and saw the dark form.

He became pale as death, and then, springing up, exclaimed:

"Ah, there she is again! There she is again!"

Nini Moustache walked to the middle of the terrace and stood still, trembling, and with eyes cast to the ground.

She was silent and awaited with impatience the young man's first words.

At the same time she fervently prayed to God that these first words would be cruel to her, that is, happy for Ursula!

If his passion for Nini had not yet entirely died out,

if he asked her to love him again, he would be pronouncing eternal separation from Ursula!

Celine knew, though, for Madame Rozel had told her so, that Ursula loved Jacquemin.

The latter, as was remarked before, had at sight of his first love arisen, pale with excitement.

"There you are again!" he exclaimed. "What do you wish here?"

Nini Moustache made no reply.

"Did the miserable scoundrel love you?" continued Jacquemin. "Then let me tell you he does not exist any more. The contempt he felt for himself killed him. You will only find here a remorseful heart, which is ready to do any penance to make the past good again. What do you wish here?" he again repeated as he saw her stretch out her arms. "Do you want to stain this pure soul through contact with you?"

Ursula stopped him.

"Not a word more, Louis!" she exclaimed.

She then added in a lower voice:

"Why do you wish to insult her? Think of her grief, if she loved you."

These words were only a breath, a murmur, the rustling of a withered leaf on the ground. Celine heard them though, and replied:

"I thank you."

She then staggered toward the staircase of the terrace.

She was determined to carry out the *whole* sacrifice.

The Countess of Monte-Cristo had not thought it necessary to tell Ursula how closely related she was to Celine, and Celine obeyed the countess in all things.

She wished to leave this house as she had entered it, spurned by Jacquemin and not known by Ursula. Her name should never be pronounced here, and the children of the young couple should never know that they had a second mother, far away, who prayed for them.

Yes, she would resign herself to this eternal solitude of the heart.

And did she not deserve it? Does not the just law of repentance say: "An eye for an eye, a tooth for a tooth?"

Whom had she sinned against?

Her father, her brother—she already called Louis her brother—and through her brother and through the daughter of her father she was to be punished.

Staggering at every step, Celine slowly walked away, and Ursula, as she followed her with her eyes, could not help pitying her.

She looked at Louis to see what impression had been made on his face.

He was grave and calm, like a person who had done his duty without weakness and from conviction.

"She suffers greatly?" said Ursula to him.

He shrugged his shoulders and replied:

"She is acting!"

That word was the last stroke. It pierced Nini Moustache to the heart. The unfortunate girl, though, did not move a muscle, but without turning her face she slowly descended the terrace stairs.

At that moment a merry couple ascended them.

"Well?" they both asked simultaneously.

"Well," replied Celine, "everything is done for now."

"I thought so," exclaimed Clement; "I knew that Louis would do his duty."

"Then," added Rosa—"then it behooves us to do ours."

And with that they both took one of Celine's arms and forced her to return with them to the terrace.

"What do you wish? What do you still wish with me?" stammered Celine, in affright.

"We wish," said Clement, "justice to be done, and that those who cursed you so long should learn to love you anew—of course in a different way," he laughingly added.

"We desire," said Madame Rozel, "the happiness of our dear Ursula to be complete, and that she should become acquainted with the mysterious cousin whom she so often blessed in the solitude of her heart."

"What! Madame Morel!" exclaimed Ursula.

"Here she is!" replied Rosa, as she forced Celine into Ursula's arms.

Clement, in the meanwhile, had taken Louis Jacquemin aside and spoken earnestly to him.

"We must not be stricter than God, Louis," he said. "You have courageously undergone the trials we made for you, and you see that we do not begrudge you your reward. Well, Celine has suffered more, for she was a greater sinner. But now she is worthy the respect of any honorable man. *Your* reward—the reward I promised you in the name of her whose instrument I am—was love and happiness. The reward which was promised to *her* was: first, your reform, for which she worked as well as we did; secondly, your forgiveness; and, thirdly, the love of her sister."

"What? Ursula—"

"Is Celine's sister. I ask you, Louis, do you wish to

leave our work half finished, and do you not wish to do something for us, who have done so much for you?"

Jacquemin thoughtfully listened to this revelation.

He then went, without saying a word, to where Ursula and Celine stood.

Celine stood with downcast eyes, and did not have the courage to look at Ursula.

The latter could only stammer:

"Oh, madame—oh, my sister!—how shall I express my gratitude to you?

Louis clasped one of Celine's hands in his, and Ursula's in the other, and in a gentle voice said:

"Ursula, my dear bride, embrace Celine, our sister."

Oh, how beautiful, how magnificent it was that morning in the Rose Garden!

CHAPTER XI

LETTERS FROM THE RETREAT

EVER since Lila had been received in his house by the Count de Puysaie, circumstances, even those which were entirely independent of each other, seemed to so group themselves that all his troubles ceased and all his cares were silenced.

It was as if an invisible providential hand conducted things—that mysterious hand which, according to popular saying, makes one lucky incident follow the other, just as in the case of ill luck, which never comes alone.

In the first place all his debts had been paid.

Most of these debts were really made for Nini Moustache. His other debts were also quite heavy. The sale of the mansion, though, produced sufficient to cover them. A buyer appeared in the person of the lawyer Durantin, the same one who had purchased Nini's small house in Madame Lamouroux's name.

This Madame Lamouroux appeared to be a rich widow who bought one property after the other.

One morning, just as the count was going to Lila's room, as was his custom every morning, he found a sealed envelope on the marble of his dressing-case.

How did this letter get there?

The count could not explain it to himself.

With the exception of his valet and his two daughters no one entered this room.

Cyprienne and Lila, when he asked them, did not seem to understand what he was talking about, and Florent positively asserted he knew nothing about the letter.

Florent had been brought up in the place, his faithfulness was above suspicion, and Loredan had to believe his words.

Besides, one likes to receive good news, no matter where it comes from, and this mysterious note contained the best news the Count de Puysaie could hope for.

The contents of the envelope were composed, in the first place, of two legal papers—the consent to Cyprienne's marriage with Baron Matifay and the cancellation of a mortgage which the countess held on the house.

Then followed a letter, signed by Hortense, and which read as follows:

"LOREDAN—You have done me great harm; but I forgive you, as I wish you to forgive me for the harm I did you. The most culpable has been neither you nor I. If I fled from your house it was because I feared to prove unfaithful to my vow, and because I did not wish for your, mine, and all the world's sake, that you should ever learn the name of the real culprit.

"I forgive you because you have suffered a great deal, and I hope that you have forgiven me, too, for I swear to you I have suffered much also.

"I know that you need the inclosed two papers, and I send them to you. By leaving my home, I have forfeited all my rights in Cyprienne. Therefore decide her fate yourself; but know and believe that the voices which come from the grave do not lie!

"*Cyprienne is your daughter!*

"All efforts you make to find me will prove fruitless. Give up all idea of seeing me again, and try to forget me. The thought that I am a source of grief or trouble to you makes me uneasy.

"As for me, I shall not lose sight of you, and my heart, my deeply bowed heart, shares all your wishes and all your joys.

"Good-by, and retain for me the tender recollection one feels for those long since dead.   HORTENSE."

No one, we have said, could have told the count how this letter had been brought into the house and laid upon the table in his room.

Cyprienne alone could have given some clew to it, though a very indistinct one.

She could only have said that she, too, had found a letter that morning in her jewel casket.

But then she would have been obliged to show the note to her father, and that was impossible.

The letter she received was also signed "Hortense," and was, besides, dated from a mysterious place, the Retreat.

"Oh, my daughter!" the letter read, "do not judge me; do not condemn me; wait and hope!

"We are, as you know, in hands which are not alone more powerful than our own, but also divinely good.

"I have been promised that you would be saved, and I have as much confidence in that promise as if it came from God himself. You will be saved.

"Do not believe, therefore, that I am betraying you to-day.

"Your father will speak to you again about that hated marriage with Baron Matifay. The sacrifice is a cruel one, but yet you must obey it.

"It will seem very peculiar to you, and it seems so to me too. This marriage, the thought alone of which filled us with despair, is, nevertheless, the only mode which remains to you to arrive at freedom and happiness.

"How so? Why? I do not know myself. I believe it though, because they told me so, the friends whom I know to be good, and who can do anything."

That night at the family dinner Loredan seemed to be more taken up with his thoughts than he had been for some time, and Lila's caresses failed to arouse him.

From time to time he looked stealthily at Cyprienne, and the latter, who, without his opening his mouth, knew very well what he wished to say, turned her eyes away.

The count hesitated.

The solemn assurance: "Cyprienne is your daughter," upset his conviction.

He had resolved, in case she showed the slightest repugnance to a renewal of the marriage project with Matifay, not to use the slightest force.

Loredan finally broke the silence.

"I have heard from your mother, Cyprienne," he said.

Cyprienne blushed, and cast down her eyes.

She had to pretend not to know anything; she had to lie.

"Will we see her soon, papa?" she asked.

"I cannot say, my poor child," he replied. "She

speaks in her letter about you, and your marriage, against which she has nothing to say.''

Loredan, who became more and more embarrassed, made several pauses as he spoke, to give his daughter an opportunity to interrupt him.

Cyprienne let him speak though.

She comprehended that the moment had come, and said:

''I have promised to obey, papa, and I will obey.''

''Without its costing you any restraint?''

''Yes, without its costing me much restraint.''

Loredan hastily arose from the table.

''Cyprienne,'' he cried, ''you are an angel, and deserve a better father than I am. Thanks to this little demon'' —and he raised Lila in his arms to kiss her—''thanks to your sacrifice, Cyprienne, all my griefs are forgotten, all my mistakes made good again. Yes, my children, I shall have to thank you for everything, and do not imagine I shall ever forget it. Yes, I shall work for you and yours, I will become rich and happy again. By the way, Cyprienne, you know that your first-born will bear my name as Count of Puysaie? I vow to you, though, that the boy will have to wait long before he will inherit from me, for I feel as hale and healthy to-day between you two as if I could live a hundred years yet!''

CHAPTER XII

PREPARATIONS

FOR more than two months the Monte-Cristo mansion stood empty.

The handsome countess had disappeared the way she came, without leaving any trace behind her.

Her intimate friends, the Vicomte de la Cruz for instance, maintained that she was travelling in Germany *incognito*.

The *incognito* must have been strictly kept, for the newspapers had not a line about her journey.

One day, however, the doors of the house opened wide, and a crowd of carpenters, upholsterers and decorators streamed in.

Baron Matifay was in love, and did not find anything too good for his dear Cyprienne. The magnificence of the Monte-Cristo mansion did not satisfy him.

Aurelie's plan had succeeded.

Upon the advice of Colonel Fritz, the baron had discontinued work on the house in the Chaussee d'Antin.

All the arrangements in the house were intrusted to the care of Clement.

Clement was only a jeweller, but still he knew everything connected with decorative art.

The former wood-chopper was a great poet.

That is, a poet in the widest sense of the word; a poet from instinct.

He was a painter, musician, and poet.

For that reason Baron Matifay had chosen Clement to superintend the decorating of the house.

Little by little everything in the house was changed.

Only one portion was spared, out of respect to Cyprienne—the hothouse and the adjoining pavilion, which the countess had reserved for herself when she let the place.

From morning to night Clement came and went, and walked up and down the stairs in feverish haste. He made it a point of honor to have everything beautiful and tasty.

In a short while everything was arranged.

The weeks passed, and the day appointed for the marriage drew near. In four days the handsome, youthful Cyprienne was to put on the orange-flowers, and lay her hand in that of a man who was not Don Jose.

And she was to swear that she loved that man, that she would obey him, and look up to him as her lord and master.

When Don Jose thought of that his heart was ready to burst in his bosom, but he had to smile, and when Cyprienne saw this smile, she regained new hope.

One day Cyprienne, in company with her father and her sixty-year-old bridegroom, rode in a carriage to the palace which was to be her future home.

She strode through the whole house, and pretended to take the greatest interest in everything.

They then went into the garden.

It was already getting dark.

Cyprienne, who had suddenly become melancholy, let her father talk with the baron, and went to the hothouse alone.

Nothing was changed there.

Cyprienne seated herself on the same bench where she —ah! what a long time had elapsed since that day—had for the first and only time conversed with Don Jose.

What had they then said to each other?

The words themselves she did not remember, but their echo remained in her heart.

On that day she had heard from his own lips of the danger which threatened her, and of the mysterious obstacle which separated her from Don Jose.

Yes, nothing was changed in this place, which she had entered for the first time with such heart-beatings and had left with such great uneasiness in her mind.

This was to be her retreat; the spot to which she could flee in the hours of solitude and sadness, and dream of her quickly lost happiness.

The night became darker and darker, and the first rays of the moon shone through the big glass window upon the flowers and leaves.

Suddenly an indistinct sparkle could be seen behind a group of Indian fig-trees. It seemed to be the reflection of a light burning in some other place.

Who could come at this hour in the still uninhabited mansion?

Was it, perhaps, thieves after the rich booty stored there?

That was certainly the most simple thought, but Cyprienne had another.

She immediately thought of some unknown friend.

Where did the light come from?

In the meanwhile the reflection became brighter; it did not last long before it resembled a star, and came toward Cyprienne.

Cyprienne could now distinguish two dark shadows, one of which carried a lantern in the hand.

It was a woman enveloped in a dark capuchin and a man.

The man was Don Jose.

The woman threw her veil aside as she passed by Cyprienne.

It was the Countess of Monte-Cristo.

They both spoke softly to one another.

Don Jose said:

"I thank you, Helene! Yes, now that I know your plan I am convinced that she is saved."

With blind confidence and unspeakable joy Cyprienne repeated to herself:

"I am saved!"

The light was extinguished, the shadows disappeared, and in the garden the count's voice was heard calling:

"Cyprienne! Cyprienne! Where are you, Cyprienne?"

CHAPTER XIII

THE MARRIAGE

THAT night Cyprienne's sleep was lulled by peaceful dreams, in which she seemed to hear the chirping of whole swarms of winged hopes.

She saw in the distance the light of the hothouse sparkle like a star, and heard dearly loved voices murmur:

"She is saved! She is saved!"

And the next day, and the one following, Don Jose did not make his appearance at the Puysaie palace.

The vicomte's absence, which at any other time would have brought Cyprienne to the verge of despair, was to-day the basis of new hope.

"He is working for me, that is the reason he cannot come," she thought.

She knew from experience the way and the manner the unknown friends worked, and she awaited every moment some unexpected incident which would foil everything, just as happened before when her mother fled.

The coming and going of any one, a frown of her father's, a postponement of Matifay's daily visits—all this made her heart beat higher, and she said to herself:

"Is it that?"

Unfortunately it was nothing, and every evening the poor girl said to herself:

"Well, then, it will be to-morrow."

Foolish hope! Vain waiting!

The next day passed as the one before, and, holding tight to her belief, she still said to herself:

"To-morrow—to-morrow!"

In that way the last week, the last day, and then the last night passed.

That night Cyprienne slept very little, but wept a great deal. She wished the night would last forever, and with melancholy feelings she awaited the coming day.

But she even struggled against this melancholy.

"Something will surely happen this morning."

The morning passed, and when she got into the carriage which was to bring her to the sacrifice, she thought:

"Perhaps at the mayor's office."

How charming is the fable of the Knight Bluebeard! How natural are the hearts pictured there clinging fast to hope! How persistently the question is repeated:

"Sister Anna, my sister Anna, don't you see anything?"

In the fable, sister Anna finally sees a knight covered with clouds of dust and riding at full speed. But Cyprienne, less fortunate than Anna, saw nothing.

She only saw the mayor, with his scarf of office, and then the altar, in the church, with the burning wax candles upon it.

The organ reverberated, the chorus of the opera sang, and the spectators declared they had never attended a finer wedding.

"Sister Anna, my sister Anna, don't you see any-thing?"

Ah, what was the use of it now? Even had the horse-men come on their foam-covered steeds, and drawn their naked swords out of their scabbards, they would have been too late.

The poor heart of sister Anna was dead.

Yes, dead—dead to every joy, dead to every hope, dead to all love.

Don Jose had deceived her. What had the unknown friends done to save her?

Nothing.

Ah, if Don Jose had only made the slightest attempt, even though it proved unsuccessful, Cyprienne would have blessed him.

But nothing, nothing, nothing!

At the moment of the struggle he had not even been seen. The poor girl was too uneasy anyway, on that day, to see anything.

Otherwise she would have noticed a handsome young man, just as pale as she was, standing in the shadow of a pillar.

No, Don Jose had not fled from the struggle and the pain. He was there, he looked the enemy in the face, he bared his heart to the pain, as the soldier his breast to the bullets.

This marriage was necessary, and he allowed it to take place, waiting bravely for the result of the game in which the Countess of Monte-Cristo was his partner.

Was she going to win the game? He hoped so. He might lose it, too, and then he would lose Cyprienne at the same time, and, in fact, forever, for she would certainly hate him for his lying promises and accuse him of treason.

He possessed a brave, manly heart; but still this struggle almost overcame his strength. Beads of perspiration rolled like tears down his cheeks.

This fear was more bitter and painful than that which he had felt in the grave where the treasure of the house of Rancogne was buried.

When the last sounds of the solemn song died away, and the organ played an accompaniment to the breaking up of the procession, every one rushed to the entrances to see the bride step into the carriage.

Don Jose, however, did not move from the spot, but leaned against the pillar.

Just like Cyprienne, he said to himself:

"Now, all is over."

There he stood, isolated and easy to be seen.

Although Cyprienne did not notice him, another person did—Colonel Fritz.

Pale, exhausted, with white lips, as if they had been dipped in vinegar and gall, the Vicomte de la Cruz looked so different from what he generally did that the colonel, in surprise, stood still and observed him closely.

He seemed to desire to address him, but, suddenly changing his mind, he hid behind a group of curiosity-seekers, and did not lose sight of Don Jose.

When Cyprienne, with downcast eyes and pale as death, passed by on the arm of Matifay, a gleam of rage shone in the vicomte's eyes, and the colonel read therein Don Jose's love for Cyprienne and his hatred of Matifay.

In the meanwhile the procession had gradually come out of the church, and the magnificent carriages rode up one after the other to bring the newly married couple and the wedding guests back to the house.

Just as Matifay placed his hand in that of his bride to help her into the carriage, he exclaimed:

"Where is your prayer-book?"

Cyprienne looked at her empty hands.

"I must have left it in the vestry," she replied.

A prayer-book costing five hundred francs! Millionnaires do not make much ado about money, still they do not like to throw it away.

"We must find the book again," exclaimed Matifay.

A little delay occurred now, and several spectators hurried back to the church.

In a few moments a man dressed like a well-to-do workman strode through the crowd.

In his hand he held the costly book.

"Here it is," he said; "I saw where madame laid it down before she signed the marriage contract."

Matifay took a five-franc piece from his pocket.

The workman, however, who was none other than our friend Jacquemin, refused to take the money.

"Thank you," he said; "the book belongs to madame, and I only ask the pleasure of handing it back to her. I think it will bring me luck in my love."

These words were, perhaps, a little bold. Jacquemin's face, however, was so open-hearted that Cyprienne smiled and took the book.

"Thank you, sir," she said.

The book lay in a richly embroidered cover, and as Cyprienne mechanically drew it out, she felt, with secret trembling, the sharp point of a note which stuck between the binding of the book and the cover.

This note, no doubt, contained an explanation of the peculiar inactivity of her unknown friends.

Matifay was sitting opposite to her, however, and she could not open the note before she reached home.

As soon as she got out of the carriage she hurried to her boudoir. The note contained only one line—a line which quieted all anger. It read as follows:

"Do not complain of any one. Be brave. You are saved.

"THE COUNTESS OF MONTE-CRISTO."

CHAPTER XIV

A RAY, A SPARKLE, A SHADOW

CYPRIENNE'S first movement, after she had read this laconic epistle, was a feeling of intense joy, not so much on account of the assurance, "You are 'saved," but because it proved her suspicions to be unjust.

How painful it is to be obliged to accuse persons we love.

Cyprienne had no rest; she could not stay anywhere, and it seemed to her that if this anxiety did not soon end she would die.

A few hours before, when she thought her misfortune sealed, she had been calmer.

Cyprienne did not count the days alone now, but the hours, and at the end of dinner the minutes.

But still nothing occurred—nothing.

Cyprienne thought now that the unknown friends urged her in their note to defend herself. That was her definition of, "Be brave."

These were her thoughts a few moments before the ball began.

Leaning against a chair, she stood there as indifferent to everything that surrounded her as if she were not the heroine of the *fête*.

She shuddered and blushed.

A burning hot hand was laid upon her shoulder.

She turned quickly around and saw Baron Matifay smiling at her. The musicians had already taken their seats on the music stand, and the bridegroom came to ask her for the first dance, as was his right.

"Be brave!" Cyprienne repeatedly said to herself, and placed her small, aristocratic hand in the broad palm of the baron.

During the continuation of the quadrille she collected herself again, and considered what course she should pursue.

Her resolve was soon made.

Matifay had promised to treat her as his daughter. She would remind him of that promise. She would throw herself at his feet, and beg him to pity and have mercy on her.

With frightened look she stealthily glanced at him, and a cold shudder ran down her back. She saw that any hope for mercy would be useless.

"Ah," she now thought, "I am lost."

The terrible quiet of a determined resolve settled on her heart like an icy fog, and she said to herself:

"I will commit suicide."

In the meanwhile the orchestra was playing merry tunes, and the toilets of the ladies sparkled and shone in the brilliancy of the dazzling light.

A little while after it was noticed that Cyprienne had left the ballroom, and the baron had disappeared too.

The festival, nevertheless, went on.

Suddenly, however, in the midst of a quadrille, a terrible cry was heard, and every one rushed to the doors of the drawing-room. All wished to know what had happened.

Several, indeed, gave utterance to the secret thought which lay in every one's mind, and asked:

"Who is being murdered here?"

The cry seemed to have come either from Cyprienne's room or from Matifay's.

One bolder than the rest took a light in his hand and went into the hallway which led from the baron's room to Cyprienne's. He soon returned with a pale face and trembling lips.

"The baron!" he stammered.

"Well, what's the matter with him?" asked forty voices at once.

"He lies in there."

And he pointed with his finger to the entrance to the hallway.

He lay stretched on the floor, the candlestick broken in pieces near him, and the melted wax still sticking to his face and clothes.

Downstairs in the parlor the rumor had already spread that the baron had really been murdered, and several persons had immediately rushed to conclusions.

Two different stories were told.

Some said the baron had been murdered by his young wife, while the others said it was the wife's lover who had done the deed. But the baron was not murdered at all.

He had merely fallen down in consequence of a congestion of the brain or something similar.

Dr. Ozam, who was one of the guests, had the hallway cleared, the doors locked, and then began to examine the baron's condition. He soon saw that Matifay was not dead, but had only fainted. He had him placed on a sofa, and prescribed the necessary remedies.

Cyprienne, who looked a thousand times prettier now, with her flowing hair and pale face, stood at her husband's couch.

What seemed to be a natural occurrence to the doctor and the others was, in her opinion, the work of the unknown friends, and she said to herself:

"Are they, then, so powerful that they can even produce apoplexy and death?"

In a little while Matifay raised himself up and pointed to a point in the wall.

"There!—there!" he cried.

One of the persons present went to the spot pointed out, and rapped on it with his finger. The sound was faint and the wall massive.

"Then it must have been a vision," said Matifay, who was quieted again by this experiment.

"What kind of a vision?" asked Dr. Ozam, gently.

Matifay did not answer the question.

The patient was brought to his room, but though his condition was not an alarming one, he did not wish to remain alone. The nurse who waited on him noticed that he moved his lips in his sleep like a person praying, and that a name continually occurred in that prayer:

"Helene! Helene!"

CHAPTER XV

AT MADAME LAMOUROUX'S

THE room is warm and comfortable. A brisk fire burns in the fireplace. We are in the same room where we introduced the reader to Ursula, namely, in the room of the widow, Madame Lamouroux.

Not a sound can be heard but the irregular crackling of the fire and the breathing of a sleeping child.

Poor Pippiona!

She sleeps, smiles, and dreams!

For a fortnight she has been in this condition.

She has suffered so much that it seems to her now that she is in Paradise.

For a fortnight, since that terrible night when she saw her poor Mistigris lying on the ground with his head crushed in, her life had been but a dream—one of those dreams out of which one desires never to awake.

Sometimes, when she opens her eyes, she sees three pitying faces bending over her couch.

The first one is that of an old lady with long gray hair, and dressed in black.

The second is the intelligent and handsome one of a man of forty, with a high bald forehead, but whose eyes sparkle with the fire of youth.

The third is the brown face of a young man of twenty-five, as handsome as that of the archangel who placed his foot on the neck of the prostrate Satan.

Pippiona cannot give names to these protecting beings. They are for her three mysterious beings who people her sleep—three beneficent genii.

Her feverish brain is still weak!

Our readers, on the other hand, have already recognized the Widow Lamouroux, Dr. Ozam, and Joseph.

Pippiona sleeps and does not wish to awake. She is afraid of chasing these divine creatures away and finding herself again in Cinella's miserable room, shuddering from cold under her thin cover and surrounded by a darkness which fills her with fear.

Yet her memory gradually comes back to her.

She sees herself crouching on the icy floor and holding poor Mistigris in her arms.

That animal, we must reflect, was for her a doll, a friend, almost a child.

The death of the poor cat was, for the deserted girl, who had never known a being that loved her, what the death of a pet child is for a mother.

Suddenly, however—here the dream ends and the vision begins—suddenly the miserable attic becomes light, and the handsomest young man she had ever seen entered the dirty room.

That was only a dream, was it not? How could it be possible that such a gentleman could have strayed into Cinella's miserable hut?

This handsome young man was at the same time very good, and spoke and looked in a way Pippiona had never heard or seen before.

And then—oh, then—what joy!—then Pippiona felt

herself enveloped in a soft, warm cloak, raised up by two strong arms, and carried away to a spot where it was beautiful and so warm.

She then saw nothing more but the three faces—the lady with the gray hair, the scientist with the thoughtful brow, and the handsome young man.

Pippiona did not wish to awake out of this dream, for she feared she would find herself back again in the horrible reality.

She slowly turned around in bed, forced her eyes to remain closed, and let her fancy have free rein.

Thanks to the artificial reality which sleep gives to every dream picture, it seemed to her as if these pictures were reality itself.

In this way the lady with the gray hair became, in the romance, her mother.

Her mother! What a word full of unknown tenderness.

A mother! She knew just as little what a mother was as what a seraph is, but she divined that it must be something good.

According to that conclusion, the lady with the gray hair must be her mother.

She could not form any distinct conception of the handsome young man, and did not know why her thoughts always turned to him.

When the man with the bald forehead bent over her, she became calm. Her pulse beat slower, and a refreshing breath chased delirium and dizziness from her forehead.

If it was the lady with the gray hair, she felt tempted, though she did not dare do it, to throw her arms about her and passionately press her to her heart.

But if it was the brown young man, she became frightened. This fear, though, gave her pleasure at the same time; her blood rushed back to her heart, and she murmured:

"It is he!"

In this way Pippiona slept and dreamed in the semi-obscurity of the room, which was faintly lighted up by the flickering gleam of the wood fire.

A door was slightly opened, and a form holding a lamp in the hand glided softly over the carpet. The lamp was carefully placed in a corner of the fireplace, and the intruder walked to the head of the bed, and bent over, as if to listen to Pippiona's breathing. The light from the lamp now fell full on her face.

Dazed and aroused from her sleep, Pippiona opened her eyes, and saw Jose's sympathetic face almost touching her own.

Jose looked the same as when Pippiona saw him for the first time. He wore a black frockcoat of the latest fashion, a fine velvet vest, a satin necktie with a diamond pin, tight cashmere trousers, and fine shoes.

He came from Cyprienne's wedding, and was very sad. Yet, in spite of this sadness, he smiled.

"Well," he said, in a cheery tone, "it looks as if you are getting better?"

"You are good!" murmured Pippiona.

"You are good!" These were the first words she had addressed to Don Jose, and she was so excited that she could not say anything more.

Jose drew up a chair, and seated himself close to the bed.

"Poor little one!" he murmured.

She turned her head aside, and looked at him with her blue eyes.

The look spoke more than a hundred words, and Jose understood its meaning, for with almost paternal emotion he tenderly pressed her to his heart.

"You have suffered a great deal, but your sufferings are over now."

Pale as death she sank back in his arms.

Her whole soul seemed to lie in the tone with which she said:

"Thank you."

"You are getting much better," continued Jose; "but you still need quiet. Try to sleep."

"No, no," she naively replied; "I feel all right as I am. Permit me to look at you."

"To look at me!" he responded, in surprise.

"Yes," replied the child, with her natural candor, "you are good, you are handsome, and I love you."

In the mouth of a child these words have no deep meaning, and Pippiona was still a child.

"If you love me," replied Don Jose, "you must prove it to me by doing as the physician ordered, and especially not speak, as it tires you. Since you are not able to sleep, I will read something to you, if you desire it."

He arose as he said this to get a book which lay on the mantel-piece.

"No," said Pippiona, "speak to me instead. I like to hear your voice, but when you utter the thoughts of others, it seems to me as if you are not speaking yourself."

"Well, then, I will tell you a story. Shall I?"

"Just as you wish," said Pippiona; "only speak to me."

Jose suddenly had an idea.

Why should he not make use of this opportunity to reawaken in the child's memory the former incidents of her life?

The attempt would probably be a vain one. That this poor foster-daughter of a wandering acrobat should be the daughter of the Countess Helene de Rancogne was hardly to be expected. Yet Jose felt an inward suspicion, an indistinct hope, and it was not the first time that he thought of this curious meeting.

He had never believed that Pippiona was really Cinella's daughter. There was too wide a difference between this blond young girl and the Neapolitan acrobat.

The delicate form of her feet and hands, her neck and her features, proved her to be of aristocratic birth.

What accident had placed this tender infant in Cinella's hands?

Blanche de Rancogne had died in Naples.

From Naples Pippiona had come to Paris.

"I will tell you a story, then," said Jose.

Pippiona turned attentively toward him, so as not to lose a word or a look.

"There was once upon a time," began Jose, "a little girl called Blanche."

"Bianca," murmured Pippiona, half aloud.

"In Italy they say Bianca," corrected Jose, "but in France they say Blanche, and the little girl whose story I am going to relate to you was French."

"Blanche had no mother, and she was intrusted to the care of a wicked man who kept her locked up in a dark, solitary house.

"The house was an old castle, with big, half-ruined

towers, which stood in the midst of a black pond, and was surrounded by high woody hills.

"In this house an incessant noise of iron hammers and melting metals was kept up.

"At night the whole building was lighted up, and half-naked, perspiring men sprung here and there between the flames, like the lost souls in Hades.

"All this made little Blanche frightened."

Until now Pippiona had listened to the voice of the story-teller without paying much attention to the meaning of the words he spoke. This description, however, suddenly seemed to awake in her something like the recollection of scenes she had perhaps seen in another life.

She raised herself on her elbows and opened her big eyes still wider, as if she were trying to behold a vision of the past.

Jose noticed this movement and his heart beat higher.

Nevertheless he continued his story in the same quiet tone:

"The little Blanche was sick, very sick, but in her bed she still heard the loud noise of the hammers and the dull whir of the machines. Men dressed in black stepped up to her bed, felt of her wrists, looked in her eyes, and then conversed with each other in a corner of the room in low tones.

"One morning, however, the merry crack of the whip and the tinkling of bells were heard under her window; she was wrapped up in a woollen blanket and carried, half dead as she was, to a handsome carriage, where her guardian seated himself beside her.

"This guardian, Pippiona, was a scoundrel. He tried

though to make Blanche have a good opinion of him, but she did not love him.

"In the first place he was very ugly! He had a pale, wrinkled face with little eyes like those of a snake, dirty blond hair and large gold spectacles, behind which hid his glassy, fixed look."

Poor Jose revenged himself, by drawing this portrait of Matifay, for the marriage of his rival with pretty Cyprienne.

Was it his sharp tone or did Pippiona's memory at length awaken?

She trembled, and her pale lips twitched as if she wished to speak.

"The whip cracked," continued Jose, "the guard cried 'Forward!' and away they went. Through the carriage window, little Blanche saw the trees, houses and meadows fly past. They rode through big noisy cities and small bright villages.

"The sky became bluer, the sun warmer, the air clearer.

"Then they went on the sea, the vast, sleepy sea with its azure waves, which shook the ship like a cradle.

"They reached a beautiful country; whose white houses stood in the shadow of olive and orange trees, and above all this showed a sky of almost black blue and from which the dazzling sun incessantly poured down."

Jose interrupted himself. The door had opened for the second time and Madame Lamouroux had entered the room.

The bed curtains prevented Pippiona from seeing her, and Madame Lamouroux placed her finger on her mouth to make Jose understand that he should not betray her.

The little one seemed to be deeply moved by the simple tale, and impatiently awaited the continuation.

Jose though was silent.

"Well," exclaimed Pippiona eagerly, "how does the story end?"

Jose smiled and answered:

"If you possess any imagination, you can tell me yourself the conclusion of little Blanche's story in your own way."

CHAPTER XVI

PIPPIONA GOES ON WITH THE STORY

MADAME LAMOUROUX stood still on the thresh-hold of the room.

She awaited Pippiona's first words as one awaits a verdict of life or death.

At length Pippiona broke the silence.

"Ah," she said, "I cannot relate anything."

"Only try," said Jose, gently.

"I am not smart enough, and do not know how to imagine a story. Yet while you were speaking a strange feeling overcame me. I thought you were telling my own history.

"It was, no doubt, folly, for these recollections are so faint and weak that they have only left on me the indistinct impression of a dream. Yet I have somewhere seen the flaming house where the noise is incessant, and of which you spoke.

"Yes, I remember the pond covered with reeds.

"I also remember the high woody hills and the gray sky, in which clouds of smoke continually hung.

"I remember everything, the carriage, the tinkling of the bells, the landscape, the sea, the beautiful blue sky, which was to me like the revelation of another world."

Madame Lamouroux clasped her hands in an ecstasy of delight and stammered:

"Almighty God, it is she!"

Perhaps on Madame Lamouroux's account, Jose interrupted the little one and said:

"You said you had no imagination, Pippiona. You see now that you were mistaken, since a purely imaginary story could make such an impression on you."

Madame Lamouroux had too quickly seized upon a hope which might be deceptive, and Jose wished to spare her a possible disappointment.

His simple observation fell like a wet blanket upon Pippiona as well as Madame Lamouroux.

"Yes, that's true!" murmured the little one; "I have been led by your recital to think I had already seen all those pictures.

"But you must not think ill of me for it. What is left to the unfortunate but dreams?

"My name is Bianca, too, and when I heard you pronounce that name I hoped—

"Cinella told me many times that I was entitled to great wealth through my birth, and I for a moment thought that God had given me back everything at once —health, wealth, and a mother.

"What we wish we easily believe, and I would feel so happy if I had to thank you for everything."

After she said this she sank back on her pillow, and silence ensued.

Jose's voice arose again, and he said:

"Well, Pippiona, how about the end of the story?"

The little one quickly raised herself up again and replied:

"I cannot invent the end of the story, but yours seems to be in so high a degree the commencement of mine that I only need to tell you the conclusion of the latter.

"As far as I can think back I see myself playing and running about in the harbor of Naples, with other children of my age.

"At that time I thought I was Cinella's daughter, and did not feel at all unhappy.

"About this time Cinella, to his own and my misfortune, made the acquaintance of Monna Feretti.

"Monna was a big, strong girl, black as a raven, bold as a lion, and very handsome as people said.

"I, for my part, did not know whether she was or not; I was afraid of her.

"At night I was often woke up by quarrels between the two.

"By day, while Cinella ran about the city to earn the money Monna demanded with avaricious greediness, she was alone in the house with me.

"Those were the hours which I feared above all.

"When Cinella was present she restrained herself, but as soon as he was absent she whipped me for nothing at all.

"I did not dare to complain to Cinella, for she threatened to kill me if I said a word.

"During the time Cinella was absent, Monna sometimes received the visits of a tall young man, who was called Tommaso. Tommaso was just as good and friendly to me as Cinella, and that is why I think Monna hated me.

"I remember that Tommaso one day gave me a necklace made of red wooden beads. Although it was a trivial present, Monna treated me terribly that day.

"If she did not strike me, she called me names, made fun over my blond hair, called me a French foundling, and so forth.

"Beatings were almost preferable to her slanderous remarks.

"But, still, through that I learned that I was not Cinella's daughter.

"What is the use of telling you all my sufferings? Every day renewed them, and they resembled those of the day before.

"I gradually grew up, and one fine morning Monna said I must earn my own bread now. For that purpose she hung a basket with flowers around my neck, and drove me into the street.

"At night my basket had to be empty, and my pockets filled with copper coins; even if that was the case Monna always complained that I did not bring enough home.

"In this way she achieved her purpose of getting rid of me by day, and whipping me at night.

"Neither Cinella nor Tommaso interfered any more to save me, for they knew that it would only anger Monna still more.

"This continual harsh treatment made me timid, almost silly.

"At that time they began to give me the name of Pippiona, so that my real name of Bianca was almost forgotten.

"One day I was suddenly released from Monna's hands.

"It happened in this way.

"Cinella was a Neapolitan, Tommaso a Corsican.

Both, governed by Monna, pretended to be friends, but at heart they despised each other. Only the Neapolitan was too cowardly to strike first, and Tommaso thought too little of Cinella to take him for a serious enemy.

"Cinella pretended not to notice his contempt, but it increased his rage so much the more.

"One night, while Cinella was absent, and the Corsican, according to custom, wished to visit Monna, he was killed by three dagger thrusts almost under her window.

"The stabs were made by a skilful hand, for Tommaso fell down dead without a murmur.

"I slept in a small, dark room which was separated from Monna's by a piece of boarding.

"Some one came cautiously up the stairs. Monna opened the door a little and asked:

"'Is that you, Tommaso?'

"'No,' replied Cinella's voice, 'it is not your Tommaso. Your Tommaso will not come back. Miserable woman, you have deceived me! You must die too.'

"And the door closed with a bang.

"It did not take long before I heard a gasp. Cinella was, no doubt, holding his hand over the unfortunate woman's mouth to prevent her from crying out. Feet were stamped, furniture overturned, and now and then came a cry for mercy. Oh, it was terrible!

"I would gladly have gotten up and gone to Monna's assistance, but I could not. All my limbs were paralyzed with fear, and I trembled violently.

"At length I heard a last hollow gasp.

"Then all was still."

Pippiona paused a moment to gain breath.

Trembling and silently praying, Madame Lamouroux waited for the continuation of the story.

Suppose Pippiona should turn out to be her daughter!

After a while the little one continued:

"For five minutes all was silent as the grave. I became frightened myself. I could not tell but that Cinella might kill me, too, to hide his double crime.

"A stealthy tread made the old withered boards in the neighboring room creak.

"Cinella had taken off his shoes so as to make as little noise as possible, but fear so increased my sense of hearing that I believe I could have heard a spider weaving its web.

"Half raised up on my miserable couch, I kept my eye continually directed at the door of my room. I thought every moment I should see it open, and the blade of a dagger glitter.

"It was not long before I heard a hand feeling around the boarding.

"I thought all was over now.

"I crawled under my quilt, made myself as small as possible, and pretended to be asleep.

"'Perhaps,' I said to myself, 'perhaps if he sees me asleep, he will think I did not hear or see anything, and will let me live.'

"Cinella soon after entered my room. I did not turn around to see him, but I guessed he had drawn near to me and bent over me, for I felt his hot breath on my cheek.

"Twice he softly called to me.

"'Pippiona! Pippiona!'

"I gave no answer.

"He grasped me by the shoulder.

" 'All is over now,' I said to myself.

"Yet I had courage enough not to make an outcry.

" 'Come, Pippiona,' he continued, 'get up and dress yourself. I committed a crime. We must depart at once.'

"This time he shook me so roughly that I could no longer pretend to be sleeping.

"There was no time then for explanations. Without speaking a word, I got up and hurriedly dressed my-self.

"Cinella, meanwhile, stood at the door, watched the stairs, turned round every minute, and impatiently cried:

" 'Hurry up! Hurry up!'

"Ten minutes later we hurried out of the house, stepping over Tommaso's body on the way.

"It was still pitch-dark, and we had to be far from the city before daylight.

"Cinella knew a good many hiding-places in the suburbs of Naples, and had more than one friend or accomplice. He therefore thought he could easily escape the clutches of the police.

"Besides that, the police were in a certain sense glad to get rid of Tommaso and Monna. They consequently did not trouble themselves to pursue the murderer.

"In this way we reached the Roman frontier without meeting with any obstacle.

"Cinella went on foot, and I rode on the back of a donkey, which he led by the bridle, like an honest peasant going to market.

"Monna was always economical with her money, and Cinella, therefore, found in her pocket a sum of money sufficient to pay our passage, by steamer, to France.

"When we reached Marseilles, Cinella used the rest of his money in buying and fixing up his Punch-and-Judy show.

"He gave performances in the streets and open squares of the city.

"Mistigris, who was small and cunning then, played along and I collected the money.

"Cinella's tricks pleased, people thought me handsome, and we did a good business.

"That was the happiest time of my life.

"Cinella had a fixed idea, though: he wished to go to Paris.

"He did not say why he wished to go there. I guessed, though, that it was on my account.

"Sometimes he looked curiously at me, and muttered between his teeth:

" 'This Pippiona, with her simple face, will perhaps make our fortune yet.'

"As soon as he had saved a little money, he bought an old horse and an old carriage, and we then journeyed through France."

Pippiona was buried in thought a few moments, and then continued again:

"I said before that you had awakened peculiar memories in me for the first time, when you related the story of little Blanche. I was mistaken, for those memories returned to me already when I made that journey with Cinella.

"Was it because Monna used to call me a French foundling? Perhaps; but no matter what the cause was, it seemed to me as if I was at length in my real home, and as the carriage rolled further and further north, I felt happier and more satisfied, as if I had returned from a long exile.

"The scenery which I saw for the first time seemed familiar to me, and often, at the turning of a street, I closed my eyes for a joke to test myself.

"I will try and see whether I still remember this neighborhood. We must find this and that, to the left a forest, to the right a ruin, and in the background of the valley a village surrounded by trees, I said to my-self.

"And, really, we found everything just as I had fore-told—in the background of the valley, the village; to the right, the ruin; and to the left, the forest.

"Twice or thrice I told my companion of my experiments, and he smiled mysteriously.

"Every time he would give his horse a sharp thrust with the whip and exclaim:

"'To Paris! To Paris!'

"Unfortunately we got there only too soon. In Paris we suffered poverty, days without bread, ice-cold nights without fire, the mocking voice of the crowd, and the insulting remarks of the passers-by.

"During the first days, Cinella wandered with feverish activity about the rich quarters of the city, only to come back at night fatigued and downhearted.

"Our savings melted away.

"One night Cinella came home drunk.

"Drink makes people wicked. Cinella gradually came to look upon me as the cause of his deceived hopes, and glared ominously at me.

"I shudderingly thought of Tommaso and Monna.

"He no longer said:

" 'You will make us rich, Pippiona.'

"He had no doubt built big plans upon me, and now that they were impossible to carry out, placed the blame on my shoulders.

"Once he came home sober and in good spirits. He had played that day in the open square in front of the Bourse.

"He tenderly embraced me, and said once more, as he used to formerly:

" 'Really, Pippiona, with your simple face, you will make us rich yet.'

"But the very next day he came home drunker and more downhearted than ever.

"The remainder of Bianca's story you know. But who can tell how the end of it will be?"

Pippiona sank back again in her white bed, closed her eyes, and, in a dreamy voice, said:

"Fables generally end with the coming of the fairy with her crystal staff. The rags disappear then, the miserable hut is transformed into a palace, and the monster into a handsome prince.

"I, for my part, saw little Blanche clasped, at the end of her trials, in her mother's arms, and smiling at her rescuer.

"Unfortunately I was mistaken. The fairy did not come, and will not come."

The voice of the poor little thing died away in a murmur; she stretched out her arms and let her small white hands fall on the silk quilt.

In a short while she was fast asleep.

Madame Lamouroux now drew near and looked lovingly at the pale face of the sleeping child.

She then turned toward Joseph, and, with an impressive gesture, commanded him to follow her.

Pippiona murmured in her sleep:

"The fairy, the good fairy will not come."

Madame Lamouroux, who stood at the threshold of the door, ready to depart, turned around once more, and replied:

"Perhaps she will come!"

CHAPTER XVII

THE SEARCH FOR CINELLA

AS SOON as Madame Lamouroux was alone with Joseph in the adjoining room, she turned toward him and said:

"Is this girl really my daughter? Do you know more about her than she has just told us? You know more, don't you? For if that was not the case, you would not have been so eager to have me take her here."

All these questions followed one another so rapidly that Joseph did not find time to answer them.

"Yes, yes," continued Madame Lamouroux, "I think I understand you. You are afraid the shock will be too great for me. That is why you sought refuge in this pious deception. At first you said: 'I offer you an illusory maternity.' I divined it though—it was a real maternity. Pippiona is my daughter; you know it, you knew it. Oh, Joseph, do not be afraid of my weakness! Have I not proved to you often enough that I am courageous? Speak one word, only one word, which will give me back my daughter."

"Ah!" murmured Joseph.

For a moment he thought of telling her a falsehood,

but he considered it unworthy of himself, and in a firm voice said:

"I know no more than you do. The resemblance between your daughter's fate and Pippiona's struck me some time ago, but I considered it accidental. To-day, however, I begin to believe in the hand of Providence."

"She is my daughter, is she not?" cried Madame Lamouroux, clinging desperately to that faint hope. "Oh, Joseph, how handsome she is! I looked at her just now while she was sleeping. She resembles George. You doubt, but a mother never doubts. I tell you it is Blanche; Blanche, whom the good Lord finally gives back to me again. Tell me, Joseph, tell me it is she!"

"I hope so," replied Joseph, "but no one can say anything positive about it but Matifay, and perhaps Cinella. Matifay won't say anything, and Cinella probably knows no more than what Pippiona told us."

Madame Lamouroux no longer listened, but hurriedly put on a brown cloak.

"What are you going to do?" asked Joseph in surprise.

"I am going to hunt up Cinella. I will ask him to tell me everything he knows, and he must answer me."

"Do you want to hunt him up at this hour?" asked Joseph.

"What has the time to do with it? I must see him at once. Another night of doubt would make me crazy."

"Well, then, let us go," said Joseph.

With these words he threw a cloak about himself, and offered his arm to Madame Lamouroux.

It was about ten o'clock at night.

A dense crowd of people still walked up and down the brilliantly lighted boulevards.

Joseph pointed to the mass of beings, and said to Madame Lamouroux:

"How are we to find any one in this crowd?"

"Let us look!" replied Madame Lamouroux, briefly.

"Then," replied Joseph, submissively, "nothing remains for us but to make a tour of the groggeries, and that will take rather long."

"That doesn't matter," said Madame Lamouroux, impatiently shrugging her shoulders, "so long as we find him."

"Let us then begin," replied Joseph, "with the café of the Blue Sash."

The café was almost empty. No one was there except Monsieur Gosse, who was just mixing himself a glass of rum.

Joseph asked a waiter. The latter said he was well acquainted with Cinella, but had not seen him in three weeks.

Joseph became thoughtful. The time was exactly as long ago as the abduction of Ursula and Pippiona.

While Joseph was speaking with the waiter, Madame Lamouroux waited in the doorway.

"Who knows," said Joseph when he had returned to her and told her of the failure of the first step—"who knows whether we shall gain anything in this way? You ought to allow me to go alone."

The poor mother resolved, however, to take part in whatever steps were taken to find her daughter, and looked so imploringly at Joseph that he was forced to immediately add:

"Well, come along, then, if you desire it; but permit me to make a few necessary preparations for this expedition, which will not be without danger in your company."

Madame Lamouroux murmured:

"Do what you think best, Joseph; only find Cinella."

This conversation had been carried on in a low voice on the street.

Joseph stepped up to a street lamp, tore a piece of paper out of his note-book, and wrote in the flickering gleam of the gas-lamp the following lines:

"This evening in half an hour, Rue Rambuteau. You as coachman with a hack, Louis in his jumper, such as he formerly wore. In haste.   JOSEPH."

This laconic note was addressed to Monsieur Clement, jeweller, Boulevard des Capucines.

It would reach the workshop before Louis Jacquemin, who had become Clement's foreman, had gone home.

The bell in the church of St. Eustache struck a quarter of eleven.

Joseph walked up to a porter, gave him the note and put him in a hack, so that he could deliver it as soon as possible.

He then took Madame Lamouroux's arm, and said:

"Let us go."

She obeyed without asking him where he was bringing her to.

Joseph turned into the Rue Rambuteau, opened a door, and entered the house which had the honor of having Monsieur and Madame Gosse as tenants.

The windows of the worthy couple were lighted up, and Bebelle was no doubt sipping a glass of Vespetro, while her monster of a husband was burning his throat, far from her, with his hot, strong rum.

Joseph hurriedly ascended the stairs.

Madame Lamouroux followed him.

When Joseph reached the last flight, he stood still in the corridor.

"It appears," he said, "that luck is in our favor and we have found our man already."

The noise of some one snoring in Cinella's room was distinctly heard.

Joseph knocked at the door.

A grunt was heard and then a voice asked:

"Who is there?"

"Can I speak to Signor Cinella?" asked Joseph, politely.

"Cinella? Doesn't live here," replied the voice, gruffly. "Go to the devil and leave me in peace."

Cinella did not live there at all, any more.

Joseph, after receiving the above categoric answer, opened the door of his own attic, lighted the lamp and bade Madame Lamouroux step in.

"You are still determined then, Helene?" he asked, for the last time.

Helene nodded assent.

"Well, then, to work!"

With these words, Joseph raised the lid of a big box which stood at the head of his bed.

This box was a perfect wardrobe of costumes.

CHAPTER XVIII

A NIGHT EXPEDITION

JOSEPH took from the box the different articles of clothing Madame Lamouroux needed to transform herself into a woman of the lowest class.

A torn dress, a cloak full of holes, shoes worn down at the heels—nothing was missing, not even the dirt which stuck to the edge of the dress.

He spread these rags out on a chair and said:

"Put these on!"

He then went into the corridor.

Without saying a word, Madame Lamouroux obeyed.

When she had finished, she knocked at the door and waited outside in her turn, until Joseph had finished with *his* toilet.

The latter consisted of a jumper stained with paint, dirty linen trousers, and an orange-yellow cap.

When he had finished he called Madame Lamouroux inside and said:

"We must wait now."

He made use of the time they had to wait by gathering up a handful of dust and sprinkling the linen of his companion with it.

He then marked with a piece of coal those large black circles under her and his own eyes, which are the distinguishing traits of an irregular and dissipated life.

After this last precaution was finished, the transformation was complete, and a person on looking at them would have taken them for one of those unmentionable couples who wander about the suburbs at night.

The man, still young, but marked by premature vice; the woman, somewhat older and still showing traces of former beauty, but dirty and the more repulsive, since one could immediately see that she had once been a beauty.

They silently observed one another and did not recognize each other.

They did not have to wait much longer.

A step was heard on the stairs, and Louis Jacquemin entered—a worthy comrade of the couple just described.

He looked now like the old Louis Jacquemin, before his moral regeneration.

"Clement is downstairs," he announced; "he dressed himself the way you desired."

"Good!" said Joseph, as he arose.

Jacquemin now noticed for the first time that Madame Lamouroux was present, and could not restrain a gesture of surprise.

"We must discover Cinella," added Joseph, "this very night."

"In that case," replied Louis, "we need only go to the Golden Drop. He generally hangs out there."

"Let us go, then, to the Golden Drop."

And all three of them went downstairs.

A hack, with Clement on the box, stood at the door.

Joseph and Madame Lamouroux got in, and Louis seated himself next to the coachman.

Then the hack rolled off at a brisk trot.

It stopped at the furthest end of the Rue du Faubourg Saint-Martin. Jacquemin jumped down from the box and opened the door.

"Get out here," he said. "Clement will follow us with the hack, so as to be at hand if necessary. We can go the rest of the way on foot."

And arm in arm they walked on, Madame Lamouroux between Joseph and Jacquemin, who gave them instructions on the way.

"You will call yourself 'Lachiffe,' madame," he said. "You are not without means, and are ready to give people a chance, now and then, to make something. Joseph is a house-painter. People of that sort like to drink, and he must imbibe freely. He is my friend August, from Angoulême. He must have people believe he made his studies in a reformatory. That makes a good impression. My own name is well known; I am proud of it, and do not need to find another. You, my friends, must know it. In the agreeable society of which I was once a member I am called Louiset. We must pretend to be slightly intoxicated."

While Jacquemin-Louiset gave these precise instructions, he gave illustrations to make them better understood.

In this way they reached La Villette, at the entrance to the Rue de Flandre.

"We shall soon be there," said Jacquemin; "the performance begins."

The three walked arm in arm again, and taking up the whole width of the sidewalk, staggered along, while

Louis Jacquemin, or, rather, Louiset, as he was now called, commenced to sing a merry drinking-song, in the chorus of which the others joined.

At the corner of a dark, unpaved and dirty lane our three friends almost fell against two men who stood conversing in low tones.

As soon as the three approached, the two men quickly drew away, but when Louis, Helene, and Joseph had passed by, they returned to the spot where they originally stood.

"They were drunk," said one of them. "You are sure, then, that he will come?"

"Yes, I am sure of it."

"And that he will go there?"

"Yes; since the day of his marriage he goes there every night."

"A funny place for a millionnaire."

"Yes, it is an incomprehensible caprice of his."

"Which, if I cared to, I could explain," thought Legigant, for he was the first speaker.

The second was Colonel Fritz.

"And," said Legigant, "your man will not consider long?"

"He hasn't a cent in his pocket, and likes to get drunk. Besides, Italians have an easy conscience, and this one is an expert at handling a knife."

"Hush! Here he comes."

A third shadow drew near; Fritz went toward it, and immediately came back to Legigant.

"It is he," he said.

"Good," replied Legigant. "Monsieur Matifay will have a bad time of it to-night."

He was satisfied with himself. The means Aurelie had proposed to get rid of the banker appeared good to him, though a little slow.

Every person possesses a certain amount of self-love, and he wished to prove to his friend by a master-stroke that he could do something without her assistance.

But what peculiar whim of Matifay's induced him to become drunk every night in the Golden Drop, like a common ragpicker?

What difference did it make? The fact existed, and it was a question of taking advantage of it.

The third person drew near, staggering slowly along.

It was Cinella.

CHAPTER XIX

"IN THE GOLDEN DROP"

THIS tavern was of a different kind from that of the café of the Blue Sash.

The red lantern of the disreputable tavern of the Golden Drop sparkled like the eye of a Cyclops at the back of a dark, dirty lane. The tavern consisted of a single large room, with a low ceiling, and smoky wooden pillars.

The tables and benches were made of wood, and were fastened to the walls. Wine was drunk here from cans, which were also attached to an iron chain.

Wine and absinthe were the drinks principally called for there.

At the back of the room was an iron railing, behind which was the bar.

A strong, muscular young man, who looked like a butcher, promenaded up and down the room.

This was the waiter, who received his pay in advance for the drinks he brought, and immediately carried the money to the cash-window, for he was never allowed to carry more than ten sous in his pocket for change.

It often happened that he had no need of these ten sous throughout the whole evening.

The guests of the Golden Drop had only small purses, but they paid well—namely, in advance.

It was a much-mixed crowd that assembled in this tavern.

At present only the lowest class of vagabonds and thieves visited the place, but a few old customers proudly recalled the time when celebrated characters used to congregate there, and new-comers were shown the tin can out of which Lacenaire was accustomed to drink.

There were honest people there, too—ragpickers and street-sweepers, who came there during their nightly rounds to drink a glass; and confirmed drunkards, who there gulped down the concentrated poison which killed quicker than at any other place.

The latter had a table to themselves, and they were called "the animals."

Much noise was not made at that table. They drank without speaking, until they fell under the table.

At this table Louis Jacquemin used to sit when he went by the name of Louiset.

Jacquemin's place, which had remained empty a long time, had found a new occupant a few days since, who, although he did not drink as much as his predecessor, was, nevertheless, a good customer.

This new guest was known under the name of "the Marquis." Marquis of ——? No one knew what, but it did not make any difference, as he was given that title only on account of his aristocratic clothing.

Luxury is something relative, and the marquis really looked like an old schoolmaster who had been unfortunate.

He continually wore a shabby broadcloth coat, a high hat, blue spectacles, and a black wig.

He came every night at half-past eleven, took his seat without speaking to any one, swallowed his glass in five draughts, which took him till half-past twelve, paid—unheard-of luxury!—in ten-sou pieces and went away, only staggering a little more than when he had come.

As, in spite of his ironical marquis' title, his whole costume was not worth over three francs, no one had yet tried to pick a quarrel with him.

This mysterious man, who drank his regular quantity of brandy at this table every night, naturally excited the curiosity of his companions.

It was now about eleven o'clock, and the marquis was consequently not there yet, when Jacquemin, Helene, and Joseph entered. The former was greeted on all sides with cries of joy.

"Good heavens! Here comes Louiset!"

"Where have you been keeping yourself?"

"You have been taking a vacation, no doubt?"

"Or been sent up for a few months?"

"Your place here has been taken."

"It is winter now, and whoever leaves his place loses it."

"The stuff is good everywhere," replied Louis, with dignity, "and, besides, I must remain with my company."

"Ah! he remains with his company."

"Who are the big boys he brings along with him?"

"Why did you not rather go to the Café Anglais with them?"

"Or to Tortoni's?"

In the meanwhile all eyes were turned upon Helene and Joseph.

"Show your face, Lachiffe," said Jacquemin. "They are looking at you."

"Confound it, Louiset, she's a beauty."

"She's a wealthy widow," said Louis, confidentially to a neighbor. "She's in love with my friend, who has got the stamps, too."

"Can we get anything to drink here or not?" asked Joseph.

All three of them played their parts to perfection. Helene, when she first entered the place, felt a cold shudder run down her back. This *rôle* was the only one of its kind that she had played in the course of her self-sacrificing mission.

Until now, Joseph and Clement had undertaken the work in the social abyss in her name.

But similar to those physicians who touch the most repulsive sores with a sure and firm hand, she, too, could observe this horrible moral misery without flinching.

The coarse language did not even reach her ear, and she felt in her heart nothing but sadness and pity.

There were women there too—yes, real women with all the coquetry, all the faults, and all the virtues of their sex—women in whose hearts would have been found the same desires, and perhaps, also, the same love, as in those of their more fortunate sisters.

Never had the Countess of Monte-Cristo felt the necessity and sublimity of her mission more than now.

The waiter brought the drinks ordered.

At the same moment a loud tumult arose, all eyes were turned toward the door, and ten voices simultaneously exclaimed:

"The marquis! The marquis!"

CHAPTER XX

"JUMP, MARQUIS, JUMP!"

THE marquis went as usual, without looking to the right or left, straight to his place.

He was already drunk. His knees cracked under the weight of his body, his pale face was covered with perspiration, but his mind was clear, and he knew everything.

He seated himself on the usual bench, took off his hat, placed his elbows on the table and his forehead upon his hand.

Though his blue spectacles and his wig almost made him unrecognizable, Joseph and Helene knew him at once.

The marquis did not have to order his drink; they already knew what he wanted. When he took his hand away from his forehead, he saw the bottle and glass standing in front of him.

He filled the latter, made a face as if he were going to take medicine, and then swallowed the poison at one gulp.

"Well done, marquis!" cried a voice in a tone of praise.

The marquis did not pay any attention to the sarcastic remark, but placed his chin in the palm of his hand. He had his face turned toward the counter, so that he could not see Helene, Joseph, and Louis Jacquemin, who sat at a table behind him.

"Yes, yes," cried another drinker, "let us rest a little, old boy. If we drink without having any thirst, we will ruin our stomachs."

"He digests," observed a shouter of a travelling menagerie. "There are other animals like him. The boa-constrictor takes three hours to digest a living squirrel, and this old man can therefore take five minutes to digest a glass of rotgut."

"That may be done, but he does not do honor to his place."

"Louiset certainly drank more."

"He swallowed the whole bottle at one gulp."

In the midst of this noise Cinella had entered unperceived, and had seated himself in the darkest corner of the room.

He was drunk, too, and very disagreeably so. He muttered indistinct words between his teeth, and repeatedly exclaimed:

"The marquis is rich—rich—rich!"

The marquis, meanwhile, mechanically seized the bottle and filled his glass a second time.

"This old fogy is as regular as a clock," remarked the drinker who had spoken once before. "He records the hour every time he drinks."

"What a pity we cannot hang him to the wall!"

"He is drinking the second glass. It is always quarter of twelve."

Helene leaned over toward Jacquemin and softly whispered some words in his ear.

"That would be wicked," he replied; "but we can try it."

The marquis had emptied the second glass like the first, and then resumed his meditative position.

Louis Jacquemin arose and approached him from behind.

"Hush! Hush!" whispered several others. "Louiset will tease the marquis a little."

"Then the latter will have to open his mouth for once."

Jacquemin laid his hand on the shoulder of the marquis, who trembled, but did not turn around.

"Well, old boy, do you never treat?" said Louis, playing off drunk.

No answer followed.

"That isn't polite, though," continued Louis; "if you take a person's place away, it's no more than right to treat him."

This time the marquis wished to answer, but could not. Fear, as well as the brandy, strangled him, and his contracted throat could only give vent to a hoarse grunting.

The whole crowd broke into loud laughter.

"My seal speaks better than that," remarked the menagerie shouter.

"If he doesn't treat," continued Jacquemin, turning to the crowd, "he can give me my place back again."

"Yes, yes!" cried twenty voices together, "he must treat the whole crowd, or else give up the seat. Treat or vacate! Treat or vacate!"

The noise became louder and louder.

The marquis felt the perspiration dripping from under his wig.

Opposite to him, on the other side of the table, was an empty seat.

"Since you won't treat," said Louis, "I will. You must give me back my seat. Sit over there, and then we can take a drink together."

The marquis got up and staggered helplessly about.

The end of the bench was occupied by drinkers half paralyzed with rum, and others lay heaped on the ground, blocking the way. The marquis looked about in a dazed way, trying to find a means of reaching the seat pointed out.

"The thing isn't as difficult as you think," cried Jacquemin, bursting into a coarse laugh. "You are a marquis, are you not? Well, then, jump, marquis!"

And with a gesture he signified to the old man that he should jump over the table.

Everybody began to laugh, and some cried out:

"That Louiset is a funny fellow! He brings life into the place."

Cinella was the only one who did not laugh. He still sat in his corner, and muttered to himself:

"The marquis is rich! Rich! Rich!"

"Jump, marquis, jump!" cried the crowd.

"Look how he staggers!"

"He will jump!"

"No, he won't jump."

The marquis thought himself lost. The cries and laughter almost deafened him.

He made an effort, and climbed upon the bench.

"Jump, marquis!"

"Turn about. He should turn around!"

Pale with fear, he turned around.

At this moment the clock, which hung behind the counter, struck the midnight hour.

The marquis immediately became, if possible, still paler. His spectacles fell, he did not himself know how, from his nose; perhaps Jacquemin had torn them down—and with fixed, wide-open eyes, and stretching his hands in front of him, he sank upon the table and muttered:

"There she is again! I see her here, too!"

Helene had raised herself to her full height, and had advanced toward the marquis.

The latter, who felt that she was always coming nearer, suddenly jumped down from the table and hurried toward the door.

But the way was blocked! What a pity the tables were fastened to the wall.

"Jump, marquis!" was cried again.

It was a grotesque and repulsive spectacle.

With a wild look in his face, and bathed in perspiration, the old man jumped over one table after the other, without being able to escape.

The menagerie shouter had picked up a broom and held it in front of the marquis, like in front of a poodle.

"Jump, marquis, jump!"

At length the unhappy man reached the door, and, half-crazed with fear, he dashed out into the dark street.

A laughing crowd ran after him, and he was far away when he still heard the cry:

"Jump, marquis, jump!"

Joseph, Louis, and Helene were among this crowd.

Cinella, too, staggered heavily along the dirty street, continually repeating to himself:

"The marquis is rich, rich, rich!"

Joseph, Helene, and Louis Jacquemin followed the marquis, in whom our readers will long since have recognized Baron Matifay. As soon as the red lantern of the Golden Drop was out of sight, they stood still on a street corner.

They did not care about Matifay; they only wanted to find Cinella.

He had left the tavern the same time they did, and, therefore, could not be far.

"Follow me," said Louis; "either I am much mistaken or else we shall get him before ten minutes have passed."

"And the hack?" asked Joseph.

"Clement has his instructions, and I know where we can find him again."

"Well, then, go on in advance!"

Louis did as requested, through all the dirty alleys and streets.

The road was not a comfortable one, but had the advantage of being the shortest.

Two or three times Louis paused to listen, and each time the night wanderers distinctly heard the noise of a footstep staggering about the gutters and the mud.

"That must be he!" said Jacquemin each time. "The wretch looked wickedly at the marquis when the latter left the Golden Drop. His knife was sticking in the pocket of his coat."

In this way they reached the furthest end of the narrow

street, at the corner of which Colonel Fritz and Legigant had conversed several hours before.

Louis ordered his two companions to stand still.

"Not a step further, and not a word more. Look down there at the turn of the street!"

It was very dark, yet Helene and Joseph saw the shadow of a man leaning close to a wall.

"That is Cinella!" whispered Jacquemin. "We must be careful now and not make a noise. I will fetch Clement, and will be back again in five minutes."

And with quick, cautious steps he disappeared in the darkness.

Baron Matifay, who knew nothing of the locality, had in the meantime chosen the longest road.

"Ah!" he murmured, as he staggered along the sidewalk, "always that vision! always she! During the first few days drink banished her; but now she comes back in spite of drink."

Cinella crouched in his corner, and when he heard the marquis's footsteps coming nearer and nearer, he thought with grim joy:

"It is he! It is he! People say he is rich, rich, rich!"

The baron was hardly ten steps away from this invisible enemy, and still repeated to himself:

"Ah, the vision! That terrible vision!"

Cinella had already placed his knife in position, prepared to rush upon the marquis.

At the same moment, however, the noise of carriage-wheels was heard in the silent street.

Cinella hesitated, and that hesitation was Matifay's salvation.

The baron went past Cinella's drawn knife without

seeing it, and staggeringly continued on his way, murmuring incessantly:

"The vision! The vision!"

Cinella was about to rush after him, when a firm hand clutched him by the neck and forced him to let go of the knife, which fell in the mud.

At the same time, two strong arms seized him around the waist and a third person put a gag in his mouth.

The hack, which had in the meanwhile advanced to within ten steps, stood still. Cinella was dragged in, a man and a woman took seats opposite to him, and the carriage drove off.

On the corner of the Rue de Flandre a second carriage, an elegant coupé, stood.

To this one the baron staggered

A lackey advanced toward him, seized him under the arm, and assisted him to get in the coach.

Hardly had Matifay seated himself in the hack than he sank into a corner and fell into a deep sleep.

The lackey climbed upon the box next to the coachman.

"Drive home, my dear Dorn," he said; "we can take the road through the rear gate."

"All right, my dear Rose," replied Dorn; "I think if these rides continue in this way we will soon know the road."

They both burst out laughing.

The coachman bent down and looked through the front window of the coupé.

"I think our master has had enough to-day, don't you think so, Rose?"

"Yes. He has been doing this since his wedding."

"A curious marriage."

And coachman and footman laughed again.

"Do you know what Miss Betty told me?"

"The English maid of the baroness?"

"Yes."

"Well, what did she say?"

The servant drew near to the coachman and murmured a few mysterious words in his ear.

"You don't say so!" exclaimed Dorn the coachman.

"It is just as I tell you," assured Rose the servant.

And then they both burst into loud laughter, which made the windows of the carriage rattle.

They knew that the baron would not awake from it.

Three days after his marriage, Matifay had begun the peculiar course of life which he had since then kept up.

Immediately after dinner he left the house like a schoolboy who has come into possession of the night key, and had himself driven to the lowest quarters of the city.

These rides always ended with the one to La Villette, and from this last station he generally came home heavily intoxicated.

Rose then carried him to his room, undressed him and put him to bed.

Rose conducted his delicate functions with great tact, and the baron next morning never found a cent in his pockets.

While Rose and Dorn conversed together on the box seat, their master snored in the interior of the coach.

The events of the night were far from his mind.

Every spark of intelligence or feeling was drowned by the quantity of alcohol he had drunk.

But after a few hours, the vision, which continually pursued him, came back to him, and followed him throughout the day to his office, to the Bourse, everywhere. At the dinner table, this vision seated itself opposite to him, and continually repeated to him:

"Here I am again! You must not forget me!"

CHAPTER XXI

DORN AND ROSE

DORN and Rose were fast friends, and their common knowledge of their master's secrets only tended to increase their friendship.

Together with Miss Betty, the English maid, they formed the aristocracy of the servants' room.

Baron Matifay's house was full of secrets, and the services which these three rendered to the banker and his young wife gave them a chance to find out some of these secrets.

Yet they knew no more than that the baron went out at night, and what Miss Betty had a chance to observe.

The chaste, prudish Englishwoman told these things only after much blushing and simpering.

As impatient and excited as the baron showed himself before his marriage, he was just as indifferent and cold since the wedding-night, when he had been found lying unconscious in front of Cyprienne's door.

He was not only indifferent to Cyprienne, but actually showed a repugnance to her.

He always refused to be alone with her, and in the presence of another only spoke as much with her as was necessary to conceal their mutual position from outsiders.

All this was extraordinary enough to arouse the curiosity of Dorn and Rose and the prudish Englishwoman; for all three suspected that their fortunes depended on a knowledge of this mystery.

For that reason they spied and overheard continually, for that reason they related to each other every morning their observations, and tried to solve the problem which bothered them.

On the morning following the night on which we have seen Matifay miraculously escape the murderous hand of Cinella, his bell rang loud and furiously at eight o'clock.

Rose, Dorn and Miss Betty were holding a conference together, and the former hastened to answer the baron's call.

"Perhaps we shall learn something new," said Dorn.

Matifay sat upright in his bed when his servant entered, his distorted features bearing witness to the horrible dreams with which his sleep had been troubled.

"Go and get Dr. Ozam at once," he said; "go quickly, take a carriage, and, if possible, bring the doctor along with you."

As soon as the servant had gone to carry out this order the baron lay down in bed again.

For the last three weeks it had been his purpose every morning to send for Dr. Ozam, but until now he had never done so.

The confidential information he had to give him was of a very delicate nature, and physicians are sometimes too curious.

They ask an explanation of the most trivial circumstance, and have a perfect mania for going to the bottom of things.

Matifay feared he would say too much.

So long as he could he had kept his terrible secret to himself. To-day, however, the struggle was too horrible, and when he thought of the fear which every night had in store for him, he felt his hair stand on end.

The poor fool! He had thought that if he married Cyprienne the terrors of his conscience would be banished from his couch, but instead of that being the case the marriage had only doubled those terrors.

Yes, only since that marriage, since the wedding-night, these terrors, so to speak, had become personified; for on the threshold of the bridal chamber the avenging spectre of Helene de Rancogne met him and barred the way.

And since then that terrible vision had risen before him every night at the same hour.

He had tried to escape from it by drinking heavily, and for a few nights he had succeeded. He already thought himself saved, and now the threatening spectre had followed him to the noisy tavern of the Golden Drop.

Intoxication, therefore, was also a failure, and something else had to be thought of.

Matifay was a sceptic.

He did not believe in the revenge of the dead, who get out of their graves to follow their murderers.

The vision which pursued him was—so he thought—nothing else but a chimera, a phantasmagoria of a disordered brain.

The obstinacy and regularity with which this vision continually reappeared made him uneasy. He placed both his hands to his head and asked himself:

"Am I losing my senses?"

The fear of becoming insane is almost always the commencement of insanity.

To secure peace once for all, he had therefore sent for Dr. Ozam.

Insanity!

The baron shudderingly murmured this word. Insanity was worse than death, for it was equivalent to ruin and shame.

A day could then come when he would let the mask fall, and loudly proclaim his own crime.

This dishonorable man—strange anomaly—thought more of his honor than of his life. He wished to remain the great citizen and the upright man.

And while he felt his secret every moment springing to his tongue, he made superhuman efforts to keep it down.

Half an hour after Rose had gone, he returned in company with the doctor.

When Matifay heard him announced, he began to hesitate once more, and had almost made up his mind to send him away again.

He collected his whole courage, however, and ordered the doctor to be sent in.

"I need only tell him what I want to," he thought, "and can break off my confidential recital as soon as I feel that it might compromise me."

Dr. Ozam entered, and the valet listened outside at the keyhole.

The physician approached the bed and felt Matifay's pulse.

The baron drew back his hand.

"I am not sick, doctor," he said.

The doctor looked at him in surprise.

"I have something which continually goes round my head," continued Matifay, "and I desire your advice about it."

"I only give physician's consultations," replied Ozam curtly.

"What I need is a physician's consultation," said Matifay.

"Then," continued the doctor, as he drew a chair to the bed and seated himself in it, "have the kindness to tell me what ails you. I am listening."

Matifay kept silent.

The moment had come. He felt the need of considering how he should express himself.

The physician waited.

"Well?" he asked at length.

"Well," replied Matifay, "I have been bothered a great deal lately by a peculiar idea. The physician of the body is, in a certain sense, if he possesses your talent, the physician of the soul, and that is why, although I am physically healthy, I sent for you."

The doctor nodded assent, but said nothing.

"Doctor," asked the banker resolutely, "in what way does a person become insane?"

CHAPTER XXII

A DOUBLE CONSULTATION

THE baron's question was a curious one, and the doctor was somewhat taken by surprise.

"A person can become insane in a great many ways," he replied. "To answer your question correctly, I must first know what form of insanity you mean."

"I mean," continued Matifay in a faint voice, "if a person has visions—or rather a vision, a single one which is always the same."

"Ah, indeed!" said the doctor, thoughtfully. "This vision appears, no doubt, at very regular intervals?"

"Yes, always at the same hour," said Matifay—"at midnight."

"Since a long time?"

"Since three weeks."

"And—excuse me for asking the question—is this vision a purely fantastical one, of the kind of which Sir Walter Scott speaks in his 'Demonology,' or has it anything to do with an event in the past life of the invalid in whose behalf you ask my advice?"

Matifay kept silent.

This was one of the questions he had determined not to answer.

Ozam arose and grasped his hat and cane.

"What are you doing there, doctor?" asked the banker.

"As soon as you conceal something from me, my advice is of no value, and I cannot do anything for your invalid."

"Oh, please stay! Ask what you will, I will answer all your questions."

Dr. Ozam took his seat again with the same unconquerable serenity.

"Just as you say," he said. "What form does the vision generally assume?"

"Always the same—that of a veiled woman in mourning."

"Is it an imaginary person, or one whom the invalid knew before?"

"A person he knew before—a person who has been dead many years."

"And does this phantom speak to him?"

"No. The woman goes past him veiled, then stands still, throws her veil back, and slowly vanishes."

"Has he ever attempted to address her?"

"No, he never tried."

"Or has he approached her—touched her—to convince himself of his delusion?"

"No, never."

"That is merely a delusion of the mind," said the doctor, as if speaking to himself; "but as the invalid has not *heard* anything yet, we may be able to cure him."

"Really, doctor? Really?" exclaimed Matifay, eagerly. "Oh, Dr. Ozam, you are one of the princes of science, a man of genius. I have great confidence in you. Do not leave me! Save me!"

"Then *you* are the invalid!" said the doctor, who became more and more thoughtful.

Matifay painfully nodded with his head.

"Affections of the brain," said the doctor, "are of such a delicate nature, that a physician must go cautiously to work. Have you ever loved the person who appears to you in such a peculiar way?"

Matifay hesitated. He was almost ready to tell a lie; he replied in a faint voice:

"No."

"Did the vision before assuming such a definite form announce itself by any preliminary symptoms? Have you not, perhaps, thought of this person? Have you not sometimes dreamed of her?"

"Yes," said Matifay. "I experienced everything just as you say it."

"One word more. Did the vision appear to you in a doze or when awake?"

"While awake! While awake!" exclaimed the banker, excitedly. "Oh, I was fully awake, I can tell you. I know positively that I did not dream on that night or the other. The first time the vision appeared to me was on my wedding day."

"The time we came up and found you lying in the corridor?"

"Yes, I saw her then for the first time," replied Matifay. "Since then I have seen her every night."

Dr. Ozam drew his chair to the table and wrote a prescription.

"The principal thing," he said, as he went on writing,

"is to think as little as possible during the day of this vision. Have this prescription made up. It will cause you to have the dreamless sleep you need. The dose is so proportioned that you will not wake up until eleven o'clock to-night. You can have your dinner sent to your private room, and I will invite myself to it. We can await the vision together."

Matifay would gladly have seized the doctor's hand and kissed it, but the latter hastily withdrew it, and not without a certain degree of repugnance.

There are instincts which do not deceive, and Dr. Ozam had never learned to respect or like "the richest and most upright man in France."

And while he went down the stairs, with his prescription in his hand, he murmured to himself:

"Behind this insanity a crime is concealed."

In the reception-room he met Rose, the valet, who had just had time to leave his post of observation at the key-hole, when he heard the doctor coming down.

The prescription was given to him, with the hint that the baron was not visible to any one throughout the day.

As it was still early in the day the doctor concluded to go to Madame Lamouroux's house, though he generally went there in the afternoon.

The confidential recital which Matifay had made to him weighed upon him, and it appeared to him as if the banker perspired crimes and strokes of conscience at every pore.

The physician had to refresh his spirits by spending a few moments at Pippiona's beside.

Unfortunately the condition of the little one was very bad, and the doctor despaired of saving her.

As the physician entered the room of his dear little patient, she was smilingly sitting upright in the midst of pillows, which supported her from all sides.

At both sides of the bed sat Joseph and Madame Lamouroux.

Joseph appeared to be in good humor.

Madame Lamouroux, on the other hand, was grave and thoughtful.

Dr. Ozam softly approached the group the three formed, felt Pippiona's emaciated arm, and said:

"Really, humanity has worked the miracle which medicine has in vain tried to accomplish. I will make you a professional nurse, Madame Lamouroux, for thanks to you Pippiona is saved."

CHAPTER XXIII

CINELLA'S CONFESSION

WE WILL go back a few hours in our story, and take it up at the moment where Baron Matifay was rescued through the intervention of Joseph, Jacquemin and Helene.

Bound hand and foot, and gagged, before he could make the slightest movement, Cinella was thrown into the hack, like a package.

He was too drunk to know anything.

Who his assailants were he knew not.

But after the fumes of the brandy had been dissipated, he began thinking of his condition.

His first feeling was one of fright when he thought of the crime he had been about to commit, before his victim was rescued.

Cinella's conscience was not a delicate one, as the story of Tommaso and Monna showed. But up till now he had only murdered through jealousy, while to-night he had been about to murder for the purpose of robbery.

From that blood and that money, at least, his hands were clean.

But, nevertheless, that did not improve his position.

His assailants belonged, no doubt, to the police department; for who but the police could have an interest in capturing a tramp like Cinella?

This supposition was the most natural, and consequently the best.

The hack rolled briskly through the Rue du Faubourg Saint-Martin, and then turned into the boulevards.

This circumstance appeared strange to Cinella.

According to his opinion, they ought to have driven through the whole of the Rue Saint-Martin to get to the central office.

It was now about two o'clock in the morning, and only a few foot passengers were seen in the street.

The carriage still followed the line of the boulevards, without paying any attention to any side streets.

Cinella could neither move nor speak, only see.

Softly and without being observed, be crawled as near as possible to the carriage window and looked at the road they were taking.

"Oh," he said to himself, after a while, "these are not police officers. I must be cautious and watch."

What could they want of him?

"We shall see," he softly said to himself.

The new conviction which formed itself in this way within him almost filled him with joy.

If so much pains had been taken to get hold of him, it was done, so he thought, because his assistance was needed, and he resolved to make as much out of it as possible.

The Italians are shrewd, and we see that Cinella almost divined the truth.

He studied his probable *rôle*, he sketched his plan like a dramatic author.

Either his abductors were enemies or friends of Pippiona. Either they had an interest in having her disappear entirely, as they tried to before in Naples, and then they would certainly buy Cinella's silence; or they had, on the contrary, the desire to acquire a positive knowledge about her personality, and then they would have to buy his testimony.

In either case there was profit for him.

The carriage had turned the corner of the boulevard and the Rue Vivienne. It stopped opposite Madame Rozel's store.

Neither Joseph nor Helene had spoken a single word during the whole ride.

The carriage door opened, and Louis Jacquemin and Clement were seen.

Helene immediately sprung out and felt around the outside of the store for the door.

The street was entirely empty; only from the Place de la Bourse could be heard the hasty steps of a belated pedestrian.

Joseph proceeded to pay Clement for the ride, and they waited until the pedestrian had turned the corner of the Boulevard Montmartre.

Then Joseph and Louis seized Cinella and carried him into the dark store, while Clement watched outside.

They then brought him up the stairs built for Madame Lamouroux, and placed him in the same room where Pippiona, only separated from him by a thin partition, lay peacefully sleeping.

The door of the store had closed again, and intense darkness reigned in the whole house.

"Now," said Cinella to himself, as he felt himself carried, like a child, in the arms of two men, "now I must keep my ears open."

We have already remarked that in the darkness of the carriage Cinella had been unable to see the features of his abductors.

At present it was far more difficult still.

The room into which he had been brought was entirely dark. He had been thrown like an inert mass on a divan, and he no longer even heard footsteps, which were deadened by the heavy carpet.

A match was rubbed against the wall and threw a faint gleam on the neighboring objects.

The gleam, which only lasted a second, was used by Cinella to take a rapid survey about him.

He saw himself in a large room with dark-colored furniture. At the background was an alcove in which stood a covered bed.

Everything was so simple, yet withal so magnificent, that Cinella had never seen anything like it.

This luxury fortified his suspicions.

He also had time—how many things one can see at a single glance—to see two persons standing in front of the divan on which he lay.

It was the man and the woman who had been sitting with him in the carriage.

Jacquemin was the one who had lighted the match and touched it to a candle.

The latter illuminated the night like a star. Cinella, however, did not make use of the circumstance to continue his observations.

His plan began now.

Above all, he had to collect his thoughts, and thoroughly prepare himself for the *rôle* on which his happiness, perhaps, depended.

His brain was not clear enough to risk a trial. He therefore pretended to be still drunk, and closed his eyes as if he were fast asleep.

His chains and a gag were taken off him, and if he did not see anything, he heard everything.

Clement had brought his hack to a place of safety, and gone back to Louis.

He helped him to free Cinella of his chains, while Helene and Joseph withdrew to a corner of the room, where they conversed in low tones.

Cinella listened attentively, hoping to catch a loud word, which would give him further information, and point out the course he had to follow.

Joseph and Helene spoke so softly, though, that their voices only reached his ear in an indistinct murmur. He only imagined he heard a name continually pronounced in their conversation—the name of Pippiona.

At length the conference seemed to be at an end, for Joseph said aloud:

"We will not be able to find out anything from this scoundrel to-night."

"Let us at least try," replied Helene.

Immediately afterward they approached the divan.

Joseph seized Cinella by the shoulder, and shook him roughly.

"Say, friend!" he exclaimed.

Cinella opened his eyes wide, uttered a groan, and immediately closed them again.

That short glance, however, had been sufficient to satisfy him that he had never seen Helene before.

As for Joseph, he thought he had met him before. But where?

He could not be the person who had given him little Pippiona in Naples.

Joseph looked very young, while that man was already then middle-aged, and must be now quite old.

This observation did not teach Cinella much, still it was something.

"You see," said Joseph to Helene, "that this man is not able to utter a single word. Let us wait until to-morrow.

"Pippiona's story has explained a good many things to me which were hitherto shrouded in mystery, and in the course of the day I will go to the Neapolitan Embassy."

In spite of his firm resolve not to move, Cinella could not help trembling a little.

"He hears us!" said Helene, who had noticed Cinella's movement. "He may be trying to overhear us."

With these words she took Joseph's arm again, and drew him to the other end of the room.

Here they began to converse together again. Clement and Louis had modestly withdrawn to the adjoining room.

This second conference lasted longer than the first. Helene seemed to persist in her intention, while Joseph attempted to keep her from carrying it out.

He did not succeed. Again soft steps were heard on the carpet, and Cinella guessed that Helene was coming toward him.

This time she addressed him:

"I do not know, Cinella, whether you hear me or

whether you are shamming drunkenness," she said. "Answer me!"

She waited a moment.

Cinella kept silent and motionless.

"Your fortune or your ruin depends on the explanations you can give us," continued Madame Lamouroux. "Your fortune if you tell the truth, your ruin if you lie to us."

Cinella snored.

"You see," said Joseph, who was really deceived by this pretended snoring. "You see, we shall learn nothing to-night. The best thing is to let him sleep off his drunk. To-morrow we will have leisure to question him."

"Ah!" exclaimed Madame Lamouroux, as she clasped both hands to her head, "you are not a mother!"

At these words, Cinella thought:

"The game is won!"

Yet he possessed sufficient self-control not to move or speak, and only answered by a snore which was stronger than the first one.

"Yes," said Helene in despair, "we will not hear anything to-day; let us wait until to-morrow."

A sudden uneasiness seized her, and she added:

"Let him not escape from us!"

"Be easy about that," replied Joseph, "I and our friends will watch. You can go to bed, Helene, and dream that Pippiona is your daughter."

How fervently Madame Lamouroux repeated the divine words:

"My daughter!"

Cinella heard the footsteps of the two glide over the

carpet. Then a door closed, and behind it a whispered conversation was carried on.

He now took the risk of opening his eyes.

The room was almost empty, and only lighted by the faint gleam of a night-lamp suspended from the ceiling. Cinella seated himself upright on the divan and listened.

The conversation behind the door still went on.

Cinella suspected that all kinds of instructions were being given to prevent an escape.

"Ha, ha!" he laughed to himself, "I haven't got any intention of running away."

He put his feet on the ground and took off his shoes so as not to make any noise when walking.

This precaution was unnecessary, for the floor was covered, as we have before stated, with a heavy carpet.

Cinella was shrewd, though, and did not wish to leave anything to chance.

With slow, cautious steps he made a survey of his prison. It was a very comfortable and finely furnished prison, in which he would gladly have passed the rest of his days.

At first he examined the exits.

At present he did not think of escaping; but who could tell whether he would not have the desire to-morrow? and a person must think of the future.

The principal door was out of the question, for that was undoubtedly watched from the outside.

The windows were barred by iron railings.

The room was—Cinella had counted the steps—on the first floor, and, as an iron railing was no obstacle to him, he resolved, in case he should feel like escaping, to take the road through the window. A shrewd man, though, must not leave anything unnoticed.

Cinella therefore opened the second door to see where it led to.

It opened into a dressing-room. All around women's dresses hung, and up above, through a crack in the wall, shone the gleam of a lighted lamp.

Cinella returned to the first room and got a chair to stand on, and see where the gleam came from. The sight he saw through the glass window was as follows:

In a large, comfortable, snow-white bed lay a young girl, a child, Pippiona, asleep.

Near her sat the woman whom he had seen before in the large room, who watched over the invalid's sleep.

"Yes," murmured Cinella, as he got down from his post of observation, "now I am convinced. I have not got into a trap here. This lady really thinks herself Pippiona's mother. These people are rich, my fortune is made."

And with this reassuring conviction Cinella lay down again on the divan. In the solitude and silence of the night Cinella combined his plans best.

He saw himself opposed to a mother who was looking for her daughter, and, rightly or wrongly, believed Pippiona was that daughter.

How had she arrived at this conviction? Through what chain of circumstances had she been led to believe it? This Cinella did not know, and he therefore had to guess it.

He did not doubt that his reward would be the greater the more he was able to strengthen this conviction! On the other hand, he knew very little about Pippiona.

A traveller, a rich Frenchman, had one day made a bargain with him, and given him, together with a large sum of money, an almost dying child to bring up. Nothing of the child's past life was told him, except that its name was Blanche.

The features of the stranger had been indelibly impressed on his memory, but those features might have changed considerably with age.

Out of this meagre material he had to build a story.

The story had to be interesting, too, and show Cinella in the light of a savior and protector.

He made use of the remaining hours of the night to plan his romance, and after he had done it to his own satisfaction, he sunk into that deep sleep which is willed to an easy conscience.

Joseph and Helene's entrance awoke him.

They had left Dr. Ozam with Pippiona, resolving to make Cinella speak, no matter what it might cost.

The Italian thought it in his interest to begin the conversation at once.

"Where am I?" he exclaimed, "and what do you want of me?"

"Only what is right," replied Madame Lamouroux. "Answer candidly and voluntarily."

"I have nothing to answer," replied Cinella, with dignity. "I do not give you permission to question me or to keep me a prisoner."

Joseph smiled.

"If we have not got your permission, Cinella, we will take it," he said; "and I advise you not to complain about this prison, because it may be changed to another one less comfortable."

"You threaten me," said Cinella, shrugging his shoulders. "I am an honest man, and have no fear of the law."

Helene interfered.

"That is not the question," she said; "I would rather have what we can get from you by force to be due to your own good-will. I can assure you that the details we shall ask of you will not harm you in any way. No matter of what nature they are, we will never make use of them to your injury, but, on the contrary, will pay you well for them."

"That's what I call talk," replied Cinella. "Ask your questions, madame, and I can then tell whether I will answer them or not."

"You are an Italian?"

"Yes, madame; Neapolitan."

"When did you leave Naples?"

"About two years ago."

"Alone?"

"No; with my daughter."

"How old is this daughter?"

"Seventeen years. Poor Pippiona is very small though and not developed for her age. She looks like fifteen."

"Pippiona! A curious name!"

"That is only a nickname. Her baptismal name is Bianca."

Question and answer followed one another rapidly.

Joseph leaned against the mantel-piece and toyed with the lambrequin.

A short pause ensued.

Madame Lamouroux considered how to continue the conversation without awakening the Italian's distrust.

"You are very poor, are you not?" she finally asked.

Cinella threw a pitying glance at his torn clothes.

"I don't look like a millionnaire, anyway," he gruffly replied. "The little one was always sick, yet helped me a great deal. She moved the audience to pity. Since I haven't got her any more, business is bad."

"What!" cried Madame Lamouroux with pretended surprise, "you haven't got your daughter any more? What has become of her, anyway?"

Cinella bit his lips and gazed distrustfully at Helene and Joseph.

"I don't know," he replied, with a deep sigh. "One night when I came home she was gone, and I have looked for her in vain ever since."

"In all the taverns, eh?" exclaimed Joseph, laughing. "Don't play the unfortunate, Cinella. You won't succeed."

"If Pippiona is your daughter," said Madame Lamouroux, "I must confess that you are a very strange father."

"That's the whole question," murmured Joseph. "Is he Pippiona's father or not? These wandering showmen often have abducted children."

"Now it's coming!" thought Cinella.

He raised his head proudly and was going to reply:

"Whom do you take me for?"

Joseph was ahead of him, though, laid his hand upon his shoulder, and said.

"I must tell you in advance, Cinella, that you will play the enraged father with as little success as the sentimental one. We look upon you as a fellow with a very wide conscience, and who is in great need of money.

Anything you may say will not change our opinion about you or your plans. You can therefore speak freely and without fear. The best thing you can do is to tell the truth. Is Pippiona your daughter?"

Cinella cast down his eyes and appeared to be hesitating, as if the confession cost him a great effort.

"No," he finally said, in a low, hollow tone.

"Then it is an abducted child?"

"No," replied Cinella again. "It was intrusted to me."

"*Who* intrusted the girl to you?" asked Helene, eagerly.

"A traveller who was a short time in Naples."

"What was his name?"

"He did not tell me."

"And you never tried to find out?"

"Yes, but in vain. No one in the city knew him, and I told you before he was only passing through Naples."

Helene let her arm fall again, and Cinella saw that he had taken a wrong course.

If he pretended not to know anything he would not get any pay for a secret he could not tell. If he, therefore, continued to deny, he had at the same time to make them believe that he, if he so desired, could tell them what they wanted.

He accordingly neutralized the meaning of his last words by a mysterious smile.

Helene noticed that smile, and new hope awoke within her.

"Yes!" she exclaimed. "You lie! You know the name of that traveller."

Cinella did not reply.

"You know him," continued the poor mother, excitedly, "but do not wish to tell me his name. You think that if you tell us the secret you won't get the promised reward. Oh, speak—what do you wish? Ask what you will; you shall have it."

Cinella kept silent again; this time from embarrassment.

How should he pronounce the name he did not know?

Helene clasped him by the hands and looked at him with tears in her eyes.

"Tell me his name!" she continued. "What good does it do you to keep silent? Are you afraid of getting into trouble by telling me? I give you my word of honor that you shall not be mixed up in this affair. Besides, I will make you rich and you can go where you wish. Ah, I do not know what I shall say. How am I to convince you? What do you demand? What do you want?"

Cinella sat upon coals.

Joseph approached and said:

"Leave him alone, Helene. Either this fellow knows nothing or else I will force him to speak before night."

CHAPTER XXIV

CHASTE LOVE

D R. OZAM had remained with Pippiona, while Joseph and Madame Lamouroux were examining Cinella.

The invalid sadly followed her friends to the door with her eyes. But when she turned around and saw the intelligent, noble face of the doctor, a smile played about her pale lips.

"Well, Pippiona," said the doctor, "I think you are much better to-day. Inside of a fortnight these poor pale cheeks will become rosy again and these eyes will shine brighter."

"They are all so kind to me!" murmured Pippiona. "It seems to me as if one not only breathes air here but life itself. Oh, what good it did me to be loved, after having been so long ill treated! I thank God that He brought me here; but what will become of me if I am sent away again?"

At this thought a tear dropped from her eyes and fell like dew upon her long blond eyelashes.

"Don't cry, Pippiona!" exclaimed the doctor, "I must forbid you to do it. If you cry you will get sick again, and I shall be compelled to give you that black medicine again which tastes so nasty."

The tear rolled down the ivory cheek of the invalid, who immediately began to smile again.

"That's right! Laugh at your doctor whenever you feel like it; only do not be sorrowful!"

Dr. Ozam paused a few seconds and then continued in loving tones:

"How can you imagine that you will be deserted after you have been brought back to new life?

"Noble hearts remain faithful to those for whom they make sacrifices, and I would not know Madame Lamouroux, if I had not the right and the duty to believe that I can assure you in her name that she will never desert you."

"Ah!" murmured Pippiona. "Then I shall always remain with her?—with her and Monsieur Joseph?"

"Why not?" asked the doctor. "Madame Lamouroux has no daughter. You can take the place of one. You will console her, you who have so often been consoled by her. Oh, fear nothing! You, my dear child, will be the one who will give the most at this exchange; I can see already that you will become a ray of sunshine in a life which until now has been gloomy and solitary!"

"What!" exclaimed Pippiona in surprise, "I could contribute to Madame Lamouroux's happiness? Ah, never, never will I be so happy as at that moment!"

A thought of a different nature suddenly seemed to awake in the girl, for she blushed deeply, and confusedly cast down her big blue eyes.

"And Monsieur Joseph?" she asked, without looking up.

"Monsieur Joseph?" repeated the doctor, "what of him?"

"Will he stay with us, too?"

"Of course! Joseph, as well as you, is an adopted child of Madame Lamouroux, and as long as she lives he will not leave her."

"Ah, that is splendid!" exclaimed Pippiona, with *naive* joy. "If he had left us, I believe I would never again have become entirely happy."

"Ah, then you love your Joseph?"

"I would be the most ungrateful creature if I did not love him," replied Pippiona.

"There, we have it!"

And with the privilege of his age and his profession, Dr. Ozam tapped his young patient lightly on the cheek.

"I owe it to him alone that I am here and that I made Madame Lamouroux's acquaintance," said Pippiona.

She then related how Joseph had carried her in his arms and brought her to this house, where she had found happiness.

"That isn't all, though," she continued; "I had a fever, I was delirious. They thought I was unconscious and could not see or hear anything. I saw and heard everything though, and I know that he often watched by me in that chair; that he cast the curtain aside every moment to see if I was sleeping; that he walked here and there on his toes, so as not to wake me; that he prepared my medicine, and when he handed it to me, he spoke in such a gentle voice that it made me forget the nasty taste of the fluid. If I was getting worse he looked melancholy, and when I became better again he brightened up. I, whom a little while before he had not even known, seemed to have become a sister, a beloved daughter, to him.

"And I should not love him! Oh, dear doctor, I would rather die than not love him."

Pippiona had arisen in bed as she spoke. Her cheeks were flushed, her eyes sparkled and her bosom heaved.

"Come, come, you little madcap, don't get so excited!" replied the doctor. "Cover your arms at once. Do you want to catch a cold? Love your Joseph as much as you please; but don't get sick again. You are looking pale. Such efforts are still too much for you."

Pippiona had indeed sunk back upon her pillow, her whole blood streamed back to her heart, and her cheeks were again as white as ivory. The cause of this sudden faintness, though, was not the one the physician pointed out.

When the invalid lay down again, she murmured three words in such a feeble voice that they did not reach the doctor's ear:

"There he comes!"

Yet no noise was heard in the room.

Did Pippiona possess the faculty of seeing through the wall?

The door was opened and Joseph entered, while Madame Lamouroux followed him.

And when the young man approached the bed, Pippiona seemed to be instilled with new life. The warm purple blood came back in her veins, the lips smiled, and the light of joy and happiness shone out of her big blue eyes.

It was a perfect transformation.

Doctor Ozam was an eminent, skilful physician, but

the honor of this cure did not belong to him. It was effected by a greater and more skilful physician—by love.

It had, of course, cost Pippiona great trouble to collect her scattered thoughts.

Her mind was still that of a child, but her heart was already that of a woman.

CHAPTER XXV

SOLITUDE BRINGS ADVICE

AGAIN Cinella found himself alone in the room which served as his prison, and his plan did not seem so easy for him to carry out now as he had at first thought.

Out of the whole story he had imagined, he had not been able to say two words, for Joseph had interrupted him from the very start.

Only one thing was required of him—a name.

Cinella regretted very much, now, that he had pretended to know this name.

If he confessed now that he did *not* know the name, he ran the danger of dissatisfying his abductors, and Joseph's last words contained an undefined threat which made him uneasy.

Although he had boldly declared he did not care a snap for the law, it would be disagreeable to him if his past career were raked up and the old affair of Tommaso and Monna gone into.

A single hope remained to him: that the person in whose power he was knew nothing of the affair.

For the present they did not seem to wish to bother

him; for after Joseph and Madame Lamouroux had gone away, the door opened again, and our friend Louis Jacquemin entered, carrying a covered basket in his hand.

In this basket were two or three appetizing dishes and several bottles of wine.

Jacquemin gravely set the table, placed the dishes and bottles upon it, and exclaimed:

"Cinella, old boy! come and eat!"

At the sound of this well-known voice Cinella opened his eyes and cried in his turn:

"What, Louiset! How did you get here?"

"Let us eat first, and then we can talk afterward. For the present, let me inform you that I am your jailer, but only for the purpose of preventing you from escaping. I ordered the cook to fix us up an extra fine dinner, and went to the cellar myself to select the wine."

While Louis said this, he seated himself, uncovered the dishes, and filled Cinella's plate, without forgetting his own.

He then began to eat with the heartiest appetite in the world, while Cinella looked stealthily at him.

"You seem to live well here," said the Italian at length.

"Oh, yes," said Jacquemin, as he filled his glass with wine. "The cooking is pretty fair, as you can see yourself."

"And the work?"

"Very easy."

"How did you get in such a good house?"

"About the same way as you did. These are curious people. They conceal themselves for the purpose of doing good, just as others hide to do evil. It's a mania."

"If these people wish to do me good," growled Cinella, "they could show it in a different way."

Jacquemin paid no attention to this remark. He filled both glasses to the brim, lifted his own aloft, and said:

"To your health, old boy!"

Cinella seized his glass, drank it down, and asked:

"What good do they intend to do me?"

"I'm sure I don't know," replied Louis. "Our benefactors are interesting themselves for you now. I heard Monsieur Joseph, when he stepped into the carriage, say to the coachman: 'To the Neapolitan Embassy!' "

Cinella became pale as death.

"What ails you?" asked Jacquemin, with naive wonder. "Has anything stuck in your throat?"

"Did you really hear him say: 'To the Neapolitan Embassy' ?"

"Yes."

Louis then added in a careless tone:

"Perhaps he wants to make inquiries about you. He did the same thing with me. But what's the use of bothering ourselves about that? I don't know anything more, and it doesn't concern me anyhow. Let us drink! Don't you think this wine magnificent?"

Cinella did not reply. Bending his head until his nose almost reached his plate, he considered.

Jacquemin smiled and said to himself:

"The stroke was a good one! What crime did the scoundrel commit in Naples?"

"As I see," he said aloud, "you are not in good humor to-day, I will therefore leave you alone, but will not take the wine with me."

With these words Louis gathered up the dishes and disappeared as quickly as he came.

Cinella was once more alone with his thoughts.

Joseph's visit to the Neapolitan Embassy was an ominous sign.

Cinella immediately thought of prison cells, chains, the galleys and things of that kind. He was angry at himself for having followed his ambitious ideas, and would now gladly tell all he knew, if he could only leave this house in freedom.

He walked up and down the room like a bear in his cage, and every five minutes went to the window to measure the distance to the ground. There could be no thought of escape this way during the daytime, for the residents of the Rue Vivienne are not in the habit of leaving their houses by way of the window.

At length in desperation he went to the door and knocked at it.

"What do you want, old boy?" asked Jacquemin's voice.

"I would like to speak to Monsieur Joseph," replied Cinella, timidly.

"Monsieur Joseph has not returned yet," replied Louis; "but as soon as he does I will send him to you."

Cinella began his cage promenade again.

It was about five o'clock in the afternoon. The streets became dark at the approach of night, and the Parisian fog made them still darker.

In the courtyard a lantern cast a melancholy light.

The darker it became in the room, the gloomier became Cinella's thoughts.

He did not think of the galleys now, but of the gallows.

And Joseph had not come back!

Cinella had now got so far as to fervently desire the interview he had formerly wished to postpone as long as possible.

At length the key turned and the door opened.

But it was not Joseph.

Louis brought the supper in the same basket he had used for the dinner.

He lighted two candles, closed the blinds, pulled down the shades, and arranged the table.

Cinella had no appetite, though, and refused to take the glass of wine Jacquemin offered him.

Cinella was conquered! Cinella refused to drink!

"Where is Monsieur Joseph?" he asked.

"Monsieur Joseph," replied Jacquemin, chewing away with all his might, "Monsieur Joseph is doing what I am —eating—and Madame likewise. He was in good humor when he came back from the Embassy. I think he arranged your affair."

This assurance made Cinella shudder, and he unconsciously placed his hand to his throat.

Jacquemin placed everything—plates, knives, forks and empty bottles—back again in his basket and moved toward the door.

"Please send Monsieur Joseph to me at once," murmured Cinella, imploringly.

From the other side of the door a loud voice exclaimed:

"Here he is, Signor Cinella! What do you wish to say to him?"

Joseph entered.

In his hand he held an envelope covered with seals

and stamps, which Cinella recognized at the first glance as coming from the Neapolitan Embassy.

"I beg your pardon," said Joseph, politely, "for not keeping you company during the day; but I can honestly swear to you that I busied myself about you every minute in the day. You refused to give us simple information, and were very wrong in doing so. I will be more candid with you, and will give you information of the fate of two persons whom you knew very well. I mean Monna Feretti, your mistress, and the Corsican Tommaso, your friend."

Cinella expected this thrust.

He did not move a muscle, his face only became a little paler. That was all.

"I see that you have my life in your power," he said.

Joseph nodded his head.

"Here is the extradition paper, signed by the Neapolitan Consul, and here is the warrant for your arrest, signed by the attorney-general," he simply said; "I am at liberty either to make use of these papers or else to throw them in the fire."

"Then," replied Cinella firmly, "you will throw the papers in the fire, for you need me."

Joseph looked at the Italian in surprise.

"Now you are talking sensibly!" he then said. "I think you will come to terms."

"The man whom you asked me about," continued Cinella, "I am not acquainted with, and if I pretended to know him, it was done merely to deceive you. Unfortunately I made a mistake, and have found my master. If you have any suspicion who he is, you have only to point him out to me, and I swear to you I will recognize him again, even in the biggest crowd. I have no interest in fooling you, for you could ruin me with a single word.''

"That is right," said Joseph. "Now tell us, first of all, how you became acquainted with Pippiona?"

He then turned toward the door and exclaimed:

"You can come in, Helene. The man is as pliable as a kid glove."

The clock struck nine P.M.

CHAPTER XXVI

THE VISION

THE clock on Baron Matifay's mantel-piece struck the ninth hour. The banker and Dr. Ozam sat at a well-filled table. No servants were present.

The doctor had ordered it so, much to Monsieur Rose's mortification.

In consequence of the wine the physician constantly poured into his host's glass, the baron was almost drunk.

From time to time a twitching of his features was noticeable, which betrayed the ominous thoughts he could not get rid of, and then his anxious gaze would be turned on the clock.

The physician observed this, raised up the glass shade which covered the clock, and stopped the pendulum.

He then sat down again at the table, and took up the conversation at the exact point he had left off.

The doctor was a man of the world and a man of wit, although a scientist.

Nothing was unknown to him, and his interesting conversation turned, inside of an hour, with wonderful facility, to all the poles of science and art.

He was more brilliant than ever this evening, although he had only one auditor, and he a very inattentive one.

His purpose was to make the latter forget the ominous hour.

The nearer it approached, the gayer and more talkative the physician became, and Matifay at length found real enjoyment in listening to him.

The dinner was nearing its end, and they were just at the third bottle of champagne.

The physician had drank very little, though he pretended to do so, leaving Matifay to do the drinking for both.

He counted upon the baron's not thinking of the vision any more, in case he was in a half-intoxicated condition.

He had no knowledge of the enormous quantities of liquor the baron had drunk lately in despair.

The hours sped on, and the banker became jollier.

The good humor of his guest had infected him too, and the doctor hoped that his presence alone would be sufficient to banish the vision.

Suddenly the baron became pale as death and listened.

"Do you hear anything, doctor?" he asked.

The doctor listened attentively.

"No, I cannot hear anything," he said.

Matifay's eyes were directed to the corridor which led to Cyprienne's room.

Beads of perspiration ran down his cheeks and forehead.

"She is coming," he murmured. "I see her coming! Do you see the door open?"

The doctor opened his eyes as wide as he could.

The door had not moved.

Dr. Ozam got up and went to the door to prove it to the baron.

"Now the door is wide open," exclaimed Matifay, as he stretched out his arms as if to chase the vision away. "There she is! Don't you see her, doctor?"

"Where?" asked the physician.

"In front of the door! She is veiled and is standing motionless."

The physician went to the spot Matifay pointed out with his finger, and stood upon it himself.

"Now she stands to your left," said the baron.

The doctor stood at the left.

"I really cannot see anything," said Dr. Ozam.

He stretched out his arms, moved them in the air, and threw his hands about, to convince Matifay that no one was there.

He did even more.

He took the baron's hand, and forced him to make the same experiment.

Matifay did it with visible repugnance, yet did not cease to see the phantom.

Through his hands he saw the terrible form come nearer, throw her veil slowly aside, and look fixedly at him. It then seemed to him as if she gradually faded away as usual, until she vanished entirely.

And as soon as the vision disappeared, Matifay's face became more cheerful, he breathed more freely, dried his forehead, and tried to smile.

The whole thing had not lasted two minutes; but to Matifay it seemed like two centuries.

The doctor pulled out his watch. It was just midnight.

That was the ominous hour!

"Well, doctor, what do you think of it?" asked the baron, still trembling with fright.

The doctor shook his head.

"You should have sent for me sooner," he then said. "Still I do not think we need give up all hope yet. You can do more to cure yourself than I can. Pass your days in the tumult and noise of business and your evenings in the theatre—in a word, try to forget."

"I will try," murmured Matifay.

"Now go to bed and try to sleep," continued the physician. "You have nothing to fear until to-morrow at the same hour. Until then we will try to think of a remedy to prevent the reappearance of the vision."

Dr. Ozam, after saying these words, opened the door, which had been locked from the inside, and called Rose, who could not have been far away, for he immediately answered the call.

But this time, too, the valet's curiosity was deceived. He found in the room into which he had not been allowed to enter throughout the whole evening nothing more than the remnants of a dinner, the doctor, who was just putting on his summer overcoat, and his master, who sat half asleep near the table.

At this same midnight hour, Joseph and Helene finally received Cinella's latest confession.

CHAPTER XXVII

CINELLA'S CONFESSION

CINELLA'S story was exactly similar to Pippiona's, and did not add anything new to what Joseph and Helene already knew.

The only important detail it contained was, that the man who gave Pippiona into strange hands in Naples was now in Paris.

Cinella had seen him one day on the Place de la Bourse, just as he was getting into his elegant victoria. The Italian attempted to run after him, but the carriage drove on too fast, and he had lost sight of him on the corner of the boulevard and the Chausee d'Antin.

The Italian described the traveller with whom he had made the contract; but, although the person he described resembled Matifay, it was still nothing positive.

Helene had to have the proof before she could really believe she had found her daughter again.

The way to become positive would have been an easy one if they had determined to bring Cinella and Matifay together, and see whether the Italian could recognize him again.

Of course this meeting must not occur by pointing out the banker to the Italian, and asking him:

"Is that the man?"

In that case, it could be foretold that Cinella, to earn his reward, would answer "Yes," at all hazards.

They would have to bring him in a large crowd of people, among whom Matifay was, and then ask him to pick out the right man.

If Cinella, without hesitating, declared the baron to be the man, then the proof was rendered, and Helene could give herself up to her joy entirely.

It was possible, though, that Cinella doubted, that he made a mistake, that he would *not* recognize Matifay again; and what pain would then be reserved for the poor mother?

Helene had suffered so much that she recoiled in terror from this experiment, which was associated with so much danger.

Yet the struggle did not last long. Helene said to herself that in such a case, where it was a question of such great joy, she must not recoil from a possible pain.

Cinella had told everything he knew. He was silent and waited.

Madame Lamouroux, who had allowed Joseph to question him, now interfered and said to Cinella:

"Let us speak about yourself now. The information you have given us, although incomplete, has its value nevertheless. What is your price for it?"

Cinella, who feared to ask either too much or too little, shrugged his shoulders and kept silent.

Helene opened a portfolio and took a package of bank-notes and a handful of gold from it.

Cinella's eyes began to sparkle.

Helene shoved the gold over to him without counting it, and placed the bank-notes on the table in front of her.

"There is something for the information you have given us up till now," she said. "Now let us continue our conversation! It is self-understood that from to-day on you forfeit all your rights in Pippiona to me. I could dispute those rights, but I prefer to buy them. How much do you ask for them, and can you write?"

"Only my name," replied Cinella.

Joseph took some writing materials and the Countess of Monte-Cristo dictated the following:

"I hereby declare that Bianca, sometime called Pippiona, is not my daughter, that I have no right to her, that I shall never ask her back again, and that I forfeit whatever interest I may have in her to Madame Lamouroux."

After Joseph had written this down, he shoved the paper over to Cinella.

"Sign," said Helene, placing five or six bank-notes next to the document.

Cinella signed his name to it.

"This is not all yet," said Madame Lamouroux.

The Italian wiped the perspiration from his face with the back of his hand. He began to fear that the gold and bank-notes, into possession of which he had so suddenly come, were only dream pictures and would evaporate into nothing.

"To-morrow," continued Helene, "you will take up your old profession again, and give your usual performances in the streets and public squares. Visit more especially the aristocratic quarters, the Tuileries and the Champs Elysees. I understand that you are very skilful in your art, and will see to it that you do not remain unnoticed. You will be asked to give performances at private parties. Do not refuse any of these invitations, for during the Carnival your Punch and Judy show must be the fashion. The money you earn in this way is yours."

Cinella wished to say something, but Helene kept on, not letting him speak.

"You mustn't forget, however, that you are in my service for the next two months, and must obey all my orders. The first of these orders is that I forbid you to get drunk. If a person gets drunk he generally says too much, and you must be silent about what has taken place between us and perhaps will take place between us. You will be constantly watched, and at the slightest sign of treason you will be denounced and sent back to Naples under police escort for the murder of poor Monna Feretti. Besides, I do not ask this obedience for a long time. On the day after the Carnival I will give you your freedom back again, and all that still lies on this table will be yours."

After uttering these words Helene gathered up the bank-notes and the gold, and threw them into the drawer again.

"I am at your service," stammered Cinella; "I will do everything you ask of me."

"I count upon it," said Helene.

She rang a bell, and Jacquemin entered.

"Have you found a residence for Cinella?"

"Yes, madame, two rooms—he sleeps in the second, I in the first, so that I can always watch him."

"That is right. Cinella, I give you Louis Jacquemin as companion and guide. He will not leave you a minute alone during the two months our compact shall last. Now go!"

As soon as the two men had gone and Joseph had taken his leave too, Madame Lamouroux turned down her lamp, and went into the room where Pippiona lay.

She still slept in the semi-darkness of the curtains. Nothing could be purer than the emaciated face of the invalid, while she lay thus in the snow-white bed.

She slept and smiled, like those children of whom it is said that they smile at the angels.

Helene remained seated a long time near the bed in silent adoration of this picture.

Pippiona's fine hand lay on the quilt, and Madame Lamouroux could not help seizing it and gently pressing it between her own.

The invalid moved a little, and her half-parted lips stammered:

"My mother—Joseph!"

This second name was merely lisped, and Helene only heard the first.

CHAPTER XXVIII

REAPPEARANCE OF THE COUNTESS OF MONTE-CRISTO

PARIS is nothing more than an immense theatre, where each one has his certain place, whether he plays a big or little part, or is only a supernumerary. On certain days the whole company steps on the boards. That happens when a new spectacular play is given, and the crowds in the streets see their favorites pass by.

Lord Larsonille is as much applauded as Frederic Lemaitre, and many a countess or marquise is a dangerous competitor to a Theresa.

The carnival, which is fast disappearing in our time, was in its fullest bloom in the reign of Louis Philippe, the citizen king.

The boulevards were crowded with maskers of all kinds.

The crowd yelled with pleasure, the street boys blew fishhorns and drums beat indiscriminately.

But the chief triumph of the day belonged to the Countess of Monte-Cristo.

Her sudden appearance on the crowded boulevards created a sensation, and was akin to the reappearance on the stage of a celebrated actor.

Carelessly leaning back in a gilded carriage, whose form reminded one of the bow of a boat, she was dressed in the costume of the wife of the Doge of Venice.

Opposite to her, in a Venetian costume of black and gold, sat the Vicomte Don Jose de la Cruz.

In the front and rear of the carriage, little negroes, dressed as pages, threw confectionery to the men and flowers to the ladies, crying at the same time at the top of their voices:

"Long live the Countess of Monte-Cristo!"

The countess smiled, and waved her hand like a queen returning to her capital after a long journey.

Suddenly she leaned over to Don Jose, and whispered something to him.

He quickly drew himself up, and both seemed to be looking at the same spot on the sidewalk.

At the end of the street stood Colonel Fritz, watching the carriage pass by with an ironical smile on his lips.

Just as the carriage was opposite to him, he laid his hand on his hat and raised it a little.

That the colonel greeted the Countess of Monte-Cristo was a simple matter. He had been a visitor to her house, and the greeting was a mere act of politeness.

The peculiar mocking smile which accompanied it gave the greeting a mysterious significance.

Immediately afterward Don Jose, in his turn, leaned over toward the countess.

He had noticed behind the colonel a second familiar face. It was none other than that of Monsieur Gosse, the public writer.

As soon as the carriage had passed by, the colonel

turned around toward the "dear little fellow," and made a gesture of approval.

"There is something new there," said Don Jose, aloud.

"The time has come," said the countess, softly. "He must die."

The colonel, meanwhile, had not left his Numa Pompilius.

As soon as the countess's carriage was out of sight, he took Monsieur Gosse along with him to a neighboring café.

"Yes, it is she," assured the public writer again, after they had seated themselves at a table.

"Ah," growled the colonel. "Legigant has betrayed me. I thought as much! And this countess?"

"Is only Aurelie," replied Gosse. "She is a false pearl."

"Without doubt one of Legigant's creatures. Let him beware, for, as sure as my name is Fritz, he will suffer for it."

A few explanatory words about the public writer's career lately will not be out of place here.

Since Legigant had paid so dearly for Colonel Fritz's two letter, Gosse naturally thought that the colonel would pay him just as much if he gave him serviceable information of the doings against him.

That was the reason why he had gone into a different camp, and, from an ally of Legigant, had become an ally of the colonel.

While he pretended not to bother about the things which took place in his house, he had nevertheless, for some time, been watching them closely.

He looked so innocent that his wife paid as little attention to him as if he had been a dog.

When Lila was still boarding with his wife, he had often seen the Countess of Monte-Cristo coming to pay the little one a visit in company with the Countess Hortense de Puysaie.

There was also an eccentric, handsome lady two or three times to see Madame Gosse on business connected with Ursula. As he found out, her name was Aurelie. Aurelie and the Countess of Monte-Cristo bore a striking resemblance to each other.

This resemblance struck the public writer, and it surprised him to see two so different yet so similar persons interested in the same intrigues.

This was all a mere suspicion; but if he had told the colonel of it, it might have been useful to him.

This was indeed the case.

The colonel recognized in the whole manner in which the intrigue was carried on the hand of Legigant.

Had he not made use of Nina in the same way to ruin Loredan?

Aurelie was probably to do him a similar service.

He had kept it a secret from the colonel, therefore it must be directed against himself.

All these theories were the more plausible as he had not seen Legigant again since his rupture with him. Whenever Legigant had any orders for him, he sent them through Dr. Toinon.

These orders the colonel had carried out without understanding their purpose, and every time he had gone to his ally and master, to ask him for an explanation, he found the doors locked.

But now, all at once, Legigant's mysterious actions were clear to him.

"He wants to betray me!" exclaimed the colonel. "So much the better; if he desires a fight, I am ready for him."

CHAPTER XXIX

FAC ET SPERA—(ACT AND HOPE)

A BALL took place that night at the Opera House. In the midst of all the noise and tumult Monsieur Gosse, still dressed as Numa Pompilius, made himself prominent through his eccentricity.

Loredan and Colonel Fritz, dressed in frock suits, sat in a box in the first balcony.

In the *foyer*, Legigant, with a false nose on, wandered among the different groups.

He was accompanied by a thin, pale man—Dr. Toinon.

The couple who created the biggest sensation were two dominos in black, with a black scarf on their shoulders.

One of the two dominos was very tall, and the other a little smaller, but very aristocratic in his bearing.

Everybody crowded and crushed to get a look at the silent couple.

Just then Numa Pompilius got into a little difficulty with the police. A small fight broke out in the centre of the hall, and the crowd, as usual, ran after the noise.

The two dominos made use of the diversion to disappear. When the noise had ceased, and order was once more restored, they were not to be found.

In the meanwhile the colonel had noticed Legigant, and had quickly left his companion to follow the former.

When the count was alone, he gazed at the sad spectacle in front of him with a mixture of melancholy and contempt. Suddenly he felt a firm hand laid upon his shoulder.

It was a feminine hand.

The count turned quickly around and saw himself face to face with the smallest of the two dominos.

He got up to allow the mask to take a seat; she refused the invitation with a wave of her hand.

"Stay here," she said, "I have only two words to say to you."

"I am sorry for that," replied Loredan, gallantly. "Two words—that is very little."

"Don't you love poor Nini Moustache any more?" asked the mask.

The count shuddered, and answered the question with another.

"Who are you?"

"Guess it if you can," replied the mask; "I cannot tell you anything further than that I am your friend— your sincere friend?"

A short pause ensued.

The mask was the first one to break it by saying:

"Do you wish to hear news of Hortense?"

"Ah!" exclaimed the count, "I must really know who you are."

"I have already told you I am your friend. Do you want a proof of it? To-morrow evening, after the ball the Baroness of Matifay gives, you will see your wife again."

Before the count could seize the mask she hurried into the corridor, and closed the doors of the box behind her.

Loredan wished to run after her, but on opening the door Colonel Fritz entered.

"Have you seen her?" asked the count.

"Whom?"

"A black domino with a black scarf on the shoulder."

"That is the one I've been following," said the colonel. "She spoke to me in the *foyer*, and escaped just as I was going to call her to account for her language."

The following had happened in the *foyer*:

The colonel, after vainly trying to find Legigant, had gone into the *foyer*, where an arm was gently thrust under his own.

"Well, colonel," murmured a voice in his ear, "are you going to leave poor Loredan alone? You are looking for friend Legigant, are you not? Friend Legigant is not here any more."

"I don't know what you mean with your Loredan and your Legigant," replied Fritz, dryly.

"You are angry? Listen; you have not got a good character!" continued the domino again. "Have you got courage?"

"I think so."

"Then go to a fencing academy to-morrow."

"And if I have no courage?" asked the colonel.

"In that case go to Belgium."

"Sir!" exclaimed the colonel.

But the arm of the black domino had already slipped from his, and he hardly saw, at the other end of the *foyer*, the satin hood of the runaway.

Colonel Fritz and Loredan hurried down the stairs and walked toward the doors.

Hardly two minutes had elapsed since their adventure, yet the door-keepers assured them that they had not seen a domino of any kind leave the hall for an hour.

Loredan and the colonel waited, therefore, at the doors.

They hoped to surely capture the black domino in this way when she left the house.

One, two, three hours passed away.

The house was gradually becoming empty.

A black domino was nowhere to be seen.

Only a tall blue one, who had a purple one on his arm, seemed to amuse himself.

A crowd had gathered about them, and remarks and counter-remarks quickly followed one another.

"Well," cried Gosse, "haven't you any joke to make about me, you long-legged slugger?"

"Good heavens!" cried the blue domino, "that is Monsieur Gosse, the dear little man! What will Bebelle say?"

At four o'clock in the morning it does not take much to make people laugh, and the spectators joyously cried:

"Ah, Gosse! Gosse! the dear little man!"

In the meanwhile the purple domino drew near to the colonel, who stood in the group, and whispered in his ear:

"*Fac et spera!*"

Colonel Fritz, although not a hero, was certainly no coward.

These mysterious warnings and threats, though, which rained upon him from all sides, excited his nerves.

He determined to see Legigant about it, and the following morning went to his office, attired in a black cravat, coat buttoned up to the chin, and a cane in his hand. He looked as dignified and distant as a second who brings a challenge.

His appearance made a deep impression upon Legigant.

"What a warlike mien, my dear colonel. Have we a serious affair on hand?"

"Perhaps," replied Fritz, curtly.

"Then," continued Legigant, "you must go to a fencing academy."

These were the same words the black domino had whispered in his ear.

The colonel thought Legigant was mocking him, and frowned.

Legigant still smiled.

"One would imagine you had a grudge against me," he said.

"Perhaps," replied Colonel Fritz again. "It depends entirely on the explanation you give me."

"An explanation!" said Legigant in surprise.

"Yes, a categorical explanation. You have bought letters from that fool Gosse which are compromising for me. What was your object in doing so?"

"To defend myself in case of necessity," replied Legigant, calmly.

"You must give me those letters back again."

"No."

"I will murder you!" cried the colonel, beside himself with rage.

"And the gallows?"

"I will denounce you! I will have you sent to the galley!"

"You cannot prove anything against me."

"What do you wish to do with the letters?" murmured the colonel.

"You would like to know, eh?" asked Legigant. "Well, I will tell you, or rather I will tell you what I *have* done with them. I sent the letters to the Count de Puysaie."

"You did that?" cried the colonel, turning pale.

"Yes."

"Do you want him to strangle us?"

"No, but I want you to kill the Count de Puysaie and give you an opportunity to do it honorably."

"But suppose he kills me?"

"That is your lookout. Have I not told you to go to a fencing academy?"

"It will be a battle of life and death."

"I hope so," replied Legigant, with savage glee.

"Suppose I refuse to fight?" said the colonel.

"I have looked out for that," replied Legigant. "You must either kill or be killed. The choice lies open to you, and I know in advance which it will be."

"Perhaps," said the colonel, gloomily. "This battle *may* result in my destruction, but—remember what I say —it will be yours, *without a doubt.*"

With these few words, spoken without any theatrical pathos, the colonel withdrew.

Legigant looked after him in surprise.

"Aurelie's shrewdness divined everything," he murmured. "That man will allow himself to be killed."

And going to his chair, he repeated the magic words: "*Fac et spera!*"

CHAPTER XXX

LITTLE MAMMA

FOR more than a fortnight Baron Matifay had not left his room except on business of great importance.

He did not go to the dining-room any more, and in the rare moments when his wife or his father-in-law was with him, he seemed to be preoccupied by a fixed idea.

Dr. Ozam alone knew of the secret, which he, however, in his position as a physician, was not at liberty to betray.

The house was now as desolate as a grave, and very few visitors came.

Yet two inhabitants of the mansion were happy—Lila and Cyprienne.

The latter, who had been forced to relinquish her love for Don Jose de la Cruz, had found an effective substitute for it in her self-sacrifice.

If the hated marriage with Baron Matifay had forced her to forfeit her love forever, she had become acquainted, through it, with a new source of tenderness—maternal love.

She looked upon Lila more in the light of a daughter than of a younger sister.

Lila, too, felt more of the affection of a real daughter to her youthful mother than of one sister to another.

On the day of the party the Baron intended giving a masked children's ball. Florent discreetly entered the room in which the count was breakfasting with his two daughters.

He brought two letters on a plate, one addressed to the Baroness Matifay and the other to Count Loredan de Puysaie.

Cyprienne hesitated to break the seal of her letter.

The count, who also held his letter unopened in his hand, began to laugh at her embarrassment.

"Is it a love letter, Cyprienne?" he asked. "Take care or I shall tell the baron."

"I think it is from the Countess of Monte-Cristo," replied Cyprienne.

"Well, then, let us see what she writes," said the count.

Cyprienne was forced to break the seal and open the letter.

Its contents were as follows:

"Although I am unable to fulfil your wish and visit your party, I still do not wish to remain an entire stranger to your pleasures. A great deal has been told me of a Punch and Judy showman, whose name I believe is Signor Cinella. I will send him to you this evening and hope he will amuse your little guests.

"COUNTESS OF MONTE-CRISTO."

Lila jumped about the room for joy.

"Ah, how magnificent!" she exclaimed. "Punch and Judy! Punch and Judy!"

The count in the meantime had also broken the seal of his letter.

Two papers fell out.

After he had read them he crumpled them together and excitedly walked up and down the room.

CHAPTER XXXI

THE ANONYMOUS LETTER

LILA and Cyprienne were surprised to see the excitement the count labored under after having read the letter.

Lila went to the window and looked down into the courtyard.

"The carriage is ready," she said.

"Well, go then," replied the count.

"And you, dear papa?"

"I cannot accompany you."

Lila wished to put her arms about his neck, to make him change his mind by flattery.

He threw her off almost gruffly, and, without saying a word, left the room.

The letter he had received, and which our readers already know, read as follows:

"COUNT—One of your most faithful friends deems it his duty to deliver to you the proofs of the dastardly betrayal of which you have been the victim. The accompanying letters will give you some details about your most intimate comrade and the meanest of all traitors."

The letter was not signed.

The papers mentioned therein consisted of two letters, which Colonel Fritz had addressed to the Countess Hortense de Puysaie and to Madame Gosse, midwife, respectively.

The first letter was the answer to the unfortunate note of Hortense, which had been the source of her whole unhappiness, and which the colonel had told the count had been written after Cyprienne's birth to the Chevalier d'Aliges.

And now the count held the proof in his hand that the note had been addressed to Colonel Fritz himself, for he had answered it.

The second document which Count Loredan de Puysaie crumpled between his fingers was a note written to the midwife, Madame Gosse, wherein Fritz told her to take care of *his daughter*.

Lila, the child he had himself brought into his own house, was the daughter of Colonel Fritz, the daughter of his worst enemy!

And all who had loved Loredan had been accomplices of this betrayal—Nini Moustache as well as Hortense de Puysaie, yes, perhaps even Cyprienne.

Cyprienne!

Ah, what remorse the count felt now that he was positive that he had sacrificed her unjustly!

Yet the only proof he had that Lila was the daughter of the colonel was the similarity of dates, which might only be an accident.

Therefore, before doing anything further in the matter, he had to satisfy himself of the truth or falsity of his suspicions.

All he had to do, then, would be to apply to Madame Gosse.

She alone would tell the truth.

Half an hour later he ascended the dark staircase of the famous house in the Rue Rambuteau.

When he reached Bebelle's door he paused.

The count knocked.

The door opened, and Loredan recoiled a step, for a mixed smell of vegetables and spirits was wafted to his nostrils.

Madame Gosse was giving a breakfast.

The goddess of the Rue Rambuteau had invited all the nymphs, or rather gossips, of the house.

The ladies were just eating the dessert.

"Can I speak to Madame Gosse?" asked the count politely.

"Yes, there she sits."

"What do you want of me?" asked Madame Gosse gruffly—she had imbibed a little too freely. "Can't a person have peace once in a year?"

In spite of this rude reception, the count strode to the centre of the room and said:

"I must speak with Madame Gosse."

Madame Gosse arose with difficulty and advanced two steps toward Loredan.

The latter drew the two crumpled letters out of his pocket, held them under Madame Gosse's nose, and said:

"I tell you once more," he curtly remarked, "that I must speak to you, and what's more, alone. Send these ladies away."

These words caused murmurs of disapproval to run through the assembly.

CHAPTER XXXII

ULYSSES RETURNS

WITH a wave of the hand the count restored order. "Don't you know me any more?" he asked of Madame Gosse.

The neighbors immediately recognized him.

"That is the gentleman with the handsome turn-out!" exclaimed one of them.

Bebelle stammered an excuse.

"I wish to speak to you," repeated the count, "and alone."

The neighbors slowly withdrew.

As soon as the last one had gone, Loredan held Colonel Fritz's letters in front of Madame Gosse's eyes and said:

"Do you know these?"

"I couldn't help it," sobbed Bebelle, who saw that all was up, "I was forced to do it. The two demanded it."

"Who? The two?" asked Loredan.

"Yes, the two ladies," replied the midwife.

The affair became more puzzling to the count. He saw himself entangled in a plot whose object it was to force him to adopt Lila.

But what was the object sought to be accomplished by that?

One of the two ladies of whom Bebelle spoke must be Nini Moustache, but who was the other?

"Have no fear, Madame Gosse," said the count. "I know that you have only been a tool. I know the name of the real culprits."

With this assurance, the count withdrew.

Poor Bebelle still remained in the middle of the room, sobbing and crying.

On the stairs the count met a wonderful creature, climbing slowly up the stairs.

This wonderful creature was no other than Numa Pompilius, the same Numa Pompilius who had made such a sensation the night before at the masked ball in the Opera House.

But in what a condition was he now!

His tights were stained with wine and grease spots, his pasteboard nose had been split in two by a blow of the fist, and his hat was all tattered and torn.

Monsieur Gosse slowly ascended the stairs.

The classical recollections of the Latin school awoke within him.

Just as Calypso could not console herself for Ulysses' departure, Numa Pompilius as bitterly regretted the fact that he had not followed Egeria's advice.

Egeria, Calypso or Bebelle—for she was all three at once—still lay on her knees in the middle of the room.

Monsieur Gosse leaned his head on the door-post, and repeatedly sighed.

From the opposite side of the door his sighs were answered by other sighs.

Pretty soon, however, the latter sighing was transformed into sonorous snoring.

The good midwife had gone to sleep.

The public writer cautiously opened the door and peeped in.

"Poor Bebelle!" he sighed, "she did the same as I; she consoled herself."

After he had assured himself there was no present danger, he entered the room on his toes.

His wife lay on the floor with her red face resting on her full round arm.

The dear little man looked at her a few minutes, and then counted with a sorrowful glance the number of empty bottles which stood in a corner of the room.

"She has taken a pretty big dose!" he sighed. "That comes of grief."

He then made a speaking tube of his hands, and cried aloud:

"I say, Madame Gosse, wake up!"

Bebelle on opening her eyes now and seeing her husband's face bending over hers, had not the courage to scold or the strength to punish.

Calypso had found Ulysses again and Numa Pompilius lay once more in Egeria's arms.

CHAPTER XXXIII

CONFIDENTIAL INFORMATION

IN THE meanwhile the Count de Puysaie was hunting all over for the colonel.

He did not find him, however. We know why.

Fritz was having that last and grave interview with Legigant at that moment.

The count mechanically directed his steps to his club

Loredan had remained there a short while and was about to go away again, when the door opened and Don Jose de la Cruz entered.

He walked straight to the Count de Puysaie and offered him his hand.

"By the holy Carnival!" exclaimed Don Jose, "my lord seems to have it all to himself to-day. England has conquered Paris with an army of masks. If I could find a companion, I would get out of the reach of this noisy tumult as far as possible."

"You find me in the same humor," said the count, "and if you need a companion I am at your service. We can have horses saddled."

"My horse," said the vicomte, "is near here. In fifteen minutes we can be in the saddle. Where shall we go to?"

"Anywhere you wish," said Loredan, "it's all the same to me."

They descended the broad stairs together.

A groom, with two thoroughbreds already saddled, awaited them at the porch.

They both leaped into the saddle and rode in the direction of the quays.

"Then," said Don Jose, "we are friends, are we not?"

"Yes," replied the count, "and I intend to put your friendship to a proof to-day."

"I am glad to hear it!" exclaimed Don Jose, laughing.

"I am mixed up in an affair of honor," began Loredan.

Don Jose made a gesture of surprise.

"It is a duel of life and death, Don Jose," continued the count. "Do you want to be my second?"

"Yes," replied Don Jose, simply.

"I shall count upon you. Do not fail to be at the party my daughter gives to-night, at the Matifay mansion."

"I will be there," replied the vicomte.

Just as they were ascending the steep hill of Passy, a closed carriage slowly drove down.

The count thought he heard a half-smothered cry, and then his name was uttered by a voice he believed he had heard before.

"Perhaps I was mistaken," he murmured, "but did not the black domino promise me I would see her again to-night?"

CHAPTER XXXIV

A CHILDREN'S PARTY

THE ball the "little mamma" gave in honor of Lila was at its height.

Loredan was among the guests, but when his glance fell upon Lila his features became clouded.

The colonel entered, and the cloud on the count's forehead grew darker.

Loredan went to meet him.

He took Fritz by the arm and said:

"You are rather late, my friend."

The two friends walked arm-in-arm through the parlors.

At length they found themselves in the empty hothouse.

Suddenly their arms were unloosened, and each measured the other with eyes full of hate.

After a short pause the count said curtly, and without any explanatory remarks:

"You scoundrel."

The colonel's pale face became livid, but he did not move a muscle.

"You have the right to address me as you please," he said, "while I am not justified in answering you similarly. Yes, I have wronged you, and I am ready to give you satisfaction."

"In that case," said the count, "I demand the following: We will now return to the parlors. Our absence has not been noticed yet. At first we will still pretend to be good friends. Afterward we must begin a quarrel under some pretext or other."

The count thought for a moment, and then continued:

"We could, for instance, play whist. There are people who, when they lose, become excited, and utter a hasty word. You will lose and utter this hasty word. A quarrel will ensue. Your hand will be raised against me, for I must have a good ground to send you a challenge, as it is my firm purpose to kill you."

The count took the colonel's arm again, and they both returned to the other guests.

The party had meanwhile entered upon a new phase.

The dance was finished.

A Punch and Judy show had been erected in one of the parlors.

It was the one belonging to Signor Cinella.

Baron Matifay, who had not been seen the whole day, had at length consented to appear for a few moments, and do the honors of his house.

The last fourteen days had been as many years to him.

He seated himself in the chair which had been reserved for him, and gave the signal for the performance to begin.

Cyprienne, in the freshness and bloom of her beauty, seated herself next to this broken-down old man, who was her husband, and winked to Lila to come to her.

When Lila passed by Loredan she smiled coquettishly at him.

That smile was generally sufficient to banish the count's sadness, but to-day it only made him gloomier still.

He regretted that feeling of unjust hate immediately, for he called Lila back to him in a pleasant tone of voice.

The colonel looked at them both with a mournful glance.

Loredan noticed it.

In a low voice he whispered in the colonel's ear:

"Fritz, embrace your child."

The colonel clasped the little one passionately in his arms and pressed his lips to her rosy cheeks.

He then put her on the ground again, and, turning to Loredan, proudly said:

"Now, I am ready; do with me what you please."

The curtain of the Punch and Judy show had meanwhile gone up, and the enthusiastic public greeted the hunchback with enthusiastic applause.

The count and the colonel went to the card-room in which a few inveterate players still remained.

CHAPTER XXXV

BEHIND THE CURTAIN

SIGNOR CINELLA'S performance was to end the party.

Behind the curtain was a small parlor. In this parlor Cinella and the Countess of Monte-Cristo were now seated.

Yet we know that the latter had excused herself, and declared that she could not visit Baron Matifay's party.

She wore a long black dress, and her head was covered with a veil.

She was now to learn whether Pippiona was her daughter or not.

"Well, madame," said Cinella, "it is eleven o'clock."

The Countess of Monte-Cristo raised her head as if out of a dream, and said:

"Yes, that's a fact."

She threw a glance at the theatre and asked:

"Is everything ready?"

"Yes, everything."

"And do you know your instructions?"

"Yes, perfectly."

"And you will not forget to keep your eye on the spectators while you are playing?"

"I have thought of everything."

"Good," remarked the countess. "I beg you, Cinella, to recall the features of that man distinctly to your mind."

"I have been thinking of him for a week," said Cinella. "If I were a painter I could draw his portrait."

"Then you are positive that you will be able to recognize him if he is here?"

"I am sure of it. Even if he has become old and gray, even though he should wear a wig, a false beard, and spectacles, I would still be able to recognize him."

"There are a great many guests here," murmured the countess, "and you must remember that you will have to pick him out among them all."

"I would recognize him among a thousand."

"Well, then, go ahead!" said the countess.

Immediately thereafter the folding doors of the parlor were rolled open, amid the enthusiastic plaudits of the children.

On the first floor of the gayly decorated house, in Cyprienne's small private parlor, a woman wept and prayed.

It was the Countess Hortense de Puysaie.

On the morning of that day she had received a letter from the Countess of Monte-Cristo.

It had been very painful to Hortense to be forced to return to the house from which she had fled. She only knew *one* duty now, though—obedience.

The laconic note of the head of the Sisters of the Retreat contained the following words:

"To-day the fate of all your friends will be decided. The present day will see Cyprienne's deliverance, and the death of the guilty. Loredan will need courage; your forgiveness is necessary to him, and *he*, too, must forgive. Come.''

The Countess Hortense had obeyed.

Cyprienne was to be freed, but in what way? And what part was she to play in the work of deliverance?

The guilty were to be punished. Who were the guilty? And in what way were they to be punished?

Only one thing was clear to Hortense; namely, that Loredan was to receive and grant forgiveness, such as is only given and granted at the moment of death.

Was the Count de Puysaie in danger of losing his life? What was her mission to be in this tragedy?

In spite of her doubts, Hortense did not hesitate a moment.

No matter what would happen, it would be surely right, for Helene wished it.

Hortense was praying, though.

She prayed at the same time for the victims and for the headsmen, for her daughter, who was to be saved, and for the wicked, who were to be punished.

She also awaited with anxiety the moment when she would find herself face to face with the husband whose happiness she had destroyed.

What would he say to her? What should she reply?

The curtain had gone up and the show commenced.

Suddenly Cinella murmured:

''I see him!''

''Where?'' asked the countess, eagerly.

''It's the old man who is sitting in a chair next to the handsome young girl, who is holding a little child on her lap.''

Cinella, surprised at Helene's silence, turned around to see what she was doing.

The Countess of Monte-Cristo was no longer there.

Just then the clock in the large parlor struck the midnight hour.

CHAPTER XXXVI

THE INSULT

WHEN the baron heard the twelve strokes he trembled. His glance wandered here and there. That was the hour! The hour in which the terrible vision appeared to him every day.

A pressure, as light as a caress, touched his shoulder. He turned around, uttered a loud cry, and fell fainting to the ground.

The Countess of Monte-Cristo, who stood there in her mourning costume, threw a glance full of contempt and satisfied vengeance at him.

She then strode through the crowd without a word and disappeared as if she were really a phantom from another world.

When the first excitement had been allayed, every one crowded about the unconscious baron.

Dr. Ozam, who was also present, had him taken to his room, and the guests were about to depart, when loud voices were heard in the card-room.

Everything had occurred there according to Loredan's programme.

Fritz had publicly insulted him, and the two men had agreed to fight a duel on the following morning.

The Vicomte de la Cruz was the Count de Puysaie's second; the colonel had chosen his from among the spectators.

After the guests had departed, the count was alone with his second, Don Jose.

The latter appeared to be waiting for something.

"What do you want?" asked Loredan.

"My instructions," replied Don Jose.

"They are very simple: Go to these gentlemen."

"But his second?" observed the vicomte.

"If his second refuses to act, we can fight without any. Go to these gentlemen. We shall fight with pistols. Ten paces. To-morrow morning, at six o'clock, in Mendon, at the foot of the Castle Terrace."

"I will be here at five, count," said Don Jose, as he bowed and went away.

The count walked through the hallway, and quickly ascended the stairs which led to his study.

An entirely different scene had meanwhile been enacted in Cyprienne's room.

The daughter had found the mother there.

Weepingly they sank into each other's arms.

Lila looked at them in surprise.

Cyprienne then told her mother of the events which had just taken place.

"Ah!" exclaimed the countess, "I feared so! The ground for the quarrel with Colonel Fritz I know only too well. The insult was only a pretext. To prevent this duel, I sacrificed you, my poor Cyprienne, and now, in spite of my caution, it will take place anyhow."

She clasped Lila in her arms and continued:

"Ah. beloved. cruel child! Innocent cause of all our

misfortunes—may you never learn how many tears, how much blood you have caused. Oh, how terrible! In a few hours one of my daughters will be orphaned through my fault!"

When the count entered his study, he immediately busied himself with the last preparations he had to make. He seated himself at his desk, took a piece of paper and wrote:

"Hortense, my beloved wife, at the moment when I am perhaps to die—to die on account of you and for your sake—I feel an irresistible impulse to write a few words to you.

"Whether they will ever reach you I do not know, as your place of refuge is unknown to me. But no matter! It shall not be said that I have left this world without having written on this paper the three words: '*I forgive you!*' and the two others: '*Forgive me!*'

"I have no feeling of hatred in my heart any more, only immeasurable sorrow and the deep pain of perhaps going to my death without being able to embrace you for the last time."

When the count had written as far as this, he felt a hot breath on his cheek, followed by a half-suppressed sob, and turning quickly around he saw Hortense in front of him. With tear-stained eyes she read across his shoulder the lines he had just written.

The black domino's prophecy had come true.

CHAPTER XXXVII

THE WILL

DR. TOINON'S residence was furnished like that of a luxury-loving lady. The doctor loved the ladies, and they loved him too.

Very important questions were being discussed at this moment in the elegant apartment.

The second whom the colonel had at first selected from among the spectators had declined to serve, and Fritz was therefore forced to fall back upon the good doctor.

The colonel, Don Jose and Toinon were seated now in the latter's parlor.

Don Jose had laid down the Count de Puysaie's challenge—pistols, ten paces, and duel to continue until one of the two opponents was killed.

"You are satisfied, then, with the conditions I have been authorized to propose?" continued Don Jose, addressing the colonel.

"Yes," replied the colonel, gravely.

"What place do you propose?"

"Any one you please."

"At what hour?"

"You can name it, too."

"Well, then, six o'clock, at Mendon."

"We shall be there."

Don Jose's mission was ended.

The three gentlemen politely bowed to each other, and Don Jose went away.

Toinon, who had only played an unimportant part in the affair up till then, turned to the colonel when they were alone, and said:

"Are you out of your senses, Fritz? You act as if you had lost them."

"That doesn't matter," replied the colonel, curtly. "I have an idea that I shall not survive the duel."

"But why are you going to fight?" asked the physician.

"I must."

"Nonsense!" exclaimed Toinon. "You can never prove to me the necessity of a healthy young man, whom the ladies love, having two ounces of lead put in his body."

"If I refuse to fight this duel, I will be dishonored."

"Nonsense!" exclaimed the doctor again. "Prejudice, mere prejudice! A duel is immoral."

"Enough of your lamentations! If you are sleepy, go to bed and try to sleep. I will wake you when the time comes."

The doctor stammered a few words more and retired to his bedroom.

The colonel, on finding himself alone, seated himself at the writing-desk, took a few sheets of paper with the doctor's initials stamped on them, and wrote:

"COUNT—My resolve is settled. On my lips and in my heart the only kiss my daughter ever gave me still lives in recollection. I owe this kiss to your generosity.

"When you read this letter I will be dead.

"You are a man of honor, and your anger, no matter how justifiable it may be, will not outlast the grave, and that is why I make you my opponent, whom I have so shamefully betrayed, the executor of my will.

"Inclosed you will find two letters. Send them to their addresses. This is the last wish of your unworthy friend,

"COLONEL FRITZ."

The first of the inclosed letters read as follows:

"LILA—My, child, my daughter!

"Without knowing it, you have pronounced my sentence.

"Since the day you showed your repugnance to me, life has become unbearable to me.

"You were right, beloved child. Your instinct warned you. I am a scoundrel; I am not worthy of being a father.

"My child, I leave you a duty.

"You must try to the best of your ability to make good again the harm I have done.

"I have made your poor mother very unhappy! I do not know whether she can ever be consoled, but I depend upon you!

"Oh! beloved child, whom I only clasped a second in my arms! The duty I burden you with is a heavy one. You are my happiness, and at the same time my punishment."

The contents of the second letter inclosed was as follows:

"Hortense—I do not know whether you will ever forgive me, but I shall retain the illusion to the last, and believe in it.

"I treated you shamefully; yet I loved you.

"When you read these lines, nothing will be left of Colonel Fritz but a mortal covering riddled with balls.

"I do not dare to ask you to shed a tear for me. Only think of me sometimes, and when you pray at night for the unfortunate and the guilty, do not except me from your prayer."

When the colonel had finished these two letters he looked at the clock.

It was five o'clock in the morning.

CHAPTER XXXVIII

THE LAST INTERVIEW

THE count sprang up in surprise. His face became pale and purple by turns.

"You here!" he said, in such a low voice that Hortense barely heard him.

Silent, with arms hanging down at her sides and eyes directed at the floor, Hortense stood there, like a condemned person awaiting the sentence of death.

Loredan, at this sight, stretched out his arms, and Hortense, bursting into tears, threw herself into them.

She then clasped her arms about his neck, laid her head on his shoulder, and he kissed her on her forehead and blond hair.

"Ah, fool! Cruel fool!" he murmured.

It was not a reproach only a complaint.

She accepted it as such, for her embrace became more fervent still.

He gently released himself.

"I cannot and will not reproach you at this moment, Hortense," he said. "Why should we imbitter the last hours which we will perhaps pass together?"

"Then it is really true?" she asked. "This duel!"

"This duel is necessary; you know that as well as I do. That man and I cannot live at the same time."

"Oh, how horrible!" exclaimed the countess, covering her face with her hands.

"Suppose I do die, what of it?" sighed the count.

"But I do not want you to die!" exclaimed Hortense. "I do not want you to die. This duel is a crime. What should I do with my grief? You say you pardon me, but at the same time you revenge yourself in the most cruel way."

"You have nothing to do with all this, Hortense. If I fall, you must not believe that you are responsible for my death. I am not going to fight with the man that deceived you, but with the intimate friend who betrayed me."

He took her hand, and forced her to take a seat on a chair.

"Hortense," he continued, "I have sacrificed Cyprienne, our daughter, to my ambition and my ruined finances. Later on I adopted Lila, and, although I was brought to do so by trickery, I herewith sanction the step again. I have made you in my will my sole heir."

Hortense was moved to tears.

"Do not weep, Hortense!" he said. "We could have been happy, but let us think no more of it! Let us think rather of the happiness of others, more especially of Cyprienne."

He paused a short while, and then continued:

"Did you have a more serious reason than the repugnance you had for the baron, when you opposed the marriage?"

Hortense cast her eyes to the floor, and gave no answer.

"I have always been a bad father of a family," continued Loredan, "and I have now only a few hours in which to occupy myself with the happiness of my folks. Therefore answer me at once and candidly."

Hortense bowed her head.

"Yes," she murmured.

"Cyprienne was in love, wasn't she?" asked the count.

"Yes," replied Hortense, again.

"You knew it then, and instead of opposing my will, you preferred not to say anything to me about it."

"You hated her," replied Hortense. "Would you have changed your mind on account of it, if you had known that she was in love?"

"Perhaps," said Loredan, thoughtfully; "but that is past now, the evil is done. The baron's health is ruined, the next crisis will carry him off, and I want Cyprienne to be happy yet. Do you know the name of the man she loves?"

"Yes, I know him. He is the most accomplished gentleman, and the noblest man, I have ever known."

"And what is his name?"

"Vicomte Jose de la Cruz."

"The selection is a good one, and I sanction it the more, since I believe Don Jose loves Cyprienne too. I lay my whole authority in your hands, Hortense. Remember that it is my most earnest wish that this marriage should take place. Now let us speak of you."

"Of me!" exclaimed Hortense; "my life is also at an end."

"No," replied Loredan, "your life is not at an end, for you are a mother."

The first rays of the dawning day shone pale and uncertain through the curtains.

The clock struck five, and three knocks were heard at the door.

The count quickly arose.

Hortense did the same.

"The hour has come," he murmured. "Farewell, Hortense—farewell, my beloved wife, and once more forgive me as I forgive you."

Hortense could not utter a word. It seemed to her as if her heart must break; she had not even the strength to cry.

With firm step Loredan walked to the door to open it and let Don Jose de la Cruz in.

"The carriage is downstairs," said the latter. "As the second of our opponent is a physician, I have not deemed it necessary to take another one."

"Yes, that would have been entirely unnecessary," remarked Loredan, gloomily.

Only now Don Jose noticed the presence of the countess.

He feared he had said too much, and bit his lip.

The count noticed it.

"You can speak," he said; "my wife knows all."

Hortense rushed upon him to hold him back. He cast her hand aside, and exclaimed:

"Come, Don Jose! I am ready!"

"You are going," exclaimed the countess; "you are going without embracing your daughter!"

"You are right! I did not wish to make her uneasy, but I think this kiss—perhaps the last one—will do me good."

The countess hurried through a side door, and a few moments later came back with Cyprienne. The count nervously clasped his weeping daughter to his bosom.

He then turned with a gentle smile to his wife, and said:

"I have two daughters, Hortense. I have only embraced one. Embrace the other yourself in my name."

CHAPTER XXXIX

MEMENTO QUIA PULVIS ES [1]

AFTER the carriage had rolled away, Cyprienne and her unhappy mother sank into each other's arms, and burst into tears.

They both went to Cyprienne's room.

There they sat opposite to each other, not daring either to look at or speak to each other.

In a small adjoining room Lila peacefully slept, not knowing that before the day was out she would be an orphan.

Hortense stood for a long time at her bedside and watched her sleeping.

Cyprienne had followed her mother.

The countess looked at the little sleeper with a mournful gaze, which seemed to say:

"You will have many trials to sustain some time. You will suffer as I have suffered. Then come to me; I am Resignation."

Cyprienne, who smiled through her tears, seemed to be saying in her turn:

"There is no sorrow which is not followed by joy, no suffering without consolation. If your heart is broke, then call me. I am Hope."

---

[1] Remember, because you are dust.

After a while Lila opened her big, blue eyes and smiled at her "little mamma."

"Is it late already?" she asked.

"Yes, Lila, you must get up now," replied Cyprienne, gently; "to-day is Ash Wednesday."

The countess and her daughter now began to dress the little one.

They put a black dress on her, as if she were already in mourning for her father.

Outside a gray fog seemed to envelop every object in mourning.

The streets were deserted.

The Countess of Puysaie, Cyprienne and Lila went on foot through the Champs-Elysees and then up the Rue de la Madeleine.

The Church of the Madeleine had been open only a few minutes and was almost empty.

Hortense and Cyprienne knelt in the darkest corner of the chapel.

"Listen, Lila," murmured Cyprienne in the little one's ear, "we must pray to-day."

And the countess added:

"We must pray for those who are in danger of losing their lives."

The priest took the sacred ashes between his fingers, made the sign of the cross on his forehead, and murmured the terrible:

"*Memento quia pulvis es.*"

"Yes, dust, and only dust," sobbed Hortense, and thought of the two men who were young and strong but yesterday, and who at this moment might perhaps be both lying on the ground stretched in death.

"*Et in pulverem reverteris!*" [1]

And all three prayed earnestly and fervently.

At this very hour a second prayer, just as earnest and fervent as this one, ascended to heaven.

It was the prayer of the Countess of Monte-Cristo.

But it was not a prayer of sorrow; it was one of joy.

Helene had recovered her child! Pippiona was really her daughter!

What more did she wish now?

Nothing.

Matifay! Legigant! Toinon! What did she care for these three soundrels?

Her daughter!

She never grew tired of repeating these two loved words, which she had so often stammered in her solitude.

Memento quis pulvis es!

Poor woman! She forgot that every joy has its evil, that every light throws a shadow!

Go, poor mother, go and kneel beside Cyprienne, Hortense, and Lila.

Joy is pride, too, and the present day is one of humility. Bow your head! Do not forget, in the intoxication of your joy, the conditions of human nature, whose slave you are!

Do not thank God alone, but implore him not to desert you.

Ah! All earthly joys resemble the fruit which, as the legend runs, one finds on the banks of the Dead Sea— outside fresh and red, inside ashes.

Et in pulverem reverteris.

---

[1] And return again to dust.

CHAPTER XL

THE DUEL

THE morning dawned. It was a cold, nasty, gloomy morning.

Two carriages slowly drove up the hill which leads to the forest of Mendon.

When they reached the top of the hill the carriages stopped, and four men got out.

From one of the carriages Count Loredan de Puysaie and the Vicomte Don Jose de la Cruz, and from the other, Colonel Fritz and Dr. Toinon.

The two parties greeted each other, and then Don Jose advanced a few steps.

Dr. Toinon followed his example, and the two seconds spoke together a while; the doctor then strode over to the carriages and gave the coachmen his instructions, by pointing out with his finger the roads they were to take.

The four men then went on foot to the thick bushes which line the left-hand side of the road.

Don Jose walked on in advance. On one arm he led the count, and in the other he carried a pistol case.

The four men went into the forest, and walked about twenty minutes under the tall chestnut trees.

Daylight finally shone through the branches, and they came to a small, open space.

This was the place.

The sun just rose above the horizon and shone through the fog, like a ball of fire.

"You have selected a good spot," said the count to Don Jose. "It is a nice place to die in."

Colonel Fritz and Toinon followed behind the two others.

Toinon was very red and the colonel very pale.

The latter approached the count and said:

"Count, do you think I am a coward?"

"No," replied the count briefly.

"Then," continued the colonel, "you will not view the step I am about to take in any other light than the proper one."

The count turned away with a look of disgust, and said to Don Jose:

"Load the pistols."

The colonel's lips twitched nervously when he heard this order.

"If you have anything more to say to me," said the count, gruffly, "then do it at once. I am in a hurry."

"Then we really are to fight a duel?"

"Have you doubted it?"

"A man of honor like you wish to stake your life against that of a miserable scoundrel like myself?"

"Hate is stronger than contempt," said the count.

"I beg you, count, consider—consider once more."

"I just told you that I did not think you a coward. Your present behavior could really induce me to suspect that you are afraid."

"Afraid—yes," murmured the colonel softly, "but not of death. What difference does my death make? There is merely one scoundrel less in the world then, that's all. But the thought that you might be killed by me is what moves me."

"Are you ready, Don Jose?" asked the count.

"Oh, one minute more! one minute more!" continued the colonel imploringly. "You want me to disappear; I can understand your motive: you have a right to it. Do you want me to emigrate? I will go wherever you wish to send me. You shall never hear from me again."

"You are indeed a coward," said the Count de Puysaie, shrugging his shoulders.

"Do you want me to die?" continued Fritz. "I will shed my blood, I give you my word of honor, I will kill myself, but do not put me in danger of becoming a murderer."

"Enough, enough!" said the count; "you cannot convince me or change my mind. Let us do what remains for us to do."

Toinon measured the paces, and made them as large as possible.

After the distance had been settled, Don Jose threw a coin in the air to decide which places the opponents were to choose.

He then loaded the pistols.

The weapons were ready.

The vicomte walked between the count and the colonel and handed each of them a pistol.

"Forward!" said Don Jose.

The pistols were aimed. A single report rang out, and the colonel shivered violently.

The count had aimed well; his ball had grazed his opponent's cheek.

A few inches further to the left, and the colonel would have been a dead man.

He quietly held up his pistol and fired in the air.

The Comte de Puysaie frowned.

"You are playing the generous man," he said ironically; "I can tell you in advance that you are wrong, for I shall not do so. Don Jose, load the pistols again."

The colonel's face became livid with fear.

With tightly clinched teeth and trembling lips, he muttered to himself:

"No, I do not wish to die!"

With shivering hand he seized the pistol which Don Jose handed to him.

This time two reports rang out simultaneously.

The count's ball had struck first, and Fritz, tumbling back, had fired into the air again, without, however, having intended to do so this time.

The lead had penetrated his breast.

He sank into the grass, and the blood rushed in streams out of his double wound.

"Let us go!" said the count, without even casting a look at his opponent.

Fritz uttered a low groan, and stretched out his arms as if to call the count back.

The latter turned around.

Toinon, who knelt at the side of the colonel, unbuttoned his coat.

A crumpled letter covered with bloodstains fell on the grass.

The letter was addressed to the Count de Puysaie.

"To me!" asked the latter in surprise.

The colonel nodded, and said:

"To you!"

Loredan took the letter, and broke the seal.

With a glance, he read the contents of the will, which we already know.

He then drew near to the dying man, and said:

"What you wish shall be done."

Fritz cast a look full of gratitude at him.

"Let us go!" said the count once more to Don Jose.

The latter turned to Dr. Toinon, and promised to send him assistance as soon as he reached the carriages, which were waiting at the foot of the hill.

The Count de Puysaie walked silently along at the side of his young friend.

As they descended the steep acclivity, which they had ascended but a few moments before, the count said to his companion:

"That man was a great scoundrel, but still he was human."

Those were the only words through which he let Don Jose into his secret.

. . . .

The mass in the church of the Madeleine was over, and with the cross of ashes on their forehead, Hortense, Cyprienne and Lila had returned home.

As the moment approached when they were finally to hear the result of the duel, their souls were bowed still lower by the weight of anxious uneasiness.

Who would come back? The colonel or the count? Or would either of the two come back?

As often as a carriage rolled along the street, they hurried to the window.

Lila did not know the reason for this fear, which she nevertheless shared, and her questioning look wandered continually from the "little mamma" to Hortense.

At last the iron gate was thrown open. Cyprienne leaned out of the window, and could not suppress a cry of joy.

It was the count, who returned alone, safe and sound.

Don Jose had remained on the field to assist Dr. Toinon.

The count, without saying a word, walked straight toward Lila, raised her in his arms, kissed her and murmured:

"Poor child!"

He then embraced his wife and Cyprienne.

"He is punished!" he said.

He then handed Hortense and Lila two letters stained with blood.

"He was a great scoundrel," said the count, "yet I feel that I have neither the courage nor the right to prevent him from receiving his daughter's embrace."

Just then another carriage rolled through the gate.

It was Don Jose de la Cruz, who had returned after having accompanied Dr. Toinon and the dying colonel to the latter's home.

"Here," said Don Jose to the count—"here is the address you wanted."

And he handed the count a piece of paper, on which were the words:

"Fritz, Rue des Macons—Sorbonne."

"This address, Hortense," said the count, "is for you. Do as your conscience tells you."

CHAPTER XLI

THE OTHER SIDE OF A GILDED LIFE

WE ARE in a narrow dirty room of a house in the Sorbonne quarter.

The room is not whitewashed, and the floor is trodden down and full of holes.

Three straw chairs, a wooden table, a bureau and a bed with a thin mattress and a straw pillow, are all the furniture in the place.

This hovel was Colonel Fritz's home.

A costly *necessaire* of carved silver stands open near a pitcher with a broken handle, and sparkles in the red gleam of a tallow candle, which is stuck in a leaden holder.

When a person is invited to castles he must appear to be rich.

Fritz had probably not eaten any breakfast for six months, so as to be able to buy this *necessaire*.

Clothes of the most modern cut hung on pegs attached to the wall, and in the half open drawers of the old bureau holland linen sparkled.

A cigar case, which cost one hundred francs, lay next to radish peels and bread crusts.

The most terrible poverty is that which conceals itself behind a luxurious exterior.

Through what miracle of shrewdness, force of will and energy, had the colonel succeeded in playing this comedy so long without having his secret found out? If he was not invited to dinner, he did not dine at all. How could he converse, smile, dance, and play the agreeable gentleman, when hunger was gnawing at his vitals?

This was just his strength. If you scratched the man, the actor appeared above the surface.

In society he was on the stage, and moved and acted in accordance with his part.

This miserable room, on the other hand, was the little apartment behind the scenes, where he dressed and painted, where he was no longer the handsome Colonel Fritz, but Florestan, the vagabond of Brussels.

He had not permitted any human eye to penetrate his secret.

Even Legigant did not know to what depths of poverty and misery his comrade had fallen.

Colonel Fritz was proud, and never complained.

Fritz suspected—and those who knew Legigant had to admit that he was right—that Legigant, if he knew of his poverty, would only throw him a bone from the booty.

To-day, however, the play was nearing its end.

Death was about to cry:

"Down with the curtain!"

What did Fritz care now whether his secret was known or not?

Lying on the mattress, his face red with fever and nervously clutching the bedcover with his hands, he gasped and groaned.

Dr. Toinon moved up and down the room, made bandages and mixed drinks.

"Give me something to drink!" stammered Fritz; "it burns in my breast as if I had swallowed hot coals."

Toinon poured the contents of a vial in a glass, mixed it with lukewarm water, and cautiously held it to the lips of the patient, who drank eagerly.

"Ah, that's good," he murmured.

He then lay down again.

Toinon shook his head.

"He will not live till morning," he murmured.

Fritz now remained perfectly quiet.

Dr. Toinon's drink gave the patient sleep but not rest.

From time to time a shudder ran through his whole frame, and reddish froth came to his lips.

Suddenly he sprang up.

Dr. Toinon in vain tried to hold him.

He slipped out of his hands with the elasticity of an eel; sprang out of bed, and ran about the room in his bare feet, while the perspiration dripped from his forehead. It did not last long, however, before he sank exhausted to the ground.

With great trouble and effort Dr. Toinon carried him back to his couch.

Here he lay tranquil.

Only his lips moved, and he uttered unintelligible words. Dr. Toinon listened intently, and became convinced that his patient was trying to pray.

In this way the hours sped on, and it became night. Toinon noiselessly opened the door of the attic, and cautiously descended the dark stairs.

He was totally exhausted, and desired to sleep a few hours.

He begged the janitress, who usually attended to the

colonel's wants, to go up two or three times, and let him know if his patient's condition suddenly changed for the worse.

He then went away without troubling his conscience at leaving his friend Fritz alone.

The janitress promised to do everything Dr. Toinon asked; but no sooner had he gone than she went to bed again and growled:

"I haven't the slightest intention of running up the stairs at night on account of that man. What do I care for the poverty-stricken fellow, who can't even afford to keep a nurse; never comes home at night until after twelve, and doesn't want to pay anything for having the door opened!"

In the colonel's little room, meanwhile, coldness and darkness reigned.

No mother, no wife, no daughter, will close the dying man's eyes.

All the ties of love he had formed had been torn asunder by himself.

He wished to live alone, let him then die alone!

.   .   .   .

The rolling of a carriage was heard in the narrow street.

The street door was opened and then shut again.

Then light, cautious steps came up the creaking stairs and paused in front of the door, which was slightly ajar.

A gleam of light fell through this opening into the room.

"Here it is, madame," said the voice of the janitress. And a veiled lady in black entered the attic room.

A girl, also dressed in mourning, stepped into the room with her.

The patient's sleep resembled a fainting fit.

He did not notice the entrance of the peculiar visitors.

"Leave us alone," said the lady in black.

Then the two—the lady and the child—silently knelt beside the deathbed.

CHAPTER XLII

THE ANGELS OF DEATH

THE dawning day still found Hortense and Lila in the same attitude.

Kneeling on the floor, Hortense read the prayer for the dead.

At the sound of her voice the colonel opened his eyes a little.

He thought his dream continued, for he saw the victims praying for the headsman.

He made a great effort to sit upright.

He stretched out his hand, to convince himself, by contact, that it was no dream, and in a voice wherein fear and joy struggled with each other, he murmured:

"Hortense!"

The Countess of Puysaie slowly raised her eyes from her book.

"You!" continued the colonel—"you here! Ah, then you forgive me too."

Hortense pointed with her finger toward heaven and earnestly replied:

"Do not punish, saith the Lord, and you will not be punished yourself."

"And my daughter?"

Hortense arose and made Lila visible through this movement.

The wounded man held out his arms to his daughter.

"Lila," said Hortense, "embrace your father."

"Ah!" exclaimed Fritz, "I gladly die now, and am happy—happy through you, you consoling angels!"

Lila seated herself on the bed, and the colonel pressed his child fervently to his heart.

"I owe this last consolation to you, madame, and to the count!" said the colonel, after a pause. "There are hearts, then, which are capable of such generosity. Ah, if it were permitted me to live longer, all my efforts would be made for you too!"

He was silent for a while, and then continued:

"But no! It is better thus! It is better that I die! Of what good am I on earth now? You will try to forget me, you will perhaps be happy yet. If I could take this hope with me to the grave, I believe I would find forgiveness in heaven too."

"Have confidence in eternal mercy," replied the countess in a gentle voice. "You will be forgiven as we have forgiven you."

"What! Has Loredan forgiven me?"

"My presence here must prove to you that he has banished all hatred from his heart, even though he has forgotten nothing."

"And my letters?"

"He delivered them to Lila and me, and Lila will conscientiously obey her father's last wishes. Let us pray now again. The moment is grave."

And once more Hortense and Lila knelt down and prayed.

Dr. Toinon, on visiting his patient early next morning, was surprised at his unusual tranquillity.

He had no hope, for the colonel was irretrievably lost; still the physician had not expected such a mild death agony.

In answer to the glances Hortense directed at him, he said:

"I cannot do anything more."

He spoke these words in a very low voice, but the colonel heard them.

"Yes," he said with a faint smile, "the physician of the body cannot do me any more good; I only need the healer of the soul."

Upon a look from the countess, Toinon went away, and a few minutes later the priest entered.

This messenger of divine mercy heard the unhappy man's confession, and then spoke the sacred words which absolve all sins in heaven and on earth.

A few minutes later the last struggle began. The hand which held Lila's in a firm clasp, hung listless, and the lips of the dying man moved as if in prayer.

Night, dark night came, and with it the angel of death entered the room.

CHAPTER XLIII

BLANCHE

IN ANOTHER sick room, of which our readers already know, joy and happiness reigned supreme.

Helene could not get tired of embracing Pippiona, her daughter, and kissed her again and again.

She made her tell her sufferings a hundred times a day.

And when Pippiona had finished, the Countess of Monte-Cristo would begin to speak of her hopes.

Thereupon an unbroken vow of plans for the future followed, all beginning with the words:

"When you get well again—"

The effect of joy is, indeed, wonderful; Pippiona's convalescence made visible progress.

Every day found her stronger and fresher.

It was to be expected that she would get up in a few weeks, and walk about the room supported on her mother's arm.

In the meanwhile spring came, beautiful spring with its blue sky, flowers, green meadows, chirping birds, and many-colored butterflies.

Then they intended to go to the country and seek a place of refuge in a small house, with white walls at the back of a large garden.

Then they wished to be alone. They had to pay up for lost time, and that could only be done by living entirely alone for a few months.

It would be hard to tell which of these two souls, whether that of the daughter or that of the mother, clung the most to these beautiful dreams.

At night the Countess of Monte-Cristo would get up to observe and admire her beloved Blanche.

She often sat hours at a time at the bedside of the convalescent, and hardly dared to breathe for fear of waking Pippiona out of her sleep.

When she was not at her side, she was troubled by sudden doubts and fears.

"If it should all be a deception," she would then say to herself, "if all this happiness were only a dream! If this child, which I have imagined to have found again, did not exist at all!"

And then she hurried back to Blanche and embraced her, to convince herself of the actuality of her happiness.

Blanche had thrown both her arms about her mother's neck.

"You love me, don't you!" asked Helene, for the hundredth time.

"Yes. Do you still doubt it?"

"Do you love me above everything?"

Blanche hesitated.

Helene felt her heart contract, and threatening her daughter with her finger, she said:

"There, you see now that you do not love me, for you are hiding something from me."

Blanche gazed at her mother with big blue eyes.

She then said:

"I am not concealing anything from you. What have I to conceal?"

In thoughtful tones she added after a while:

"I am thinking in vain of anything I could conceal from you. Yes, I think I love you above everything. At least, I don't know of any one I love more than you."

"Perhaps," murmured the Countess of Monte-Cristo, "there is some one to-day whom you love so much as you love me, and you will love that person even more to-morrow."

Blanche cast down her eyes and made no reply.

"I was right," thought Helene to herself, "love has awakened."

This thought made her shudder.

Love had awakened, but when and for whom?

Up till now Blanche had lived in the society of Cinella, Monna, Tommaso, in a society of acrobats, murderers and thieves.

Had she learned to love in *this* society?

Ah, if Blanche had succumbed to that horrible fate!

What would then become of the beautiful dreams Helene had indulged in?

"At least," she said aloud, "at least you do not regret anything which your past life offered you?"

"Why should I regret anything?" replied Blanche, candidly. "I always suffered."

"There are sufferings one learns to love."

Blanche sorrowfully shook her head.

"There may have been one among your former comrades," continued Helene, pursuing her idea, "who was friendlier and more affectionate to you than the others.

At present you do not regret him, but a day may come when you might.''

Blanche's eyes opened so wide, and with such an expression of surprise in them, that it clearly showed how incomprehensible her mother's words were to her.

The latter was put at ease by this look.

"I see,'' she murmured, "that this poor little heart belongs to me alone.''

Then she added aloud:

"You must not be angry at my question, dear child. Other mothers are happy. They have always had their child before them, and its heart never harbored a thought which was not known to them. I, on the other hand, do not know the thoughts of your heart. I do not know what trials you have undergone. You are almost a stranger to me, and yet are so closely allied to me that you are almost a portion of my own self.''

At this moment the door of the room was opened, and Joseph's voice asked:

"Can I come in?''

At the sound of Joseph's voice Blanche trembled violently, a blush suffused her cheeks, and she clung close to her mother.

The latter looked at her in surprise.

The thought suddenly awoke in her:

"Is this the one she loves?''

She turned toward the door behind which Jose waited, and said:

"In a few minutes, Don Jose.''

She then turned to her daughter again, and said:

"Oh, my Blanche! have confidence in me, and leave the care of making you happy to me. Tell me all your thoughts, all your griefs, if you have any. Unlock your heart, so that I can read therein the secrets which you yourself may not be aware of.

"A mother's eye penetrates the future, and I already feel that the moment is approaching when you will be lost to me again. On the day you will feel this also; come without fear to me and confess everything to me, as to your best friend. Why should you not be candid? You know that I have no other desire than to see you happy."

Blanche hid her face in her mother's bosom, and replied in a low, almost indistinct voice:

"I swear to you, mother, that I have nothing to conceal from you."

"Are you sure of it?" asked the countess, doubtingly.

"Yes, perfectly sure."

"Then," thought Helene to herself, and thoroughly reassured, "I must have been mistaken."

At the same time she arose, opened the door, and exclaimed:

"You can come in, Don Jose."

Joseph entered.

He was very serious, almost gloomy.

He had just witnessed the duel between the Count de Puysaie and Colonel Fritz.

"Well?" asked Helene, as she turned her questioning look toward him.

"It is over," he replied, in a low voice; "Fritz has received the wages of his sins."

"Good!" said the Countess of Monte-Cristo. "Is that all you have to tell me? You can tell me now all the details."

"I have," said Don Jose, "a visitor to announce to you that is not for you alone, but rather for Mademoiselle Blanche."

He smiled as he said this, and this smile was reflected on the countess's stern face.

"Really, Don Jose," she said, "you are a treasure; you think of everything. Come here, little one. Blanche asks after you every day."

These words were directed to a person who had timidly paused at the threshold of the door.

Blanche raised herself up in bed, stretched out her arms, and exclaimed:

"My dear, good Ursula!"

Ursula was already at her side, and was already being overwhelmed with caresses by the invalid.

"Thank you, Don Jose," said Helene. "You could not have given me more pleasure."

Joseph's arrival reminded her, however, that her work was not done yet.

"Now that you have found your good and pretty nurse again," she said, turning to Blanche, "I am no longer uneasy. I can leave you for a short while. You are old friends. I will leave you alone together. Still I beg you, Ursula, do not allow our patient to talk too much."

"Have no fear, madame."

"Come, Joseph, and tell me all about the duel."

The countess and Joseph left the room, and the two young girls remained alone together.

"Now that I have you by me, I feel entirely happy!" exclaimed Blanche.

She was buried in thought a moment and then murmured:

"Was that what ailed me? Yes, it must have been that. For I am not ungrateful. I feel that. I love Madame Lamouroux, my mother, with all the strength of my soul, and yet—can I tell it to you, Ursula?—there is a void in my heart. There is something still missing to me. Isn't that funny?"

Ursula smiled, as young girls usually smile when they begin to understand the affairs of the heart.

"A few months ago I should have been as much surprised at it as you!" she murmured; "to-day, though, I understand its meaning."

She silently thought of Louis Jacquemin, and said to herself:

"Love is what she misses."

"But now," continued Blanche, "I am satisfied, and why should I not be, since I see every one that I love beside me—my mother, Dr. Ozam, you, Ursula, and—"

She hesitated a moment, and then added in a low voice:

"And Joseph?"

Her hesitation did not last long, and the change in her voice was very slight.

Still Ursula had noticed both.

What the Countess of Monte-Cristo could not discover, Ursula guessed at the first glance. She read Blanche's secret, the secret which Blanche, no doubt, did not know herself.

The poor girl loved Joseph, or was about to love him.

Blanche was still young, and could not feel any serious passion for Joseph.

But if this indistinct need were permitted to take root,

it would, perhaps, be transformed in a very short while into real love.

And what sorrows, what struggles were in store for every one, especially for Blanche herself.

Ursula, who was not only Cyprienne's confidant, but Joseph's also, knew of their mutual love.

She therefore considered it her duty to inform Blanche of it.

All these reflections passed rapidly through Ursula's brain, and she replied to Blanche's last remark as follows:

"You must accustom yourself to the thought, Blanche, of not always seeing these persons about you. Your mother, of course, will never leave you, and Dr. Ozam will always be at your side in case you need him. Joseph and I will only be too glad to do you a service at all times. Still, this cannot always remain thus. You are now entirely restored, and we must turn to others who need our care more than you do. Besides, each of us has his special duty, which cannot be neglected."

Ursula paused a moment, and then continued:

"I tell you all this from mere love for you, for I would like to guard you against hopes and dreams which will never be realized. Therefore, it is better to crush and nip them in the bud."

"What you tell me, Ursula," replied Blanche, "is very cruel. I know, though, that your intentions are good, and I thank you for it. You tell me all that on account of Joseph?"

Ursula nodded assent.

Blanche placed her hand over her forehead and eyes.

"It seems to me," she then said, "as if your voice awakened me, and since you spoke to me I read my thoughts clearly. Oh, you are right! I thank you for your candor. Then Joseph—"

"Loves a pure girl, handsome as an angel, and worthy of him. Do you wish to be an obstacle to this love? I guessed that you loved Joseph, and I considered it my duty to warn you. You know so little of him yet that the sacrifice cannot be a cruel one; but what is easy to-day might be impossible to-morrow."

"Easy to-day!" murmured Blanche, with the smile of a martyr. "You are right, Ursula. It is easy, indeed, to-day. Your advice is good, and I shall heed it."

Joseph meanwhile had told the Countess of Monte-Cristo all about the duel between the Count de Puysaie and Colonel Fritz.

When Joseph had finished, she begged him to send Ursula to her, so that she could tell her all the news from the rose garden.

Joseph was to take Ursula's place by Blanche meanwhile.

They were alone in the room, and Blanche, whose thoughts were still busy with Ursula's last words, kept silent.

Joseph was also silent.

Blanche was the first to break the silence.

Ursula had either told her too much or too little, and she wished to hear her sentence out of Joseph's own mouth.

"What ails you," she asked, "you are looking so gloomy!"

"If a person is engaged in a life-and-death struggle," replied Joseph, "as your mother and I, days come when the mind is troubled."

"And is this one of those days?" asked Blanche, gently.

Joseph did not answer this question, and continued:

"There are hours when one grows tired of being alone, and when one seeks congenial souls, a friend who understands our grief and consoles us."

"Have you not got me?" asked Blanche, smiling; "am I not your sister?"

Joseph thankfully seized the little hand Blanche offered him.

"Yes, dear sister," he cried; "yes, you shall be the friend to whom I shall in the future relate my joys and sorrows. Where could I find a more agreeable consoler and confidant than you?",

He placed Blanche's hand to his lips as he said this.

"Go on," she said, "I await the commencement of the terrible confession."

"I am in love," replied Joseph, simply.

Blanche trembled. She was now to receive positive assurance.

"And you are loved in return?" she asked.

"I think so," replied Joseph, modestly.

"Then," said Blanche, with a forced smile, "I cannot see why you should be unhappy."

"Ah, I am the unhappiest man in the world!"

And now he told everything from the commencement —how beautiful Cyprienne looked the first time he saw her in the Countess of Monte-Cristo's parlors; the meeting in the hothouse, and then that mournful day when Joseph, hiding behind a pillar, had witnessed Cyprienne's marriage to Baron Matifay.

Pale and breathless, Blanche listened to the tale. The

more fervently Joseph's passion for Cyprienne was expressed, the more the poor girl had to make superhuman efforts not to lose her strength and betray herself.

She thought, she felt, she knew!

Her uneasiness during the last few days, her sudden starts, the trembling of her lips, the beating of her heart —all was clear to her now.

Ursula was right. She loved Joseph.

In this weak body, though, lived the courage of a heroine.

"I am nothing but a sickly person," she said. "I am not fated ever to enjoy the happiness of marriage. I will be your sister. Cyprienne will enjoy the pleasure which life and society offer; I will only sit at the fireside, rock the children, and sing them to sleep with the beautiful Italian songs I know."

Joseph did not divine the real cause of the mournful character of Blanche's words; he had no suspicion of the cruelty he inflicted through his confidential remarks. He could not grow tired of speaking about Cyprienne, and went right on with his story.

Blanche listened to him like a martyr.

"Ah, how he loves her!" she thought.

Joseph still went on. Suddenly, however, he stopped.

Helene entered, quickly drew near to him, and muttered in a voice which sent a cold shudder down his back:

"Silence, unhappy man! You are killing her. She loves you!"

CHAPTER XLIV

AN ANGEL DIES

SHE loves you! These muttered words filled the young man's heart with inexpressible fear. Blanche was in love with him, and he could not return this love because he loved Cyprienne.

The Countess of Monte-Cristo, in spite of the grief which moved her heart, forced herself to smile, and she seated herself at her daughter's bedside, as if to protect her against that terrible enemy, hopeless love.

"Have you conversed pleasantly?" she asked, in a gay tone.

"Yes," replied Blanche. "My brother Joseph told me his troubles, and I reassured him. We must never give up all hope, even though we feel we are dying."

"Dying!" exclaimed the Countess of Monte-Cristo, as a cold shudder ran down her back. "What a terrible word! We must not think of death, but of life."

Blanche sank back in her white bed with a sigh.

"Ah, mother," she murmured, "I am very tired! When we die, we perhaps sleep."

"Banish such foolish thoughts!" exclaimed the Countess of Monte-Cristo. "You *must not* die! How can you speak of death at the moment when you have been given back to me, and when we shall all be happy?"

With gleaming eyes, she turned toward Joseph, and said:

"Do you hear, Joseph? This wicked child speaks of dying."

And in a lower tone, she added:

"Are you really going to let my daughter die?"

He did not dare to raise his eyes. His face was pale as death.

A terrible struggle raged within him.

It was a question of losing Cyprienne forever, or to let the only child of the sainted woman die.

"My life belongs to you, Helene," he finally murmured; "do with it as you wish!"

The Countess of Monte-Cristo enthusiastically seized Joseph's hand and exclaimed:

"I accept this sacrifice in my name and in that of Blanche. Joseph, you are the noblest man in the world. You are my beloved son!"

She passionately embraced him, and he murmured:

"My heart is dead. I have nothing to hope for on earth any more. My happiness was your work, Helene. You gave it to me; you take it from me again—your will be done!"

The Countess of Monte-Cristo and Joseph spoke softly to each other a short time yet, and Blanche watched, with curious eyes, this, to her, silent but not incomprehensible scene.

She divine that Joseph was bringing her, at this moment, a new sacrifice, the greatest his noble soul was capable of.

But she, too, formed an invincible resolve—the resolve to conceal her love, and if necessary to deny it.

She did not wish to possess, at any price, this noble heart, which she would have to rob another of.

When, therefore, after Joseph had gone away, and the Countess of Monte-Cristo returned to her daughter, her eyes sparkling with hope, Blanche was the first to speak.

"Mamma," she said, "my brother Joseph is very sad."

"Yes," replied the Countess of Monte-Cristo, gently. "I've noticed it a long time, and was uneasy about it. Joseph is sad because his heart is empty. If he is loved he will be happy again."

"You think his heart is empty?" replied Blanche, with a doubtful smile, full of mournful irony. "You only say that, mother. I think that his heart is not empty, but, on the contrary, too full. Do you know the girl my brother Joseph loves?"

Only mothers know how to tell pious lies.

"Yes, I know her," said the countess, "and perhaps she is not far from here."

Blanche smiled again, in the same way as before.

"An obstacle separates him from her, he told me," continued Blanche. "Do you know the nature of the obstacle, mamma?"

"Yes," replied Helene, "your will would be sufficient to remove it."

"Then it will certainly be removed," replied Blanche, "for it is my most fervent wish to see my brother Joseph happy with his Cyprienne."

"With his Cyprienne?" repeated the Countess of Monte-Cristo, with pretended surprise. "Who is Cyprienne?"

Blanche raised herself up in bed, and looked at her mother with the same gentle, ironical look.

"You don't want to tell me, mamma," she began, "but I know it already. The girl my brother Joseph loves is not named Blanche, but Cyprienne. What difference can it make to poor Pippiona, who must die anyway, whether Don Jose's happy bride is named Blanche or Cyprienne? Pippiona is a poor girl, whom he would never have thought of falling in love with. And as for Blanche, who was to be so handsome, so rich, so fabulously happy, neither you, nor he, nor any one will ever know her. Ah, that poor Blanche might have become jealous; poor Pippiona knows, however, that she has not that right."

"Ah, there you see, now," exclaimed Helene, despairingly, "that you love Joseph!"

"That is true," replied Blanche. "I love him very much, almost as much as I do you; but what is love? Pippiona is still too young, too insignificant and poor, to be really in love. Blanche, of course, would have loved, and would have been loved."

"Do not talk that way!" cried the poor mother. "You will break my heart!"

"If I loved my brother Joseph," continued Blanche, in a more serious tone, "the way a bride loves her intended, I would be sad if I heard that he loved another.

"Look and see if I am crying! On the contrary, I have never felt so happy as I do now."

She became as white as the muslin of her dress, but continued nevertheless:

"Yes, I am happy, very happy. I don't know, but I feel bad all of a sudden."

She sank back exhausted on her pillow, adding in explanation: "Joy tires."

The Countess of Monte-Cristo observed this affecting resignation with silent wonder.

To describe her despair would be impossible.

Blanche, her daughter, was still there, and her hand touched her; her lips could still feel on her cheeks the warm traces of former kisses; her ear heard the loved sound of her voice, and yet the unhappy mother felt as if she were embracing a phantom, and as if this voice were but a distant echo from another world.

Blanche possessed now in Helene's eyes the nebulous brilliancy of a spirit. Her fixed look seemed to be gazing far away in the great beyond—in her voice the sound of divine harmonies trembled.

There could be no doubt any more. Love had brought her back to life, the lack of love was killing her.

But it was not a mournful death—oh, no!

About the lips of the dying girl that indescribable smile played which recalls the exiled back to their country.

She herself consoled her poor, despairing mother.

The latter did not leave her. It seemed as if she wished to sun herself in the last rays of this extinguishing soul; as if she wished to transform every hour into a day and every day into a week of that pleasure which she had known but a short time, and which she was to be deprived of again forever.

"Come, dear mother," said Blanche, "you must not cry. I am not suffering! I feel no pain. I am merely going to sleep. I am only tired, so tired!"

She paused a minute, and then continued:

"Life was a great burden to me. Yet I do not complain. The two months I have lived with you more than counterbalance a lifetime of misery. Why do you cry? I am not going to leave you. God is good. If I have committed any fault He will forgive me; He will open His paradise to me, but I shall say to Him: 'No, my God, I do not wish to wander about your garden where the stars bloom. Permit me to choose my own Paradise.' And my Paradise, dear mother, will be to stay by you, by you! Always to live in your thoughts, to hear and answer you, and to softly whisper with your soul. When the flower fills the garden with its perfume, and you hold it to your lips, then I will be the flower and I will receive the kiss. I will transform myself into the ray which gives light, into the spirit which floats past, into the murmur which greets your ear. The wind which plays with your hair will be my caress, the perfume which rises from the blooming lilies to your window will be my breath, and the distant melody which moves you to tears will be my voice."

The Countess of Monte-Cristo listened to the heart-rending consolation of her dying daughter with aching heart and eyes streaming with tears.

"No, no!" she exclaimed, "angel of heaven, do not fly from me! What will become of me if I do not see you any more, if I do not hear the music of your voice any more, if I cannot kiss your eyes any more, or drink in your smile! Oh, heavenly nourishment of my heart, bread of my soul! Shall the barely commenced meal be ended already? I am hungering and thirsting for your caresses. Is God only an unjust, capricious tyrant? Why did he give you back to me, if he takes you away from me again so soon?"

Blanche raised her voice and said, in a pious, almost stern tone:

"Mother, do not blaspheme! Do not be angry with God! Your rage and your blasphemy will separate us forever. I know very well that you will not be able to live without me, but that is what makes me, at this moment, so joyous and calm. So long as you remain on the earth I will be the companion of your exile; later on, when you follow the will of our Father in heaven, and likewise close your eyes in death, then I shall stand at your bedside, and our two hearts, intoxicated with joy, united forever, will fly aloft to heaven."

The night was beautiful, and the sky radiant with stars.

The invalid had fallen asleep, and in her dream she appeared to be speaking with some one who could not be seen.

Suddenly, her weak, emaciated limbs trembled, she opened her eyes wide, and called her mother, who stood at the window.

The poor mother approached the bed, and Blanche, seizing her hand, said in a faint voice:

"The moments I still have to stay with you are few. I wish every one to be here to say good-by to me forever. All—do you hear? Especially you, the good doctor, Ursula, Cyprienne, and Joseph."

This last name was spoken lower than the others. It was Blanche's last sigh—her last earthly plaint.

From that moment on she belonged entirely to heaven. They were all there, all whom Blanche wished to see assembled about her deathbed—Helene, Dr. Ozam, Ursula, Cyprienne, and Joseph.

The curtains were drawn together, the lamp was covered with a shade and the light turned down half.

All was silent.

All was still.

Only now and then a low moan, a sob, or a sigh, was heard.

Blanche had wished Cyprienne to advance close to her—Cyprienne and Joseph, the only man for whom her heart had beat, and her rival, whom she called "sister."

She turned her humid eyes toward them, and said, with a divine smile:

"Your happiness will not make you forget me, will it?"

She then looked at Cyprienne and sighed.

"You are very handsome! I can see your soul; it is still more beautiful than your face. You are good, my sister, and I love you."

She had drawn her emaciated hand from under the quilt and offered it to Cyprienne, who pressed it to her lips and knelt down beside the bed.

"You are a saint, Blanche!" stammered Cyprienne.

Blanche held her pale lips close to Cyprienne's ear, and said in a voice weak as a whisper:

"I love you. Love him for my sake."

"Ah, dear, dear sister!" exclaimed Cyprienne, bursting into tears.

"I will be your sister," replied Blanche, "in heaven!"

She let go of Cyprienne's hand, and with a glance she called Joseph to her side.

"You must know, too, my friend," she then said, "that I loved you dearly. The violet in the grass sometimes sighs, if it is not noticed. It is angry at the hand which despises it; at the eye which did not know how to discover it. That is why it exhales its perfume. It means to say

by it: 'I am here, think of me!' I was like the little violet.
You passed by. You did not see me, and that is why I
die. Still be blessed, Joseph, for causing me this pain; it
is very cruel, and yet so sweet! The little violet is withered; it hangs loosely on its stem, but its last perfume
belongs to you!"

She seized Cyprienne's hand again, and that of Joseph,
and placed them in each other.

"And now you, my good doctor," she continued, after
Joseph and Cyprienne had stepped aside, "you are a
learned man, an experienced physician, and would, without doubt, have saved me if my sickness had not been
here."

She laid her hand on her heart.

"You would not have done me a service anyway if you
had saved me. What should I have done here? I would
only have had to suffer."

She looked at Cyprienne and Joseph, and added:

"To suffer or to make others suffer—one is as bad as
the other. And now, farewell, my friends; the earth seems
to be far from me already. I see your faces only through
a veil. Farewell!"

Her long eyelashes trembled, and she sank again into
that ecstatic dream, out of which she had awoke for a few
minutes.

About one o'clock in the morning she began to gasp.
This gasp put an end to all Helene's illusions and hopes.
It was the advance-guard of death!

With a cry of despair the unhappy mother sprang
upon the bed and exclaimed:

"Blanche! Blanche! Speak to me; look at me!"

·Blanche gave no answer.

From time to time the emaciated breast heaved, and in those moments the terrible gasps opened her blue lips.

The angel of death scattered violets over her cheeks and shoulders.

In vain Helene prayed, and sobbed, and kissed Blanche's cheeks, hands and shoulders.

All was useless.

Dr. Ozam drew aside the window curtain.

Once more Blanche opened her big blue eyes.

Her lips moved three times, and then her eyelashes hung down again.

Day broke and the sun shone bright and clear.

The pale, heavenly smile of which we have already spoken, played about her lips, and she murmured:

"That is the dawn. The—"

The spectators felt something like a spirit move through the room.

They guessed it was Blanche's soul which fled through the open window, and seized by pious fear, they sank down upon their knees.

Dr. Ozam, who stood next to the bed, held the smooth face of a mirror before Blanche's parted lips.

The smooth face, however, was not clouded.

CHAPTER XLV

A MOTHER'S GRIEF

THE moments which followed now were terrible. Helene threw herself upon the bed and clasped the dear corpse in her arms.

Was that really her daughter? This motionless and already cold body, these eyes which only showed the whites of the pupils, these hands nervously clutched together, these blue lips through which the tightly closed teeth could be seen.

Was that really her daughter?

She piously closed her eyes, which she had so often covered with kisses, shut her lips, and uttered a hollow groan.

She then became frantic with grief.

She did not wish to believe that Blanche was really dead, she feverishly clasped the physician's hands, and begged him for a lie.

"She is not dead, is she, doctor? Her bosom is still warm. Her heart beats under my hand. Her lips have moved. I feel her breath. Oh, she is only unconscious and you will wake her again, won't you?"

She let her arms fall down again, and murmured:

"My daughter, my beloved daughter, my poor Blanche is dead!"

At the same time she shot a glance of hatred at Cyprienne, which meant:

"For your sake she died."

The other witnesses of this scene stood dumfounded at the sight of such grief.

What could they have said?

Helene turned wildly around at them.

"Go away from here!" she cried. "I wish to be alone —alone with her."

They silently obeyed.

When the door closed behind them, the countess burst into tears.

She raised the lifeless body of her daughter on to the pillows and made the toilet of the dead.

She dressed her in white lace, and stuck flowers in her hair. She then clasped one of the dead girl's hands, and seated herself at her accustomed place near the bed.

She then spoke gently to her as she usually did, as if she could still understand her.

She said:

"Do not go away! Have you not gained good by us? Who will love you more than I? What paradise will be better than your mother's love?"

And it seemed to her as if she heard a distant voice, which answered her:

"I am here! I hear you! I am in you!"

Her illusion eased her sufferings.

She knelt down, buried her face in her hands and prayed.

In the meanwhile it had become daylight and a ray of sunlight shone through the open window and into the room.

The countess, after ending her prayer, opened her eyes and looked at her dead daughter.

The ray which toyed with Blanche's pale gold hair enveloped her head like an aureole.

The hours meanwhile sped on. The doctor came to report the death, and then the undertaker followed.

Blanche already lay in her coffin many hours, but the unhappy mother would not permit it to be shut or carried away. That whole day, the night before, and the whole of yesterday, she had spent alone with the dead girl.

It became absolutely necessary to draw her away from her dangerous contemplation.

Dr. Ozam undertook to do it.

This prince of science and noble-hearted man, of whom we have spoken so many times in the course of this story, was a big, strong, robust man about sixty years of age, with long, white hair which fell over his shoulders.

His white hair was the only external sign of his age. His figure was still handsome, his shoulders broad, his whole build strong and elastic, and his face, lighted up by big gray eyes, still had a youthful expression.

This man had undertaken to console this mother, who, like the one we read of in the holy Scriptures, did not wish to be consoled.

When he advanced toward Helene in the room, she was kneeling beside Blanche's coffin.

She had thrown aside a part of the winding-sheet which covered her daughter's forehead, as if to convince herself once more that she was really dead.

The doctor, with a mournful smile, shrugged his shoulders.

"Are you," he said, "really the courageous woman I have known, and whom I now find so weak in the face of pain?"

"What do you want of me?" asked Helene, in a daze.

"I wish," replied the doctor, firmly, "to tear you away from this grave, and to convince you of the cowardice of your grief. I wish you to remember what you once were, and that while you accept this trial with resignation, you raise yourself up again, and stronger than ever, instead of showing such weakness, which is so unworthy of you."

Helene rose up to her full height, and pointed with a sublime gesture to the coffin. She only spoke four words, but they contained a complete justification. These four words were:

"She was my daughter."

"*She was,*" repeated Dr. Ozam—"*she was* your daughter, but she is so no longer. What we see of her here is a little flesh, already slightly decomposed, nerves which no longer vibrate, eyes which no longer see, a mouth which no longer speaks, ears which no longer hear—a handful of dust."

Helene did not reply, but kept her eyes fixed on the corpse.

The doctor continued:

"Your daughter is now a corpse, in which fertile nature already permits other life to seed. In a short while this corpse will become grass, bloom as a rose, and return to the ground all the living strength it robbed it of. No, that is no longer your daughter. What we see of her here is only the delicate, handsome covering in which she walked through life, a covering which she threw off disdainfully, like a worn-out dress. If you wish to have a living remembrance of your daughter you must turn your gaze in a different direction and higher up.''

''Yes,'' replied the countess—''yes, I feel that you are right. I have undertaken a work which is beyond my strength. Yes, doctor, I was proud; I confess it in the humiliation of my heart. I said to myself: 'You will occupy the place of Providence. You will be the messenger of God!' Ah, I did not imagine that I would not only sacrifice my own life to this mission, but that of my daughter also!''

She paused a while, and then continued:

''Yes, it is true, I am egotistical. My heart is not wide enough for the limitless love of humanity it should embrace. My own grief is a greater torture to me than that which I had made it my duty to console. Yes, it is true, from the moment I dreamed of this work it was my duty to stifle every spark of ambition, and to give up all love for a being which would be dearer to me than all others. Who that wishes to love humanity with the divine love I dreamed of must only love it.''

The Countess of Monte-Cristo, exhausted, paused again a few moments before continuing. She then said:

''A few days ago a poor woman, whom Madame Lamouroux took under her protection, came here. Just like me, she had lost her only child and her heart was broken. I, on the other hand, lived in the full enjoyment of my happiness at having found my daughter again, and I listened to the poor woman's story with pity, of course, but almost with indifferent pity. And yet she suffered almost as much as I, yes, perhaps more than I do, at this moment. Yes, I confess it, the grief of that woman ought to have awakened a louder echo in my heart."

The Countess of Monte-Cristo uttered these last words with such sincere humility that the doctor was deeply affected.

He feared he had been too stern.

Did he have any right to make such reproaches? Did he have the right to demand of this despairing mother the fulfilment of a superhuman task?

The meekness with which she accepted his reproaches went to his heart and he murmured:

"You are a saint."

The Countess of Monte-Cristo smiled mournfully.

"Yes, a saint whom you have just reminded that she belongs to the weak human race. I thank you for your words, even though they have not consoled me. I cannot be so and do not wish to be so. Your words, however, have taught me that if a person possesses the pride to undertake a work like mine, then every step backward is a cowardice, almost a crime. Am I now sufficiently unhappy? Even my grief does not belong to me. I have not the right to think of it so long as there are others who suffer. My path is marked out for me like that of the Wandering Jew. I must follow it no matter where it leads to, through thorns or over precipices. Ah, how gladly I would like to live alone, away from every human face, buried entirely in my recollection and my grief. But I must go on further, always further. Although I am myself more in need of consolation than any one else, I must nevertheless stretch out my hand to the weak, and weep over strange misery, although my own is far greater. I must wander until the end of my life, until, tired and utterly exhausted, I sink into that bed out of which we never get up.''

These last words were more sighed than spoken.

The physician seized Helene's hand and pressed it in his own, as if to cry to her:

''Courage! courage!''

The countess withdrew her hand and said:

''You have recalled me to my duty. I am very sad, but resigned, and this very evening I will be brave and strong. The night, the long night on the Mount of Olives is over. Even the Saviour felt, at the moment he brought the sacrifice, that he was a human being and trembled.''

From that moment on no trace of suffering could be seen on Helene's face. It was as pale as chiselled marble, and so calm that it could have been taken for a statue of Resignation.

She did not shed another tear, and when the pall-bearers came she allowed the coffin to be carried away without a sigh or an outcry.

Her last interview with Cyprienne and Don Jose was affecting.

She clasped their hands, and led them to the coffin which was to be nailed shortly.

''Here,'' she said, ''lies everything which still remains of my heart. Without wishing to do so, my poor children, you have killed poor Blanche. I have nothing to forgive you for, for what was your crime? A love which I myself encouraged. The death of this angel shall not have been a useless one. Blanche placed your hands together, and I wish them to remain so. The only consolation my misery knows of is your happiness. On this grave I swear that Blanche's last wishes shall be conscientiously followed."

That very evening Dr. Ozam was closeted with the Countess of Monte-Cristo.

After he had left her earlier in the day, he had visited Baron Matifay.

The latter was in such a weak state that his approaching dissolution could be looked for at any moment.

"One more crisis," said the physician to Helene, "and the patient is lost."

"Then it is time to act."

Blanche's corpse was carried to the nearest church and buried without much ceremony.

Only five persons witnessed it.

From that time on Madame Lamouroux had no further need of existing, and Helene laid off forever the dark cloak which so many unfortunates had blessed.

The windows of the house in the Rue Vivienne were closed, and Helene returned to the magnificent mansion in the Chaussee d'Antin.

She became Aurelie again.

Since more than three weeks—so long Blanche had been dangerously ill—the countess had not set foot in the house, and Legigant had not allowed a day to pass without inquiring for her.

In the antechamber she found the mass of cards which had accumulated meanwhile, and a note of the same day, wherein Legigant bitterly complained of her neglect of him and asked for an interview. This letter caused Helene to smile.

"Ah," she murmured, "how impatient he is. He desires a result, no matter what kind it may be. I also wish to make an end of the affair.''

She seated herself at her desk, and wrote with a feverish hand.

On the edge of the paper could be read the words: "*Fac et spera.*"

The remainder of the day passed for the countess in a terrible struggle—the last.

Until now she had been a kind of Providence. To-day she was to be Justice, and if necessary the cold-blooded executioner of her own sentence.

Nevertheless her doubts were not as troublous as usual.

She was right when she told Cyprienne and Joseph that her heart had been killed by her daughter's death.

At certain moments it even seemed to her as if she would experience a new joy in the satisfaction of her revenge.

This revenge, which she had at first looked upon as a painful necessity, caused her pleasure now, and this was the only impression which could stir the listless fibres of her heart!

CHAPTER XLVI

FAC ET SPERA—(CONTINUATION)

THE news of Matifay's sickness spread very rapidly. His wife did not receive visitors any more. The magnificent mansion stood silent and deserted. Every night, though, there was a ray of light visible in the pavilion at the rear of the hothouse.

This ray of light had, as the reader will remember, occupied the imaginative powers of the neighbors for some days. During the absence of the Countess of Monte-Cristo, and when the house was empty, this ray had always been seen at the same hour in the uninhabited part of the house.

When Baron Matifay began to live in the house the mysterious light had disappeared. Now it was seen again, and always in that part of the house which was unoccupied.

It was whispered about that this light was nothing more than Matifay's soul, and on the day it became extinguished the banker would be dead.

If that were really the case, then the light would soon be extinguished.

Dr. Ozam had, as we have learned from a letter he wrote to the Countess of Monte-Cristo, no hope of his patient's restoration.

Matifay was now no longer able to leave his bed.

The last vision, the one at the children's ball, had entirely prostrated him.

Up till then the spectre had been satisfied to appear to him, but that time it had touched him.

The seventh hour had struck.

The countess, on her side, did not wish to hesitate any longer, but preferred to carry out the decisive stroke at once.

That is why she had thus unhesitatingly answered Legigant's note:

"You are unjust, but you are impatient, and on account of your impatience I forgive you your injustice. Everything is nearing the end. All is ready. Be at Matifay's house to-night and knock at the garden gate. It will be opened to you. Follow the guide and do not ask him any questions. This very evening the millions will be ours and you will have your reward."

On the night of that day three men and one woman were assembled in the oratory, to which we have already conducted our readers.

The lamp hung from the ceiling, and cast a pale light in the darkness as usual.

The walls were still hung in black.

On the altar were still seen, under the glass shade, the relics of Helene's loved dead, Counts George and Octave.

The woman was Helene herself; the men were Joseph, Louis Jacquemin, and Clement.

"Justice must be done now," murmured the Countess of Rancogne, with a gloomy mien, "and if I am cruel may God pardon me. Whoever has killed my heart need not ask pity of me to-day."

In the adjoining room the clock struck ten. These strokes could be heard as distinctly as if the clock were in the oratory itself.

"It is time," said the countess; "Legigant must be there."

She lighted the candle in the lamp, threw a cloak over her shoulders, and went out, followed by her three companions.

On the threshold she paused, and laying her fingers on her lips, said:

"Be perfectly silent and do not show yourselves. No movement! Not a word! We must not let this wild animal escape, for you know how dangerous it is. Let me do everything myself. When it is time I will say: '*Fac et spera*,' and you will then know what you have to do."

Thereupon she went down the stairs, walked through a long corridor, and found herself in the hothouse.

Joseph, Clement, and Louis Jacquemin had followed her.

They hid behind the plants, and nothing, not even the rustling of a leaf, betrayed their presence.

The Countess of Monte-Cristo placed the light upon the marble bench, which stood in the centre of the hothouse, and then went into the garden.

She walked with such a light step that not even the sand creaked under her feet.

Arrived at the door, she opened it and cautiously asked:

"Are you there?"

A dark masculine form immediately hurried toward her.

"Ah, are you there at last?" exclaimed the man.

"The password!" replied the Countess of Monte-Cristo.

"*Fac et spera*," replied the man.

"Good.   Come in."

Helene stepped aside and the man sprang into the garden.   The door closed noiselessly.

"Aurelie!" murmured Legigant, as he tried to seize the countess's hand.

The latter withdrew it immediately.

"Wait," she said, "it is not time yet."

And with a quick step she went toward the hothouse, followed by Legigant.

When they reached the marble bench, Helene turned suddenly around and stretched out her hand toward Legigant to command him to stand still.

He seized this hand and passionately pressed it to his lips.   It was immediately withdrawn from him, however.

"It is not time yet," said the Countess of Monte-Cristo again.

She was very pale, but as it was dark in the hothouse, Legigant did not see her pallor.

"Why," he asked, imploringly—"why shall I always wait?   If I have to wait much longer I will die."

"Calm yourself, Hercules," said Helene, with a peculiar intonation, "you shall not have to wait much longer."

At the name of Hercules, Legigant trembled violently. How did Aurelie know that was his name?   But did she not know everything?

"Come and let us have a talk together," continued Helene in a careless tone.   "In the first place, let me ask you: Are you satisfied with me?   I am so with you."

As she said this she had seated herself on the bench.

Legigant wished to sit down beside her.

She pushed him back with gentle force.

"Wait," said Aurelie again, in a faint voice. "I am satisfied with you," she added, in a firm voice; "the affair with Colonel Fritz was shrewdly conducted and brought to a rapid end. Your former accomplice is dead, and you need not share with him any more. You guarantee me for Toinon, and I must confess to you, besides, that I have good reasons not to fear him. As for me, I owe you also an account of my doings, which were perhaps at times unintelligible to you. What I have done is as follows."

The Countess of Monte-Cristo appeared for a moment to be collecting her thoughts, and then continued:

"Nini Moustache was no longer necessary to us, and would have been, on the contrary, an obstacle to us. I therefore had to withdraw her from the game, and the gratitude she owes me gives me the necessary power over her. Her sister Ursula is going to marry Louis Jacquemin, and all three of them are going to the country to live. They will be happy and will have us to thank for it. For those three, I am in a certain sense a saint."

Helene made a slight pause and then continued:

"Matifay is on his deathbed. Inside of a few months his widow will change her name and become Mme. de la Cruz. Now you know that I have all the necessary documents which prove that Jose is your son and mine. I need not tell you, either, that Don Jose is not our accomplice, but only our tool, and what is more, a tool who has been tested a thousand times. He is a foundling who does not know his parents, and whom I have always told I alone knew the secret of his birth. If I tell him, 'I am your mother, that man there is your father,' he will believe me."

"Then," cried Legigant, "nothing separates us from our aim."

"No, nothing," replied .the countess. "I believe I have foreseen everything, arranged everything, and overcome all possible obstacles. But if a person nears the result he hesitates and doubts. We fear that at the last moment something wrong may turn up. In brief, of so many persons whom I have had think and act in my way, there is only one who is unknown to me. That person is you— you, whom I have chosen as my partner in this great game. To-day the hour of solemn explanations has struck. The booty is here. We need only reach out our hands to take and divide it. But before the division, we must give each other guarantees, otherwise nothing can be done. I am not ready to allow myself to be fooled, not even by the man I love."

The Countess of Monte-Cristo was silent, but as Legigant did not reply, she continued:

"What will become of my conquest when I shall once be married to you? This fortune, of which I have richly earned my share, will fall into your hands. I have given myself a master, perhaps a tyrant. I am defenceless opposed to you. I am not like other women, Legigant. I do not want to be a passive, obedient wife. I must possess weapons against you, and that is why I count upon you."

"Upon me?" asked Legigant, in surprise.

"Yes, only upon you. What difference does it make? Were I to tear our sealed union, would I not injure myself? Were I to plunge you into destruction, would I not have to share the same fate? I only fear that you might think some day of crushing me. If I make you my husband, I deliver myself over to you with bound hands. You must do the same."

"But how shall I do it?" asked Legigant.

"It is very simple. Keep no secret from me; tell me the story of your life; tell me who you really are; in a word, show me the face which your mask conceals."

A terrible struggle went on in the heart of the wretch. What Aurelie asked of him was nothing else but his honor, his life.

The Countess of Monte-Cristo seized him by the hand, and let him take a seat beside her.

"Have we not," she said in a low voice, "agreed not to have any secrets between us, that we should only be one soul in two bodies? Everything in the future must be in common between us, and your confessions will not change my opinion of you, no matter what they are."

"Well, then, question me," replied Legigant.

"Above all," said the countess, "what is your real name?"

"Hercules Champion."

"Ah," replied Aurelie, "that name already explains a great deal to me. Your name is Hercules Champion, and you are a cousin of the Countess of Rancogne. I read that name in the reports of the trial. Do you think the countess was guilty? Matifay's actions were very suspicious. But what did you do? What share did you have in Count George's death, in that of his brother Octave, and in the conviction of his widow?"

Legigant was silent.

"Three men were mixed up in it," continued Aurelie: "a financier, Matifay; a scientific man, Dr. Toinon, and an ambitious man, you. The scientific man delivered the poison, the financier ruined the business, and your head planned the whole thing."

Legigant made a protesting gesture.

"Oh, you need not conceal anything from me," continued Aurelie. "I am a peculiar woman. I admire strength wherever I find it. To secure your aim, the death of two men and the conviction of an innocent woman was necessary to you—what of it? I like to see a man go straight ahead regardless of consequences. Yes, I confess I love you, because of your energy and dauntless courage."

"Yes, yes," said Legigant; "since I must be such a man for you to love me, I confess it. Yes, I did everything. I was the head which made use of those hands as its tools. Matifay, who is a coward, is troubled by remorse. I, on the contrary, who am strong, fear nothing. Toinon is a common scoundrel, and did nothing more than mix a little arsenic in the count's medicine. Without me those stupid people would not have made anything, but have ended their lives like common criminals, on the galleys. And you?" asked Legigant—"you, to whom I reveal the terrible secret of my life to-day, will you tell me your secret likewise?"

"Do you wish to know my secret?" said Aurelie, in a peculiar voice.

At the same time she arose, withdrew her hand from Legigant's grasp and added:

"If you wish to know my secret then follow me."

CHAPTER XLVII

LEGIGANT FEELS A HAND

THE Countess of Monte-Cristo walked up the dark, narrow stairs and Legigant followed behind her.

As he stumbled against each step the countess held her hand out to him, to lead him.

The hand was cold as marble.

After he had gone up about twenty steps Legigant noticed a faint ray of light which proceeded from under a door.

The door opened noiselessly, and Legigant stood amazed at the curious spectacle before him.

He found himself on the threshold of the oratory, into which we have already conducted our readers twice.

Helene turned quickly around to him.

"Since you wish to know who I am, come in," she said.

She had thrown her veil aside and Legigant recognized the pale face, which he had one day seen in Aurelie's boudoir.

He felt that he was lost, but tried in vain to utter an outcry.

The door had already closed behind him, and just at the moment he was about to throw himself upon the dead persons who persisted in stepping out of their graves, a heavy hand was laid upon his shoulder. He sank upon a chair, as if weighed down by a terrible burden.

The hand hurriedly ran over his face and bound something tight behind his head.

Legigant was gagged.

"You want to know who I am," said the countess in a low voice. "You shall be satisfied at once. I am the avenging spectre of your crime, I am the remorse which cannot be killed. I am the condemned woman of the Criminal Court of Limoges, the sacrificed innocent, the inconsolable widow whom you have robbed of her husband, the mother whose daughter is dead. This man here"—with these words the countess pointed to Don Jose, who stood beside the chair upon which Legigant lay bound and gagged—"is the weak boy who foiled your devilish plans, the faithful companion of my sorrows and my revenge, the trusted helpmate who always served me, who always loved me."

Legigant could not reply; his looks, though, betrayed the terrible fear and fright which tortured him.

"God is just," continued the Countess of Monte-Cristo. "We were very weak. A woman without a name, without a country, and a poor peasant boy. You were strong. You possessed money, reputation—everything. Yet this woman and this boy stand here to-day to decide your fate."

She raised up her hand, and the room became suddenly dark. The light in the lamp went out, and the persons in the room were for a few moments wrapped in dense darkness.

Suddenly Legigant saw a ray of light shine in front of him as if the wall was transparent.

This light became gradually brighter, and Legigant then saw through the wall a horrible spectacle.

He looked into a large, luxuriously furnished room. In this room lay a sick man in a dark alcove.

The clock struck the midnight hour.

As if the sick man had seen a similar phantasmagoria on his part as Legigant, he slowly raised himself upon his elbows and stretched out his arms, as if to chase away a terrible vision.

His lips appeared to wish to express loud cries for help, but were not able to stammer anything but the word:

"Mercy!"

Legigant recognized Matifay.

Helene stood in the centre of the room.

With a solemn, stern gesture, she stretched out her arm toward the banker and answered:

"No!"

The baron wrung his hands in terror.

This was the first time the vision had spoken to him, and he recognized the voice just as he had recognized the face.

"What shall I do?" he asked.

"Confess your crime!" replied the vision.

"I will confess it! I will confess it!" exclaimed Matifay.

"Then do so at once!" exclaimed the voice again.

At the same time the vision pointed with the hand toward the baron's writing desk.

Matifay made a superhuman effort to get out of bed.

"I cannot," he murmured.

"You must!" exclaimed the voice again. "So long as you do not write, I will remain here."

Again the baron tried to raise himself up. After repeated trials, he finally succeeded in putting his feet on the carpet.

He then clutched at the furniture, slowly threw a jacket over himself and dragged himself as far as the table.

"What shall I write?" he asked again.

"Everything you did, everything your accomplices have done."

Legigant now saw the danger of the situation.

He made extraordinary efforts to release himself of his gag, so that he could say to Matifay:

"You are being deceived! You think you are seeing a spectre—a shadow from the grave. The woman who is playing this terrible *rôle* is no spectre though, but a living being. Banish your fear. Now that we know her, when she has thrown off the mask, the victory is no longer doubtful for us."

He tried to roll off his chair, but Don Jose's hands were laid once more on his shoulders.

And close to his ear the stern voice of the young man whispered:

"Listen, Hercules Champion—!"

"You must reveal everything, write everything, and sign everything," continued the Countess of Monte-Cristo. "Your punishment, Matifay, is already complete. The dead woman has touched your forehead. God permitted this miracle. But let me tell you that she will not return to her grave until her memory is free from taint, and the honor of her name re-established. Write!"

Matifay wiped the perspiration from his face with the sleeve of his jacket.

He thought to himself:

"It is nothing else than a delusion brought about by my sickness. This form does not really exist, the voice is only that of my spirit. A little more courage and all will soon be over."

This man was used to having himself called the richest and most upright man in France.

And now he was to write his own sentence, and with a single stroke of the pen, in a day, in an hour, to destroy a whole lifetime of patience and hypocrisy.

He already could hear the people whispering to one another:

"Have you heard the news? That millionnaire was a scoundrel. His uprightness was only sham. That honorable patriarch is a common murderer."

And the proofs of all these statements he was to deliver himself; he was to write them down and sign them with his own name, at the command of a phantom which, without a doubt, existed only in his sickly imagination.

"No," he exclaimed, as he suddenly threw the pen away, "I will not write that!"

Legigant uttered a deep sigh of relief.

CHAPTER XLVIII

CONTINUATION OF THE PRECEDING

THE courage which Matifay displayed was that of a coward who is driven in a corner.

He thought of his physician's advice: "Go straight toward the vision; convince yourself of its non-existence, and then, perhaps, you will be saved."

He hurriedly stood up and proceeded to follow Dr. Ozam's advice.

Hardly had he gone a few paces than he had to stand still so as not to lose his balance.

The physical effort he made was almost as superhuman a one as the moral. At every step he felt his knees crack; he had to stand still to wipe off the perspiration which dripped from his forehead. He would then rest a few seconds in a chair, if he found any on his way, or, if that were not the case, on the carpet.

If he would then have refreshed himself a little, he would get up again and continue his pursuit of the vision.

The latter remained motionless and silent in the same position—and, oh, happiness! the nearer Matifay came to her, the paler and more transparent she became.

The physician was right, then. This vision of his

feverish brain disappeared when tested by a firm, resolute mind.

If Matifay could come close to her, she would probably vanish altogether.

Suddenly it appeared to the baron as if the vision were gradually fading away—first, the lower part of the dress, then the knees, then the waist, and finally the whole body.

He uttered a sigh of relief.

A faint voice, however, which seemed to come from another world, spoke close to the baron's ear.

It only said one word:

"Write!"

Matifay stretched out his trembling hands so as not to allow the vision to appear again; and to calm himself by the sound of his own voice, he exclaimed:

"Delusion of the brain! Remnant of a foolish delirium! The spectre does not exist any more, I do not see it any longer!"

"Write!" replied the voice.

This time it sounded loud and piercing.

Matifay recoiled a step backward, and a similar phenomenon as before, only in reverse order, immediately showed itself. In proportion as the banker drew away, the vision reappeared. Gradually the black veil, the pale forehead, the fixed eyes, the firmly closed mouth, then the bust and the angrily outstretched hand were seen again.

In a word the whole vision was seen again.

Matifay, completely dumfounded, sank back again into the chair he had left but a few moments before.

"Write!" said the voice for the third time.

Matifay leaned over the table and wrote.

This lasted very long.

From time to time he paused to dry his forehead. He would then turn round to see if the vision was still there.

If that was not the case, he would have dropped his pen and paper and run away.

The vision, however, was still there, and every time the baron turned his eyes toward it, it seemed to say to him by look and gesture:

"Write!"

When he was at length done, his exhausted hand let the pen fall, and the voice of the vision sounded again, saying:

"That is right! You have made your crime good again as far as you were able. May God forgive you as I forgive you."

With that the vision vanished.

An indescribable feeling of comfort penetrated Matifay's soul.

Was this already an effect of the forgiveness Helene had promised him?

For a moment he felt tempted to seize what he had written, and to throw it in the flames.

He did not dare to do it, however, for he remembered the terrors he had just experienced.

"She has forgiven me," he said to himself, "and she will not come back again now. Ah, if she came back again!"

Far from destroying the paper, he folded it instead carefully together, put it in an envelope, sealed it, and placed it on the table, so that it could be seen at once by any one entering the room.

He then got up to return to his bed, but was forced to lean against the table with his hands for fear of falling.

His feet cracked under him, and everything went around in a circle with him.

He felt a pressure on his breast as if he would choke; he felt as if he had been drawn into a stream and was being whirled toward the sea, the limitless sea, with terrific rapidity.

He heard already the roar of the ocean striking on his ear. And the waves rose higher and higher, and under their icy coldness his feet, lungs, and heart froze. With great difficulty he raised himself to his full height, stretched out his arms, as if to stem the tide which bore him toward infinity, uttered a hoarse cry, staggered, and fell forward with the upper portion of his body on the table.

He was dead.

In the oratory the Countess of Monte-Cristo ·still stood next to Joseph, Jacquemin and Clement.

Everything which went on in the baron's room could be seen from this, by means of an opening in the wall.

When Matifay sank down, the countess turned to the three witnesses of this scene, and said:

"We have nothing to do here any more. Right has triumphed."

Legigant had not lost his time during the last portion of the scene we have just described.

At first convinced that he need expect no mercy from Helene and her companions, and that his efforts to undeceive Matifay would be useless, he had sunk into a state of stupor and downheartedness.

Now all was over.

The game was lost, and instead of winning riches he must prepare to meet the gallows or the galleys.

Bound hand and foot, with a gag in his mouth, all movement or outcry was impossible.

And even if he had been able to speak and move, what resistance could he make against three strong men?

But gradually new hope woke within him.

"If I were only free, we would see!" he said to himself. "The game is desperate, I confess, but still I shall not give it up until the day the chain and ball is fastened to my feet."

We have often seen Legigant weak, even cowardly.

Even Fritz had inspired him with fear.

But at the same time there lay an untamable strength in Legigant's soul, if there was no physical danger to brook.

If any.one had threatened him with the fist he would have turned pale and submitted. But now, when he was threatened with the gallows or the galleys, he felt no fear, and his whole resoluteness reawoke.

As soon as the momentary fright was over he said to himself:

"I must regain my freedom, first of all, and then I shall see what else can be done."

From that moment on he betrayed neither impatience nor fear.

Even his captors, Louis and Clement, who stood at either side of his chair, were surprised at his indifference.

During that whole time, he was thinking; yes, he did more. he acted.

Clement had bound him. The knots were tight, and **it** would not have been easy to loosen them.

Legigant was sly.

The knots were not tied so closely as not to allow the right hand a slight movement.

This movement was Legigant's hope.

In his right vest pocket he had a penknife. This knife he wished to get into his possession without attracting his captor's attention.

He turned his arm so that he could reach the upper part of his pocket.

After he got so far he had to pause. His hand could not be forced to go any further and penetrate into the interior of the pocket.

Legigant now changed his plan. Instead of getting into the pocket from the top, he tried it from the bottom.

With his pointed finger nails he tore and ripped open the seam and lining of the vest. A single hole, the length of his finger, would be sufficient. Since he had no other tool than the hand above named, the work lasted long.

To rip up three stitches took him almost an hour.

At length he succeeded, and his index finger touched the penknife.

He pulled it through the opening with the same patience, and let it slip into his half-closed hand.

A great part of the work was done, but there was still more yet.

In the first place he had to open the knife. For that purpose both hands were necessary. The spring was strong, and the knife itself so little as to be difficult to handle.

Nevertheless, after another half hour of patient labor the blade was opened.

Now the thick rope which bound his hands had to be cut, or rather filed through.

If he only got one hand free the other knots would be easy to loosen.

Louis and Clement watched Legigant's movements carefully: the oratory, however, was very dark, and that was in the prisoner's favor.

Every time Helene spoke, or Matifay answered her, Legigant worked away.

The hempen rope was already half cut through, although his hands did not appear to have moved any.

Legigant could, as soon as he was free, and the chains about his feet were loosened, spring right into the midst of his frightened captors, and make use of their momentary surprise to escape. Instead of that he kept as motionless as ever, and his wrists as close together as if they were still bound.

He did not wish to leave anything to chance, and therefore waited for a favorable opportunity.

The success of his first attempt made him hope that he would find himself, in a very few moments, outside of this house and able to act freely.

What should he do then? He did not know.

How could he neutralize the effects of Matifay's confession? That confession was his ruin, and no matter how much he thought over it, he could find no means of destroying it.

Besides, the baron, rooted to the spot by the Countess of Monte-Cristo's glance, continued to write this confession, which contained Toinon and Legigant's condemnation together with his own.

When he had finished, Helene turned to Joseph, Clement and Louis.

"Leave me," she said; "I do not need you here any longer. Only God alone shall be a witness of what passes between that man and me."

Joseph wished to make a timid observation, but Helene repeated once more:

"Leave me!"

She spoke these two words with such authority that they almost sounded like a command.

"You can be happy yet," continued the countess. "Think of your happiness. My work from to-day on will become a gloomy and terrible one, and it does not seem proper to me to have you mixed up in it."

Deep silence reigned, while she, with bowed head, seemed to forget the presence of the three young men, who were waiting for her last orders.

When she raised her head again she saw Joseph and his two companions still standing in front of her, and for the third time she repeated almost angrily:

"Leave me, and don't come here under any pretext whatever! What will happen here even you must not know, and from this day on this chapel of death will really become a graveyard."

CHAPTER XLIX

LEGIGANT'S REVENGE

A S Joseph, Clement and Louis left the room, Legigant attentively listened to the noise of their footsteps, which gradually died away upon the stairs.

Still he did not move; not even after he was perfectly sure that they were really away, and too far off to be able to hear him.

He waited.

His two hands, which he voluntarily held close to each other, seemed to be still tightly bound. He had, meanwhile, also freed his feet.

The Countess of Monte-Cristo did not notice any of Legigant's doings.

Thoughtful and dreamy she sat for a long time in the faint light of the hanging lamp which lighted up the oratory.

At last she arose and walked up to her prisoner.

"Do you remember the day, Hercules," she asked, "when you stood at the bed of suffering of a woman about to give birth to a child, and spoke like a tyrant to her? You only left this woman one choice, either to commit a great crime, or to remain innocent but to have public shame heaped upon her. Her choice was not doubtful, she chose shame."

Legigant replied with a hollow grunt, which might have been meant to signify assent.

"Since then," continued Helene, "this woman has courageously struggled and suffered. She did more, she tried, if not to forgive, at least to forget. She almost succeeded in this; she had almost lost the recollection of her existence, and cared very little for revenge. What fate caused you to come anew in her way? She only wished to forgive. You force her, however, to punish."

Legigant remained silent yet.

"You were uncompromising," continued Helene again, "and yet I would have been, until a week ago, merciful. But to-day I will be so no longer. If I look within me, I only find uncompromising justice. I am forced along by a higher power like the bullet by powder, and woe to all who wish to stop me. The day of mercy is past. Your sentence has been pronounced."

With slow steps she approached the altar upon which lay the relics of her vanished happiness, and then she turned again to the prisoner, who still lay motionless in his chair.

"If I have had you brought here," she said, "it is because I do not wish to forgive! If a trace of cowardly pity awakened in my heart, the voice of recollection would at once arise and condemn me. I would hear that of George, whom you poisoned; that of Octave, whom you hounded to his death in the moor of Noirmont. No, no; no pity! Just as the spectre of Helene de Rancogne appeared a while ago to Matifay, just the same way the beloved dead appeared to me and cried out: 'Punish these scoundrels!'"

There was still no answer.

"Listen," continued Helene, as she advanced toward Champion again, and folded her arms across her bosom. "Justice and revenge now signify the same thing. Matifay died an unnatural death. I killed him. You, Champion, have done worse things. You tortured me, I who took you into my house. You made me experience all the terrors of death. Death would be too mild, too quick a punishment for you. You will, of course, die, but suffer torture beforehand. Ah! you do not know the tortures of the night I spent here, praying, weeping and wringing my hands. You do not know how often the dear departed ones appeared to me, and said: 'But, Helene, we are not revenged yet, have you forgotten us?'

"No, dear shades, I have not forgotten you, I bring you your prey; seize on him. Since his soul is not open to remorse, fill it with fear and fright. He shall be forced to spend his last days in your company. These sacred remnants of his victims will be so many objects of fear. At the moment his eyes are about to close forever, he shall not turn them from these terrors, and the last thing he shall see before his death will be a representation of his crime."

After she had uttered this adjuration in solemn tones, she turned once more to Legigant, and added:

"Here you will die. Do not attempt to find a means of escape. I have taken all precautions. Your gag will stifle your cries. You will remain here alone with your victims. You are strong, Legigant; we shall see whether this iron heart won't break in this night and in this silence. For this lamp will die out in the same way as your life, and then you will, tortured by hunger and despair, see the shades of your victims close to you. I know they will come. They have always answered my call, but have never looked angrily at *me*. They have always brought *me* courage and consolation. To *you*, on the contrary, they will only bring horror, madness, and despair—this oratory will be your prison.''

She said all this coldly and slowly, as if it were a bitter pleasure to her to describe to her enemy the tortures which awaited him. She described to him, day for day, hour for hour, the tortures she had destined for him.

Legigant, on his part, had gradually raised himself up. The loosened ropes had slipped from off his hands on to his knees and from his knees to the floor.

Suddenly he tore his gag off and sprung into the middle of the room. With his big fists he seized Helene's hands, and face to face, eye to eye, he cried with sparkling eyes:

''The death you just described to me is a horrible one, and I, who am a scoundrel, could not have invented it. The saints and pious ones possess more imagination. You are the one who will suffer this death.''

Dumfounded by this unexpected turn of affairs, the Countess of Monte-Cristo stood silent and motionless.

As soon as the first fright was over she tried to cry out. Legigant laughed maliciously.

''That won't do you any good,'' he said; ''have you not had the kindness to tell me that you took all precautions? I consider you far too smart to think that you could have forgotten a single one. It was your purpose to have me starve. How humane! I had nothing to reply to that and kept silent. Now, however, I am the stronger. Forward!''

While Legigant was speaking, he forced Helene into a chair, and forced her to sit down.

He then bound her in the same way he had been bound. Half dead with fright, she allowed him to do what he pleased without making the slightest resistance.

Of what avail could any kind of resistance she could make be against Legigant's superior strength?

The scene which followed now was the exact counterpart of the one which preceded it.

Just as Legigant a few moments before, the Countess of Monte-Cristo now felt herself lost.

All the measures she had taken to prevent Legigant's flight now turned against herself.

No one except Joseph knew the secret at the entrance to the oratory, and he had received, as we know, strict orders not to come back again.

Was it to be expected that he would become uneasy at Helene's disappearance and come back in spite of the orders?

Helene could not hope for this. She had accustomed him to her long absences, without his ever knowing where she was staying.

If he became uneasy at last it would then be probably too late.

All these thoughts darted through the Countess of Monte-Cristo's brain like lightning.

Legigant had in the meantime bound the gag in her mouth, and he now looked curiously at the altar.

"You thought you could frighten a Legigant with such tinsel," he said, in contemptuous tones.

In spite of his contempt for what he called tinsel, he looked observantly at it.

A person must not neglect anything. Perhaps he might find among these things which Helene looked upon as relics a weapon.

While he glanced at the objects in this way his eyes fell on a sealed envelope, the address of which consisted of one word.

This word read:

"Joseph!"

And below on one side of the envelope was the notice:

"This envelope must not be opened before the heir of Rancogne returns to Noirmont."

His first success had intoxicated Legigant. He no longer doubted anything.

"If the devil allows me to live I will be the heir of Rancogne. Of course I am not at Noirmont yet, but it won't do any harm if we know some things in advance."

With these words he took the envelope and broke the seal.

The very first words he read caused him to utter a cry of surprise and joy.

"That can do me good service," he murmured.

And he quickly put the paper in his pocket.

He then returned to the Countess of Monte-Cristo, bowed with ironical politeness to her and said:

"I thank you for the respect you have for my talent. You thought then that you could catch poor Legigant like a rat in the trap? Fortunately the rat has long teeth, it gnawed the trap in two. You are very smart, my child, but, like all women, you are too anxious to shine with your smartness. If you had, instead of bringing me to this interesting place to witness the death of that stupid baron, merely given me a new promise, I would be sleeping now on both ears, and the stupid old fool would in the meantime have signed the paper without my knowledge. A simple letter from you or from the interesting Don Jose to the district-attorney, and to-morrow I would be in jail. There could be no defence on my part, the farce would be at an end. Thanks to you, I know the danger which threatens me. I am warned. In a case of necessity I need only take a trip to Belgium."

The Countess of Monte-Cristo listened quietly to him.

Legigant drew a chair close to her, and seated himself beside her.

He then said:

"You had the kindness, a little while ago, to tell me what plans you had with respect to me. It would be ungrateful in me if I did not return such affecting confidence. Did you not say a few hours ago, downstairs in the hot-house, that between two good friends there must be no secrets?"

He paused a moment, and then continued:

"I confess that at the first moment I saw myself free I came very near weakening. I was about to give up the game and make good my escape. But you have done me a greater service in bringing me here than I at first thought. You have not only warned me of the danger which threatened me, but also given me the means to avert it."

With these words he pulled out the paper he had placed in his pocket, and waved it in the countess's face.

"I can tell you everything," he continued, "since you will most likely never leave this place again. This paper contains, first of all, something which neutralizes the dear baron's confession, and besides that, the weapon which will give me an opportunity to continue the struggle again, with almost the same chance of success as before. Yes, thanks to this weapon, if I do not conquer, I will be able at least to disarrange your plans a little. What did you wish to do, pious angel? You wished to make every one happy, didn't you? This thing here, though, I assure you, will be a heavy blow for Don Jose; he must become my Colonel Fritz, as he was yours."

The poor gagged Helene could not answer; she slowly shook her head, though, as if to say:

"Do not count on it!"

"Good," exclaimed Legigant, as he arose. "You think our hero will not be weak. So much the worse for him. But I am talking instead of acting. Farewell, my pretty lady. I leave you in the society of the agreeable shades whose companionship *you* had promised *me*. You have been living from your recollections, you said? Well, then, try and die from them as gently as possible. This is my last word."

After Legigant had said this, he turned his steps to the iron door, about which Helene had spoken, locked it, and put the key in his pocket.

Instead of going direct toward the boulevard, he first walked up the Champs-Elysees to the quays.

Arrived at the Concorde Bridge, he leaned over and threw the key to the oratory into the Seine.

He then wended his way to the Tuileries.

It was now bright daylight, but in the oratory not a ray of sunshine penetrated. Only the flickering gleam of the hanging lamp fell upon the Countess of Monte-Cristo, who lay unconscious in her chair.

CHAPTER L

MATIFAY'S CONFESSION

WHEN Rose, the valet, went up to his master's room next morning as usual, he found him dead.

Matifay lay with the upper part of his body on the table, and everything clearly proved that his death was sudden and unexpected.

Every one in the house rushed up on hearing the valet's loud cries. Cyprienne was almost the first one to enter.

The baron had been already placed upon his bed. On the same place which the head of the dead man had occupied on the table, Cyprienne found an envelope, with the address:

"To the Baroness of Matifay *nee* Puysaie."

Further down were the words doubly underscored:

"To be opened by her personally."

This letter, the ink of which was still fresh, must contain the baron's last thoughts.

These last thoughts had been for Cyprienne.

She was affected by that, and did not feel any more the instinctive repugnance her husband usually inspired her with.

She complained of herself now; she almost regretted that she had not been more attentive and gentle.

"Ah," she sighed, "if he had only consented to look upon me as a daughter."

The news of the baron's death had, meanwhile, spread over the whole house, like a flash of lightning.

Loredan and Hortense hurried to the room, and both tried to induce Cyprienne to leave the death-chamber.

Cyprienne, though, did not wish to go away until she had seen her husband's face once more.

The spectacle was a terrible one. The face was thick, bloated, and decomposition had already set in.

The blue-black lips were parted, as if to utter a cry of terror, and the glazed eyes seemed to be still observing Helene's avenging spirit.

In spite of her firm resolve, Cyprienne could not stand the sight, and pressing the letter, which was addressed to her, to her bosom, she sought refuge again in her room.

Here she was sure of not being surprised, and broke the seal of the envelope.

Her heart beat rapidly. What was she going to learn?

At the very first words she turned pale. At the commencement of the written pages were the words:

"This is my confession."

The confession was a long one. It contained eight closely written pages.

The letter read as follows:

"I address this confession to you, Cyprienne, so that you can make whatever use of it your conscience dictates to you.

"You have been, without knowing it, my ruin and my

victim at the same time. My punishment began from the day on which you were forced to take my name. My intention was to bring joy and peace into the house with you; you brought me, though, only remorse and despair.

"God is just. Through you I hoped to forget; he forced me, however, to remember through you.

"This cannot have been the work of chance. When a person is near his death, he understands a great many things which were until then obscure to him.

"The very evening you entered my house I began to feel remorse. Without doubt you were destined to be my judge. Perhaps I became, in spite of the degradation to which I had sunk, better through contact with your sacred purity.

"The scales fell from my eyes and I comprehended the whole depth of my crimes.

"These crimes you shall now become acquainted with. Will you permit them to be made public? I feel I have not the right to ask this clemency, for it would fall back upon you, because, as ill-luck will have it, you bear the same name as I.

"Whatever you do depends entirely on yourself, and I do not demand a public step which will dishonor you. I do not think that this is the purpose of the supernatural being who stands since many months at my bedside, and whose mysterious voice forces me now to write this.

"Ah, that woman, the first of my victims, as you have been the last, has known undeserved suffering and unjust contempt. It will, therefore, not be her wish to burden you likewise."

Upon this preliminary Matifay's actual confession followed, a complete confession, whose terrible details are already known to us.

As Cyprienne read on and, so to speak, saw the mournful story of Helene de Rancogne pass before her eyes, she felt she was becoming paler and paler.

She imagined she was laboring under a terrible dream. Her throat almost glued together.

The monosyllable "dead" was in almost every line of this terrible report.

Count George dead, his brother Octave dead, the Countess Helene dead, Joseph, the little shepherd, also dead.

At least this was to be suspected, for he had not been seen again, and, according to the report, he had been pursued by the murderer Limaille.

Blanche, finally, that angel, that doubly sacred orphan, was also dead.

"Dead! All dead!" repeated Cyprienne; "dead through him! And I was the wife of that man! I have borne his name, and bear it still!"

Madame Jacquemin, who still acted as Cyprienne's maid, entered the room softly and surprised her young mistress at this tragical reading.

Cyprienne quickly shoved Matifay's letter into a drawer which stood open near at hand.

"What's new?" she asked.

Madame Jacquemin only answered by pronouncing a name.

"The Vicomte de la Cruz."

The Vicomte de la Cruz! Don Jose! Had a higher instinct, an inward voice, told him that she was suffering, since he had come to her at once?

"Let him come in! Let him come in!" exclaimed Cyprienne, eagerly.

As soon as he entered, she weepingly rushed toward him.

"Ah!" she exclaimed, "why did I not listen to you? Why did I not fly as you advised me to? You were right, Don Jose, that man was a monster!"

CHAPTER LI

A RAY OF SUNSHINE

IN a serious tone of voice Don Jose replied: "He is dead, and God alone has the right to condemn him."

Cyprienne cast her eyes on the ground, and gradually a slight flush suffused her pale cheeks.

At length she raised her childish-pious gaze and looked straight at Don Jose's thoughtful face.

"You have always been my best friend," she said. "You have the right to know all."

With these words, she took the letter out of the drawer into which she had thrown it, and handed it to Don Jose.

The latter gently pushed her hand away and said:

"I know all that the letter contains."

"All?" repeated Cyprienne, becoming pale again— "all? And you did not use any means, even if it had been force itself, to hinder me from marrying that wretch?"

Don Jose smiled mysteriously.

"The marriage was necessary," he said.

"Necessary! How so? Why?"

This time Don Jose did not reply, but asked a question himself:

"What are you going to do now?"

"You ask me that?" replied Cyprienne. "I will make the confession of the great criminal, who chose me as the administrator of his will, public. His repentance must be a complete one, and all his crimes must be made good again, as far as it is possible. Is not honor the highest virtue? Since it is not in my power to give the poor victims their lives back again, at least this poor Countess of Rancogne must be given back the honor which was stolen from her."

"And then?" asked Don Jose, again.

"Then," continued Cyprienne, "then I will discover the relatives of the victims and return them this money, which comes from an unclean source and which fills me with repugnance."

"There are no relatives living," said Don Jose.

"Then the money shall become the legacy of the poor."

"And then?"

Cyprienne kept silent, cast down her eyes, and blushed again.

The struggle was a short one. After a few moments she raised her head again, and, in a firm voice, replied:

"I will not get married again, Vicomte de la Cruz. I do not wish to make any one the companion of my voluntary poverty."

"I am rich," observed Don Jose, smiling again.

"I do not wish either," continued Cyprienne, "to burden any one with the undeserved shame which, in consequence of my husband's crimes, it will henceforth be my lot to bear. I would only marry a man I respected, and such a man cannot, and must not, become the husband of the widow of a murderer."

Don Jose stretched out his arms, and exclaimed:

"The test has been withstood."

And then, while she, because she did not understand him, stood there motionless, timid, and trembling, he bent one knee, and said:

"Oh! do not think I have ever doubted you, Cyprienne. Before this interview commenced I knew it would end in this way. Calm yourself now, dear Cyprienne; you have withstood the numerous trials you had to go through without fear or wavering. Your sufferings are over, as well as mine. The moment of reward has come."

He seized her hand, which she allowed him to do.

"I told you at the beginning that I was poor, and that there was a secret in my life," he said. "Instead of repelling me, you replied: 'Then I love you all the more!' To-day I come to remind you of your words. You are unhappy, lonely, and dishonored, for society is so organized that one person's mistakes injure others, the innocent, and I tell you only for my own part, Cyprienne, this poverty and this shame give me a right. Do you want to be my wife?"

Cyprienne did not give any answer, but what a world of meaning lay in her gaze!

"Do you want to be my wife?" asked the young man again.

"Ah," Cyprienne's gentle, reproachful gaze seemed to say, "why did you not address this question to me before?"

He at least appeared to comprehend the meaning of that silent question, for he replied at once:

"The hour has not come yet. I could not yet devote

a whole life entirely to you, for a portion of it still belongs to another. Ah, you have no cause to be jealous,'' he quickly added, noticing that Cyprienne made a movement. "Your rival was an idea, an undertaking, a work whose secret you will find out later on, for it has been promised me that it will be revealed to you. The undertaking is now nearly ended; I am finished with my share of it. My freedom has been given back to me again. Besides, a peculiar light commences to spread itself over the secret of my life, and perhaps—''

He paused, but continued after a while:

"When you saw me for the first time again, a little while ago, your first word was an expression of remorse for not having had confidence in me. Do not fall into the same error again, but be assured that if I have not yet opened my heart to you, that if I still hide something from you, the reason for it is because I cannot act differently now. Cyprienne, I love you—I love you more than anything else in the world; yes, even more than the duty to which I devoted my whole life, and which I was almost on the point of betraying—of betraying for your sake. Yes, I was on the point of doing so, and God alone knows of the struggles which went on in my heart, on the day I saw you being conducted to the altar by that terrible monster, Matifay. I was on the point of forgetting my oath, of interrupting the ceremony, and of telling you all, of revealing everything to your father, the count, and even at the risk of a scandal of dissolving this connection.''

"Ah, why did you not do that?'' murmured the young widow.

"Fortunately I did not do so,'' replied Don Jose,

firmly. "Such a scandal would have perhaps separated us forever."

Cyprienne looked thoughtfully at him.

"All what you tell me," she said, "is very singular. But I believe you. You cannot wish me any harm. An inward voice tells me this."

"Oh, obey that inward voice!" exclaimed Don Jose; "that voice speaks the truth. Have the same confidence in me as I have in you, and a day will soon come when all the secrets which still envelop my life will be cleared up."

Suddenly a firm, sonorous voice was heard coming from the doorway, which cried:

"The vicomte will not tell you, Cyprienne, that the marriage, which he did not hinder, was necessary to bring you both together. The Vicomte de la Cruz could perhaps have married Cyprienne de Puysaie, but not an adventurer, who does not even know his own name. He will not tell you, either, that this marriage was necessary, so that the bride of the noble and chivalrous Don Jose would be enriched by the disreputable millions of Baron Matifay."

CHAPTER LII

EXPLANATIONS

AT THE sound of this voice Cyprienne and Don Jose started up in surprise.

They turned around and saw the Count de Puysaie in front of them.

Don Jose wished to open his mouth to reply, but the count restrained him with a gesture, and continued:

"Enough! I learned this morning of the shame of the unfortunate man who is now dead, and I confess that when I came here I expected to hear the news denied."

"Ah!" sighed Cyprienne, "the news is but too true."

"And you," continued the count, addressing himself to Don Jose, "you knew of this?"

"Yes."

"And you called yourself our friend without telling us anything about it?"

"Reasons which I cannot reveal to you made my silence necessary."

"Listen to me," said the count, in a gentle tone of voice. "I brought my daughter into shame and misfortune; it is, therefore, my duty to watch doubly over her. I do not condemn you; I do not even complain. Cyprienne loves you, that is clear; and I do not reproach her for it. My duty demands, however, that I should not allow myself to be blindly led by my feelings, and that is why you will permit me, Don Jose, to question you, and to beg you to answer my questions candidly."

"Question me," said Don Jose.

"This letter," continued the count, "was sent to me in the same mysterious way as another one formerly was, which had reference to my wife. I recognize the handwriting. The first letter I speak of did not deceive me. Would to God that the contents of the second were not true. Is the name of Don Jose de la Cruz really your own?"

"No, it is not."

"Where do you come from?"

"I do not know."

"And where did you get your fortune?"

"I do not possess any personal property; my apparent riches do not belong to me."

"And who is the real owner?"

"I cannot name him."

"You have pronounced your own doom," said the count. "The anonymous letter, in which I did not place any faith, contains no graver accusations than those which you have just now confirmed with your own mouth. This letter says that the marriage of my daughter with Matifay was only the result of the intrigue which you and your accomplices played. It is said in this letter that your secret purpose was to get Matifay's fortune in Cyprienne s possession, so that it would be *yours* later on."

"I never lie, count; and although I know that my

answer will injure me in your estimation, I will not conceal anything. All the allegations contained in that letter are true."

"Then what am I to think? What am I to believe?"

"I cannot tell you what to think or believe. I can only repeat to you that it is impossible for me to justify myself to-day, although I could do it easily and by a single word. I beg you, therefore, to withhold your judgment for a few days."

"Oh, father!" cried Cyprienne, sobbing, "I am convinced he is innocent."

"Yes, I am trying to believe so myself," replied the count, "for I see very well that your happiness depends on his innocence. I see that you love him, my poor child, and if he were only nameless and poor, I would at once give up my ambitious plans. I would place your hands together, and say: 'Be happy, and try to forget in your happiness the evil I have caused you.'"

The count paused a few seconds, and then continued:

"But I cannot do it yet. This young man says he is poor, and yet he throws money around with full hands. He decorates himself with a borrowed title and name, and the experience I have had with Colonel Fritz has been too hard a one for me ever to forget it. Don Jose has promised to justify himself. Let us await that justification. Until that day your love must remain in the background. You have already proved to me, my daughter, that you can stand pain, and that gives me the courage to ask this new sacrifice of you. I am only thinking of your honor and your happiness."

"Yes, I know it, father," sobbed Cyprienne. "There is no need of an order from you, for I feel myself that

I cannot act differently. Yet I swear to you that he is innocent."

"May God grant it!" murmured the count. "But this is not the only sacrifice I have to ask of you to-day, Cyprienne."

The count paused a moment, and then continued:

"You have, no doubt, thought too, my daughter, that this dishonorable fortune cannot remain in the possession of our house. If we were to keep it, after knowing from whence it came, we would, in a certain sense, make ourselves accomplices of that wretch."

"Yes, papa, that is my opinion too," replied Cyprienne. "Just as you came in before, I was telling Don Jose that I wished to return this money to the rightful heirs of the Rancogne family, or, if there were no heirs in existence, to use it for charitable purposes."

"And what did Don Jose say?" asked the count.

"He said he was perfectly satisfied. You see, papa, that he is not moved by any selfish interest; that he is, in a word, innocent."

CHAPTER LIII

LEGIGANT'S DAY'S WORK

AFTER Legigant had thrown the key of the oratory into the Seine, he lost no time.

What was he to do with the paper he had in his pocket and which he thought was of such great value?

He did not know. His plan was not yet sketched. But what he did know was that he must act quickly.

He was morally and physically certain that Helene would not come out of the cell again in which he had literally buried her.

Therefore, he had only Don Jose still to fear.

The latter did not believe that Legigant was capable of doing anything, and therefore did not surely think of disturbing him.

There was nothing more simple, then, than to take possession of the contents of the cash box in the Faubourg Montmartre, and to escape to a foreign land.

The ease with which he had secured his first success had inflamed Legigant's ambition. But a few hours before, he only desired his liberty; but now he wished to fight and conquer.

The attraction Matifay's millions exerted upon him was irresistible.

He therefore resolved to make a last attempt, even at the risk of suffering defeat.

He seated himself on a bench in the garden of the Tuileries, pulled the valuable document, upon which he set his whole hope, out of his pocket, and read it carefully.

There were several other papers attached to it, such as birth certificates, marriage contracts, and certificates of deaths.

Legigant read each paper carefully through, placed it then in his portfolio, and smilingly arose.

His plan was formed.

Without hesitating, he walked quickly in the direction of the Pointe St. Eustache.

The shop of our old friend, Gosse, was open.

When Monsieur Gosse saw the speculator coming, he shuddered; he suspected that he would be asked to lend a hand to some new deviltry.

Legigant, however, possessed the golden key which opens hearts and grants the means to drink.

The public writer, therefore, hesitated only so long as to increase the value of his services.

He remained closeted with Legigant about half an hour. The latter then left the shop and waved a letter, addressed to Count Loredan de Puysaie, in his hand.

This letter was to destroy Don Jose's influence with the count, and have a second effect, which our readers will learn later on.

As soon as Legigant had stamped the letter and brought it to the post-office, he got into a cab and had himself driven to Dr. Toinon's house.

The servant—Dr. Toinon had a servant, and a very

handsome one, too—opened the door and Legigant ran up to the doctor's bedroom.

"Come, get up!" he cried. "This is no time to sleep. Our heads are at stake!"

"What's the matter?" asked the doctor, in amazement.

"Dress yourself," replied Legigant, "and be quick about it! We can talk later on."

Toinon did as he was told.

"But," he began again, "I would like to know—"

Legigant gave him a look which stopped further utterance.

"Come! come!" exclaimed Legigant, "let us·be off. I have my carriage downstairs."

As soon as the two friends entered the office of H. Legigant & Co. they locked themselves in, so as not to be disturbed by any one. Legigant then made his friend sit beside him, and began a long story in a low voice.

This story was apparently not an agreeable one, for Toinon's cheeks became pale as death.

When Legigant had finished, Toinon bounded up as if on springs.

Legigant remained quietly seated, and, turning half around to Toinon, he asked:

"What shall we do now?"

"You can do as you please, dear friend," said the physician; "I shall order horses at once."

Legigant shrugged his shoulders.

"We have plenty of time," he said.

"You seem to take the thing easy," said Toinon, angrily. "Do you know whom you remind me of? You remind me of Jean Bart."

"Who sat on a powder magazine and calmly smoked his pipe? He puffed away with great pleasure, and the magazine did not fly in the air."

"Puff away, too, as long as you please, my friend, but puff alone. I am not a friend of smoking."

And with these words the physician made for the door.

He had already placed his hand on the knob, when Legigant called him back.

"Toinon!"

"Well?"

"Your idea is not a bad one," said Legigant, pointing with his finger to the safe, which stood in a corner of the room. "Have you got the key with you?" he added.

We must here explain in what way the firm of "H. Legigant & Co." was organized.

Legigant was the superintendent and general manager, and Toinon was not the cashier but the man that locked the safe. Colonel Fritz had been the chief broker.

As he could not touch the safe in the absence of his two companions, he had been given a great proof of the confidence felt in him, by having the key intrusted to his care.

This key he now pulled out of his pocket, and the two partners opened the safe.

It contained several hundred thousand francs, the same which Nini Moustache had one day thrown into Legigant's face.

CHAPTER LIV

THE CAFÉ BADOCHE

TOINON was dazzled at the contents of the safe.

"Let us divide," said Legigant.

Toinon immediately stretched forth his long narrow hand. With a cry of pain he quickly drew the hand back again.

"Patience!" exclaimed Legigant, who had given the doctor's fingers a crack with the ruler. "Before we begin the division we have a few words to say to each other." With these words Legigant seated himself again in his chair, and Toinon obediently sat down beside him.

Legigant spoke again in low, firm tones like a man who gives orders and prescribes conditions.

His last words were:

"All or nothing."

The poor doctor was therefore compelled to choose "all," in spite of his inborn horror of adventures and danger.

After the two partners had agreed, the division took place in the most regular way in the world.

After this was finished, the empty safe was locked again and both of them left the office.

The cab was waiting outside.

It was now about eleven o'clock.

Legigant and Toinon got into the cab and had themselves driven to the Rue de la Harpe.

In this street an establishment called the Café Badoche bloomed.

The great feature of the café and the one which immortalized it forever, was Badoche the great—the great, the only Badoche!

The man who bore this name, the former star of the "Chaumiere" and the "Prado," was in his way a kind of Delacroix or Victor Hugo.

He was physically small and lean, quick as a fly and as wrinkled as an old woman. There was a nervous shake noticeable in his limbs, and his voice was thin and cracked. Morals he had none.

Yet outside of that he was one of the best men in the world. He never refused to play a game of billiards, for he was as skilful with his hands as with his feet, and condescended to compromise his past glorious career by giving lessons in the cancan and billiards to the students.

There was only one other celebrity of any account in the café, outside of Badoche. This celebrity was named Marie Joseph Tarantas.

He was a tall, strong, broad-shouldered man, with big blue eyes. Marie Joseph Tarantas had—it was some time ago—had a youth once; one could see that in the traces of the same in the flabby features of his face.

At that time a mother had tenderly combed his blond hair, which now hung wildly over his head like a mane. That poor mother had kissed that brow, which was now prematurely wrinkled, as well as those lips now burned by alcohol, and the cheeks hollowed by dissipation and hunger.

Tarantas understood fun, but still he never liked to hear his mother spoken of.

Two or three practical jokers, who had heard of this weakness of his, hit upon the idea one day of putting him to a test with respect to it.

On that day two ribs and one arm were broken in the Café Badoche.

Tarantas was strong, strong as an ox, and also as gentle as one, that is, if he was not drunk.

Formerly, he had been intelligent, too. When a student, he had often won prizes, and great hopes were entertained of him.

At present he unfortunately tried to deaden his intelligence as much as possible, and his soul was entirely at the service of his body.

The latter flourished in an extraordinary way. Tarantas ate for ten and drank for twenty, but never paid for more than one.

Badoche, his friend, did not complain about it. On the contrary, he would rather have lost his best customers than parted with Tarantas.

Tarantas was his right bower, his executive authority; in a word, the man without whom he could not exist. Badoche ordered, and Tarantas obeyed.

If a quarrel broke out in the place, the cry was: "Where is Tarantas?"

"Here is Tarantas!" the lady cashiers would exclaim in a piercing voice.

And all would then return to their seats subdued by the mere utterance of that feared name.

If Badoche was absent, Tarantas took his place at the billiard-table. At night he was the one who looked after the "pool."

During the day, his table in the left-hand corner was never empty.

A great number of games of *ecarte* were played there, and a correspondingly large number of wines or absinthes were drunk.

Tarantas drank for four, and the losers paid for it.

That helped the business along.

Tarantas' moral and physical degradation was the work of that speculator in vice—Legigant.

CHAPTER LV

MARIE JOSEPH TARANTAS

MARIE JOSEPH TARANTAS came of a good provincial family.

His father, who had died at an early age, had left him three farms and a hunting forest.

Although quite a piece of property, it was not very valuable. Land is very cheap in Limousin.

Besides this, Marie Joseph possessed chestnut forests, green meadows, cool valleys with spring-water brooks in which the blue sky was reflected, eight pair of oxen, two hundred head of poultry, four dogs, and a brisk little brown horse.

Sometimes at night, when Marie Joseph was sitting drinking his wine, he saw all this pass before his eyes.

Then he would see his mother again, as she was then, still young and beautiful, with an expression of the most tender kindness of heart on her fine features.

Poor dazzled mother! She wished to make a great man out of her beloved son, a scientist. Marie Joseph was educated at college, which was very costly, and still further reduced the widow's meagre income.

Tarantas was afterward sent to Paris.

From this on, his career can be summed up in a few lines.

He added one more to the great regiment of persons who are ruined by laziness, carelessness and dissipation.

His property represented a capital of barely sixty thousand francs.

Marie Joseph Tarantas thought this would never become exhausted.

At the end of a year he had to confess that he had made many debts, and at the end of the second year they were still more.

The vacations he spent at his mother's house, and was always received like the master, the king of the house. The poor mother did not complain. Marie Joseph, who was not bad at heart, saw very well that things were pinched in the house more than usual.

The carriage had been sold, and Madame Tarantas went to church on foot.

In other respects, things were different, and as much as possible was saved in meat, bread, and groceries.

Marie Joseph comprehended the situation at a glance, and would, perhaps, have still held back on the brink of the abyss if he had not fallen in with Legigant immediately on his return to Paris.

The latter opened his purse to him and loaned him whatever sum the student demanded.

Hardly had six months gone by than Marie Joseph was compelled to inform his mother of a new deficit.

She complained as little now as before, but she sold one of the farms.

Acre for acre, meadow for meadow, the other two met the same fate and paid the loans of the usurer back again with one hundred per cent interest.

Joseph, who now gave himself up for lost, tried to forget his remorse in drink, and although he knew that a day would come when it would be impossible for him to continue to live in this way, he still possessed sufficient sense of shame to conceal his real condition as much as possible from his mother.

Every week he wrote her enthusiastic letters, in which he spoke of nothing but his studies, his future, of the fame and fortune he would certainly reap some day.

The good woman believed in her son, as we believe in a God.

Yet she saw herself forced one day to leave one of her beloved son's demands unsatisfied.

She now possessed nothing more than her house, and as the phrase goes, her eyes with which to weep.

She wept, the poor woman, over the lost son whom she had not seen for many years.

She wept so much that her eyes grew dim, and one day she wrote to Marie Joseph, who continually promised to visit her but never came.

"You have waited too long, my son. You will not see me again."

This simple note, humid with tears, almost stirred up the heart of the ungrateful son out of its long sleep.

If it had come some years before, it would perhaps have saved Tarantas.

Yet now it was too late. Ambition was gone, dissipation had become a habit, and reform was impossible.

Marie Joseph threw an affrighted look into the depths of his degradation, and gave up all attempts to raise himself. He, at least, swore that "the old lady" should keep her house and garden until her death.

He did still more. He had the courage to make an artificial life for himself.

Hungry and shivering, far from every loved being, wandering alone about the dirty pavements of Paris, he wished to have his mother believe that if not rich, he was in comfortable circumstances.

In the moments he wrote to her, he became the Marie Joseph he might have really become. He told her his plans for the future, his imaginary successes, and since he could not really send her the happiness, he sent her at least the illusion.

In this way two different beings lived in Marie Joseph Tarantas: Marie Joseph and Tarantas.

Marie Joseph was young, handsome, loving, beloved, pure in spirit and heart; filled with ambition and plans for the future.

Tarantas, on the other hand, was prematurely old, his mind and heart were dulled, and his head continually sunk in the sleep of intoxication and indifference. One of them was the young and handsome student, the other the common customer of the Café Badoche. There was one virtue which Tarantas still retained. He cherished no anger. All the hate he knew was directed at one man, the cause of his whole unhappiness and his remorse.

We have named Legigant.

At the moment the latter and Dr. Toinon got out of the carriage in front of the Café Badoche, the clock struck half-past eleven.

In the Quartier Latin people generally get up late. The rooms were therefore still almost empty. The waiter wiped off the tables, and the lady cashier was just finishing her breakfast.

Badoche was practicing shooting.

Marie Joseph Tarantas was seated alone at a table drinking absinthe.

No one would have dared to interrupt him during this interesting operation.

The morning was always hard for him to pass, and it did not occur to any one to speak a word to him during this time.

The reason for this was that he was still sober—that is proportionately so.

The excitement of the previous evening had calmed down in sleep. The thought of the chestnut forests, of the meadows, of the brooks, and of the wheat and rye fields. More especially he thought of the "old lady."

But when he had his necessary amount of alcohol in his stomach, his eyes sparkled and his lips smiled again. He forgot.

Suddenly the street door opened, and Marie Joseph, who held a glass of absinthe to his lips, set it down again on the marble table.

He was very pale. He had recognized the man he hated more than any one else.

Legigant, followed by Toinon, went straight toward Marie Joseph and offered him his hand.

Marie Joseph seized his glass with his right hand, as if to throw it in Legigant's face, muttered a few unintelligible words, and sat down again.

"Don't you know your friends any more?" asked Legigant. "It is certainly a long time since we have seen each other, Monsieur Tarantas."

As Legigant said this, he seated himself close to Marie Joseph, turned half around toward Badoche, and said:

"Come, old friend! Two glasses of Vermouth for my friend and me."

Badoche hurried to fill the order, and Legigant turned once more to Tarantas.

"I see how it is," he said; "you are still angry at me. I should like to know, though, what good that will do you. Business is business. It caused my heart to bleed every time you could not pay me on the day the money was due. If I had only to look out for myself I would gladly have waited, for what would we not do for a friend! But I had to have the money myself."

Marie Joseph suddenly struck the marble table with his clinched fist, causing the glasses to chink.

"What do you want of me?" he asked Legigant.

"There we have it," said Legigant. "Did I not say so, Toinon? I interest myself for this young man, because I was, without wishing to be so, the cause of his misfortune. Now, I have a good thing in hand, which, if it does not exactly make him rich, will at least doubly replace what he has lost. Instead of going to some one else who will accept my offer with gratitude, I say to myself, 'That will be something for poor Tarantas. I will hunt him up.' And now I am received in this way."

Tarantas drank his glass at one draught, and smiled cynically.

"Ha, ha, ha!" he exclaimed. "Don't speak of your kindness, Legigant. It resembles that of the wolf for the lamb."

"If you think that way, I won't disturb you any further."

With these words he arose.

"Come, Toinon," he said to the physician; "let us

leave this ungrateful man. We will find some one else who will take the hundred thousand francs I intended to have him earn.''

Tarantas opened his eyes.

''One hundred thousand francs!'' he murmured.

''Perhaps more, on no account any less,'' said Legigant, peremptorily.

''What deviltry is it that you need me for?'' stammered Marie Joseph.

Legigant shrugged his shoulders.

''Prejudices!'' he exclaimed. ''There is nothing easier or more simple than the business I have in hand; but since you refuse—''

And he pretended to walk toward the door.

''Wait!'' cried Marie Joseph.

Legigant turned around again.

''Well,'' he said, ''have you changed your mind? That pleases me, for I would rather you earned the money than any one else.''

''I would like to know first,'' murmured Tarantas, ''what the nature of the business is.''

''First let us take breakfast together,'' replied Legigant. ''I will then explain everything to you. Toinon, tell the cabman to drive up.''

''He is already here,'' replied Toinon.

''Well, then, let's go!'' exclaimed Legigant. ''Get in, comrade Tarantas; and now drive on, coachman!''

Ten minutes later, the carriage stopped in front of a barber shop, and half an hour later in front of a clothing store.

They then drove to a hat store, a linen draper's, a shoe store, and finally to a celebrated restaurant in the Palais Royal.

When the three companions entered one of the private rooms, Marie Joseph Tarantas was completely transformed.

He was now an elegant cavalier, somewhat worn out and dissipated, but still handsome.

He was, in a word, the perfect type of a gentleman.

Legigant admired his own work and said to himself:

"With such an accomplice we must succeed without a doubt."

During the last ride, Legigant had sent a messenger on in advance, to order a superb breakfast.

At sight of the fine white table-cloth, the damask napkins, the champagne bottles, and all the luxurious things he had known but a short time and lost sight of so long, Marie Joseph's face lighted up with pleasure.

"Even if we do not do any business," he said to himself, "I will at least have got a new suit and a good breakfast."

He then added aloud:

"I am beginning to think, Legigant, that I did not judge you rightly before."

"And 1 hope," replied Legigant, "that you will soon become thoroughly convinced of it. But let us sit down to table. At the dessert we will have plenty of time to talk."

They all sat down, Marie Joseph Tarantas·between Legigant and Toinon.

Marie Joseph's glass was never empty, for his two neighbors continually kept it filled.

The effect of this procedure was a different one from what they had expected, for the more wine he drank, the gloomier and more taciturn the ex-student became.

The usurer's purpose had been to make him maudlin, so as to secure his assistance in an undertaking which up to the present the reader has no knowledge of.

He knew the danger, though, of enraging the wild animal which slumbered in Marie Joseph and which was awakened by alcohol.

He therefore determined upon a new line of action.

He rang for the waiter, pointed to the half-empty champagne bottles and said:

"Take this wine away."

Then turning to Tarantas, he added:

"We must keep our senses together. We have important things to talk about."

"That's so," said Tarantas. "You had a proposition to make to me."

"Yes, and a good one too!" exclaimed Legigant.

He paused a moment and then continued:

"Dear friend, you are down a little just now, but if a person is young, intelligent and brave it doesn't make much difference. There are always ways and means left to get rich. In ruining yourself, you have also ruined your mother."

"Why do you tell me this?" asked Marie Joseph. "Have you a right to heap such reproaches upon me?"

"You are at present," continued Legigant calmly, "entirely down. You have no more hope. When a man once goes downhill, he generally goes quicker, and I am convinced that inside of two years you would be a thief or a beggar."

"Well?" asked Marie Joseph. "You certainly did not come here to tell me something I knew long ago."

"Listen!" continued Legigant. "I have come to give you, who are nothing more, who have no more hopes for the future, no rank in the world, a name, a title, and a fortune. Assent to my proposition and I will make a count of you. Say *yes*, and I will make you rich."

Tarantas thought he was dreaming.

"You still doubt me, don't you?" cried Legigant. "Look, here is something which will dispel all your doubts."

With these words he pulled out of his pocket the large envelope whose contents he had carefully read through with such satisfaction.

"Here is the birth certificate of your father and your mother—namely, the father and mother I am going to give you—here is their marriage contract, and here are the certificates of their deaths."

"And if I accepted your proposition," asked Tarantas, "what would my name then be?"

"Count Joseph de Rancogne," replied Legigant simply.

"Then," said Marie Joseph, "it is a question of a fraud—an imposture."

"I beg your pardon," said Legigant, with a smile, "but I must have you understand that our precautionary measures are taken, and that from the moment I have let you into my confidence so far, I look upon you as concerned in it. Do you know what will happen if you refuse your assistance? I have a draft upon you yet, payment of which I have not demanded because I knew you had not the money. That is the thread on which I hold you. This draft represents the last peaceful days of your mother. If I wish, the old lady, as you call her, will be poorer inside of a fortnight than the worst beggar in Limousin. Either your mother's house will be sold, or you come into possession of a handsome sum—I can say a small fortune, for we are not used to haggling with those who serve us—a fortune you will earn with a lie. Choose between them.''

"Ah!'' cried Marie Joseph, "you are a devil! What sum will you give me for this infamy?''

"Infamy is a severe word,'' said Legigant. "You must know, dear friend, that—''

"I do not wish to know anything,'' interrupted Marie Joseph. "I do not wish to be anything else in your hands but a tool. I do not know what your aim is, and do not wish to. What you tell me to do, I will do—that is all there is about it. How much are you going to pay me?''

"I believe,'' replied Legigant, "that I spoke of one hundred thousand francs.''

"No, that is too much. I do not want so much. I am a scoundrel for accepting your proposition, but up to a certain point my reasons for doing so justify me in my own eyes. I wish that my mother should die in peace, nothing more. She shall believe that my efforts have at length been crowned with success; she shall again come into possession of the property she sold piecemeal on my account. As for myself, I will hide in some corner. When we have finished with each other, Legigant, beware of ever coming across me again. I cannot promise you not to use force against you, for you have now taken everything from me, even the remnant of respect I had for myself.''

Legigant snapped his fingers, as if to say:

"You will think differently, my friend.''

He then arose and pulled out his watch.

"It is now half-past three," he said. "The appointment was made for six o'clock. We have therefore just time enough to inform the Count de Rancogne of his family affairs before the Count de Puysaie gets there. Come!"

A few seconds later the three gentlemen sat in a cab which rode quickly in the direction of the Arc de Triomphe.

CHAPTER LVI

MATIFAY'S SOUL

WHILE Legigant was so busy that forenoon, the undertakers were in possession of the Matifay mansion.

The doors of the magnificent house stood wide open, and the public streamed in to see the great citizen lying in state.

The staircases were lined with heavy folds of black mourning cloth.

The death-chamber looked like a chapel, and sparkled in the brilliancy of several hundred candles.

The death of so great a financier made as great a noise as the death of a prince.

All the stocks fell.

On the next day the remains of the great man were to be buried.

In spite of the caution which had been used, not to allow the details of the banker's insanity to become public, the attacks he had had in front of so many of his guests had been repeated to others and spoken about.

His lonely death in the middle of the night, without any witnesses, was mysterious, and gave rise to a great many legends.

One of these legends we have already spoken about.

Every night the passer-by could see the lonely light which had been called for a long time "Matifay's soul."

During the first days the light always became fainter, the preceding night it could hardly be seen, and the neighbors said as they crossed themselves:

"The baron will die."

Now the baron had really died, and as the neighbors walked past the coffin one by one, their principal thought was whether the light would be visible the following night.

In the meanwhile, the persons who ought to have been grieved most by Matifay's death, that is, Cyprienne, his wife, and the Count de Puysaie, his father-in-law, were busy with quite different thoughts.

Cyprienne felt her heart again filled with the uncertainty which had troubled her so much before. Her heart, of course, did not doubt Don Jose, but her reason.

The Count de Puysaie read again and again the anonymous letter which concerned Don Jose de la Cruz and Baron Matifay.

The letter closed with a few lines, which the count thought best not to communicate to any one.

These lines were as follows:

"The proofs of my statement, count, you will find in your own house.

"The fortune of Baron Matifay, which has come into your daughter's possession through his death, belongs to the Rancogne family. The latter possesses a representative whose identity will be clearly proved to you.

"Do you want the proof to be placed in the hands of the officials?

"I believe—and I do not doubt but what you think so likewise—that the publicity of a secret so long kept would cast a very disagreeable light upon the Puysaie family, because you were so closely connected with that scoundrel.

"If you, therefore, think the same as I do, and prefer a friendly, secret arrangement to a public examination, then be at the Rondpoint of the Champs Elysees this evening at six o'clock. A cab will await you to bring you to us. You will recognize it easily by the sky-blue livery of the coachman.

"To-night then, or if you do not accept the meeting I offer you, in the name of the last of the Rancognes, then the rest to-morrow."

Although the Count de Puysaie did not generally trust people easily, he did not hesitate a minute to go to the meeting-place the letter stated.

He had no fear of falling into a trap.

Accordingly at half-past five he left the house, and walked toward the place named.

That very hour Cyprienne received a note from Madame Rozel.

It only contained a few words:

"CYPRIENNE—I cannot get over the thought that you doubted me, even though it were only an hour.

"Will you permit me to justify myself to you alone?

Promise me that what I tell you in confidence will be kept a secret?

"If you wish this, then be in the hothouse to-night, on the same spot where we saw each other for the first time, and you shall know all."

Cyprienne pressed the paper to her lips and exclaimed:

"No, no; he is not punishable!"

CHAPTER LVII

IN THE PAVILION OF THE RUE DU BEL RESPIRO

THE place where Legigant and his friends stopped was at a small house in the Rue du Bel Respiro.

The three gentlemen sat around the fireplace, in which a fire had been quickly made, as it was very damp and cold.

Legigant spoke in low tones, and Toinon and Marie Joseph listened attentively.

He told everything that the latter must know to be able to play his part as the last of the Rancognes.

The legend Legigant had imagined was not a bad one, inasmuch as the Countess of Monte-Cristo was no longer there, and could not contradict.

We will relate this fable in its simple form, and without any of the flourishes Legigant's fertile imagination gave to it.

In the first place it was intended to whitewash Hercules Champion and Dr. Toinon, and to throw the whole burden of the crime on Matifay's shoulders.

''Search, above all, for the one the crime benefited,'' says an old rule of the criminal code. Well, the crime had not benefited either Dr. Toinon or Champion, but Matifay alone.

Therefore, Matifay was the only guilty man.

Upon this hypothesis Legigant built up the story of the night of terror, in which the death of Count Octave and the indictment against the Countess Helene had occurred, in his own way, and mingled truth and deception with such art that it was almost impossible to distinguish the one from the other.

In his story Hercules remained up to the last moment a faithful relative. It was he and Dr. Toinon who helped Octave to escape. He had foreseen the danger which threatened the young count, and since he did not learn of Limaille's ambush until the last moment, he had sent Joseph off in all haste to warn him.

The poor fellow came too late, though—he only came in time to witness his master's death, and hear Matifay's voice cry out three times:

"Shoot him, Limaille! Shoot him!"

But why had Legigant, or rather Hercules Champion— for we can give him back this name, which he intended to bear again from now on—not given this information, which vindicated his unhappy cousin?

He had not done this because Matifay was strong and he, Champion, was weak. He had also not seen Joseph return from his dangerous mission, and had to believe, therefore, that he had been lost, together with his master, on the moor.

And who would then have cared for poor Blanche de Rancogne, who had been intrusted to her worst enemy, Matifay?

Besides, he was falsely accused and ruined by Matifay, and was forced to leave France.

Yet he had not ceased to keep the fate of the poor

orphan in his mind. Through a miracle of patience he, Joseph and Toinon, the only friends which fate had left the name of Rancogne, had succeeded in finding the trail of the deserted child. It was living in Paris, in great misery, and was in the power of a common Italian named Cinella.

Here Legigant's fable became a little mixed up.

At the moment when the three unselfish defenders of the name of Rancogne tore the poor child out of the arms of its scoundrelly protector, gathered the proofs of Blanche's identity, and were about to crush Matifay under the weight of the unexpected proofs, they came across an unlooked-for mysterious obstacle.

This obstacle was Don Jose de la Cruz, who had his eye also on the banker's millions.

Blanche suddenly disappeared, and could not be found again.

If she had not disappeared, the baron's fortune would, without a doubt, have fallen again into the hands of the rightful heir, and Matifay would not have made Cyprienne de Puysaie rich by marrying her.

In a word, Don Jose de la Cruz, who had succeeded in winning Cyprienne's love by lies and intrigues, would now have married only a poor girl instead of a rich widow.

As for Joseph, the young and courageous defender of the honor of the Rancogne family, Legigant, whose unselfishness in this matter was notorious, since he had absolutely nothing to gain by the whole affair, would let the proofs he held in his hands speak for themselves.

Through these proofs it was shown that, beside the

elder branch of the Rancognes which had died out with Count George and Octave and Blanche, a younger one existed which was represented by Count Guillaume, the second son of Count Juan.

This Guillaume had brought his father's anger upon him, for making a *mesalliance*. His father had turned him out of the castle and nothing had ever been heard of him again.

It now turned out that he had left a grandscn behind him, and that this grandson was Joseph.

All this was categorically proved beyond a possible doubt: first, through the will of Guillaume, who was known in the whole neighborhood as Biasson; secondly, through the certificate of his birth and his marriage license with Jeanne, and finally through the birth certificate and marriage license of Joseph's father, who had died at an early age, and through the certificate of the birth of Joseph himself.

These were the documents Legigant had found in the oratory and which were addressed to the real Joseph.

The rolling of a carriage was heard outside in the street.

Toinon opened the window and bent out to see.

"It is he," he said to Legigant.

"In that case," said Legigant, quickly, as he showed Marie Joseph into an adjoining room, "go inside there, reflect upon your *role*, and let me attend to the preliminaries."

Toinon had gone out to meet the count, and soon returned with him.

The Count de Puysaie looked with surprise at the two faces, which were perfectly strange to him.

"With whom have I the honor of speaking?" he finally asked.

"You will have read our names in the confession of your son-in-law. My friend here is Dr. Toinon, and my name is Hercules Champion."

CHAPTER LVIII

MATIFAY'S SOUL—(CONTINUATION AND CONCLUSION)

TWO hours later, the Count de Puysaie again took leave of Legigant and Dr. Toinon.

It had been agreed between them that the false Joseph, accompanied by Toinon and Legigant, should bring him the documents next day so that he could study them at his leisure.

"Well," said Legigant, after the door had closed behind the count, "the first point is gained."

"Yes, but the second?" murmured the doctor.

"The second and last," replied Legigant, "we shall gain to-morrow."

In the meantime the count had returned home. A large crowd of people had congregated close to the gate.

Dorn, the coachman, stood gesticulating in the midst of this crowd, and all eyes were turned toward a single spot in the dark mass of the building.

Through a small opening shone a light.

This was the light which was known in the neighborhood as "Matifay's soul."

Just as the count approached he heard a woman exclaim:

"I tell you it is his soul begging us to pray for him!
It will not become extinguished until the requisite number of masses have been read for it."

"Hush! hush!" exclaimed another voice. "The count
is there, and hears us."

All were silent.

"What is the meaning of this crowd?" asked the
count, drawing near to Rose, the valet, who was among
the crowd.

Rose merely pointed with his finger to the mysterious
light.

"That is, indeed, a singular thing," said the count.
"Where can that light come from?"

The valet stammered a few words in a low voice.

"What!" exclaimed the count. "Do not tell any one
about it, and come with me now and tell me what you
have seen and heard."

With these words he entered the park with Rose, and
closed the gate in the face of the crowd.

"What is this whole story?"

"It is no story," replied the servant; "it is the truth.
For a month the light appears nightly, and we have
looked all around without discovering from whence it
comes."

"It must come from the baron's own room," said the
count, thoughtfully.

"But you know as well as I do, count, that the de-
ceased baron's room has no window from this side."

"Very strange! Very strange!" murmured the count.

He then suddenly raised his head and added:

"To judge from the few words you told me before, I
think you know more."

"Yes, I know more. I know that strange things occur in the baron's room. This evening about nine o'clock all was dark when I went up, but hardly had I opened the door, and was looking about for a match to light the candle, when I suddenly heard a deep sigh, which seemed to come from the direction of the dead baron's bed. I said to myself: 'I want to see what it is,' and lighted the candle.

"Well," asked the count, "and what did you find?"

"Nothing," replied the valet; "nothing, absolutely nothing. I looked under the bed, under the furniture, but could see nothing. Just as I was about to leave the room, though, I heard something again, close to my ear."

"What was it?" asked the count.

"What it actually was I do not know. It sounded like a sigh. The dead baron always spoke of a ghost which he continually believed he saw either in front of or beside him, and perhaps it is this ghost which sighs."

"Tell no one about this," said the count; "bring from my room a few books, writing materials, a lamp, and carry them to the baron's room. We shall see if the ghost will sigh to me, too."

"What, count? You want—" exclaimed the valet, trembling in all his limbs.

"Go!" said the count.

The valet did not wait to be told twice.

The count said to himself:

"If it were permitted to the dead to return to earth, I could hear the truth from Matıfay's soul."

Cyprienne sat on the marble bench in the hothouse and waited.

The gravel in the lane creaked beneath the tread of a cautious step.

She arose and saw Don Jose in front of her.

"Cyprienne," said Don Jose, "from this night on you are my wife in God's eyes. You have the right to read into my life. From this time on there must be no secrets between us."

A ray of light shone through the trees.

It was the light in the oratory.

Joseph pointed it out to Cyprienne.

"I will not unveil this secret," he continued; "it will be she who weeps and prays up there, she who protects us and has saved us, who will in a few moments open her arms to you and call you her daughter, as she already calls me her son; in a word, the protectress of all those who suffer, the consoler of all who weep—the Countess of Monte-Cristo."

During this conversation the lovers had returned to the hothouse, and Don Jose led Cyprienne with quick steps up the secret stairs of the oratory.

They ascended it at once.

When they reached the landing, they found the door locked.

With hands and feet, Don Jose knocked at it.

There was no answer.

"My God! my God!" he murmured. "What has happened in there?"

He quickly hurried downstairs again into the garden, and looked up at the opening in the oratory.

The light still shone, but very faint. It gradually

became weaker and weaker, until it finally went out altogether.

Don Jose became anxious.

He suspected some terrible, unknown danger.

Why he felt fear he did not know, but it was so.

He had to get into the oratory.

But how?

Suddenly he had an idea.

The mirror in the baron's room was less capable of resistance than the iron door.

Although Helene had forbidden him to come into the oratory again, an inward voice urged him on, and spoke louder than his reason:

"You must get in, let it cost what it will."

CHAPTER LIX

A NIGHT WATCH

AT THE same hour as Cyprienne and Don Jose met in the hothouse, Count Loredan de Puysaie entered Baron Matifay's room.

He placed the lamp on the table and took a seat in the same chair from which the night before Matifay had written down his terrible confession.

The Count de Puysaie had opened his book, but he only read with his eyes. After he had read twenty pages, he forgot the title of the book.

The clock had struck half-past eleven.

Immediately thereafter the count sprang up from his feet as if he had received an electrical shock.

He felt positive that he had heard a long-drawn sigh.

He walked over to the bed in which Matifay's corpse lay in state.

The body was still lying there motionless.

With one hand the count raised the cloth which covered the face of the corpse.

Matifay's eyes were closed, his lips blue and thick, but also closed. They had not uttered that sigh.

Yet the count was positive he had heard one.

He walked around the room and looked all about him.

He could not discover anything.

"I must have been mistaken," he said to himself. And with that he seated himself at the table again.

Only this time he did not try to read.

All was still; neither outside nor inside could the slightest noise be heard.

After he had waited this way for some hours, another sigh was heard; but this time it was as weak as that of a sleeping child.

Where did it come from?

That was the question.

The count searched through the room again.

The sigh, meanwhile, had turned into a loud wail.

It filled the room, and brought the count to the verge of despair.

He sank exhausted into a chair and closed his eyes, so as not to see anything more.

Again he received a shock. A door had opened behind him, a firm step sounded on the floor, and, at the same time, the rustling of a dress could be heard.

The count did not dare to look around, for he feared to see the legendary ghost in a long, white winding-sheet.

A hand was laid on his shoulder, and a calm voice asked him:

"What's going on here, count?"

It was the voice of Don Jose de la Cruz.

CHAPTER LX

THE RESCUE

THE count, on seeing who it was, breathed more freely.

"What's going on here, I don't know," he replied. "It is something demoniacal and inexplicable. Listen!"

All three—Don Jose, Cyprienne and the count—were silent, and listened.

It did not last long before they heard the sighing and groaning.

Don Jose became pale.

"It is a woman's voice," he said. "Let's to work. I have an idea that we have come just in time to prevent a great calamity, and a fearful crime. An instrument! a hammer! a saw! anything at all!"

And in wild haste he let his gaze wander about the room.

He found nothing but a coal shovel.

Breaking off the stem, he shivered with it the mirror which separated the oratory from Matifay's room into a thousand pieces.

The count and Cyprienne uttered a cry of surprise and terror.

In the middle of the dark oratory lay a human form, the form of a woman who raised herself up on her elbows, and, uttering a cry of joy, sank senseless to the ground again.

.   .   .   .

One hour later the Countess of Monte-Cristo awoke to consciousness, in Cyprienne's bed.

Her rescuers stood around her, and with a smile of gratitude she said to Don Jose:

"This is the second time, my child, that you have opened the grave for me."

The Count de Puysaie said nothing; his gaze, though, asked for an explanation.

He received it, not out of Don Jose's mouth, but out of that of the Countess Helene de Rancogne herself.

She placed the drama of Noirmont in the right light, and told him of Don Jose's nobility of soul.

He then told her, on his part, of his recent interview with Hercules Champion, and the unexpected information the latter had given him in regard to a legitimate heir of Rancogne, who was named Joseph.

The next day the house was filled with a crowd of people, who had come to attend Matifay's funeral.

Everything passed off as the master of ceremonies had prescribed.

In the meantime the Count de Puysaie, whose absence from the funeral, as well as that of all the other members of his family, had been noticed, had made the preparations he had agreed upon with the Countess of Monte-Cristo, to receive Legigant and his two companions in a worthy way.

The count's statement with regard to the heir of Rancogne had explained to Helene and Joseph the value of the sealed envelope which Hercules Champion had stolen from the altar in the oratory.

According to the wretch's assurance, this envelope contained the secret of Joseph's birth, and the latter was a scion of the noble house.

Joseph was a nephew of George and Octave, Joseph was a Rancogne.

Just as little Rosa murmured once, Helene did so now:

"The dead have a prophetic vision."

And when she recalled the scene which Joseph had so often described without attaching any particular importance to it, she repeated Biasson's prophecy:

"Even though Count Octave falls into his enemies' hands, even though the Countess Helene and the innocent child she has not yet brought into the world, fall victims to them, Rancogne will still be saved."

Yes, unfortunately that unhappy child, born on that day, poor Blanche, had fallen a victim to circumstance, for *she* ought now, instead of Cyprienne, to have knelt at the feet of her mother, *she* ought to have placed her soft, white hand into the faithful one of Count Joseph de Rancogne.

Helene's eyes filled with tears as she thought that this might have been the possible result. But when she saw Cyprienne's gentle look directed toward her, she silently added:

"We are the penitent victims; so let it be, since Rancogne is saved!"

CHAPTER LXI

THE RETRIBUTION

COUNT DE PUYSAIE awaited Legigant at the appointed hour, in his study.

In front of him, on the table, was the cash-book which contained the amount of Matifay's private fortune.

To the right of it, the documents relating to his real estate and stocks formed quite a pile. To the left, thick bundles of bank-notes and checks to bearer formed a still larger one.

The count was ready to make an accounting. At this moment he was reading once more the power of attorney his daughter had made out in his favor.

The count was alone, but at times the whisper of conversation could be heard through the half-opened hangings of the doors.

The count would then turn half around toward the side from which the conversation came, lay his finger on his lips, and utter a mysterious "Pst!"

Everything would then at once become quiet.

Suddenly the valet knocked softly at the door.

Then he opened it a little, and, like a servant who understands his occupation, announced:

"The gentlemen whom the count expects."

The gentlemen entered.

Marie Joseph formed a marked contrast to his companions.

He, alone, the least guilty one, seemed now, at the moment of the encounter, to be determined to urge it on at any price.

Toinon hid timidly behind Legigant, who had thought it advisable for this occasion to mask his eyes with a pair of large green spectacles.

The count arose; then, without leaving his chair, and, pointing with a noble, indifferent gesture to the colossal fortune he was about to restore without regret, said:

"You see, gentlemen, I have been expecting you."

Legigant could not suppress a movement of joy.

Toinon, already, instinctively stretched out his long hands.

Marie Joseph felt a blush of shame mounting to his cheeks; by an effort of the will, however, he managed to control the beating of his heart, and he became pale again.

"There only remains now," continued the count, addressing Hercules Champion specially, "to fulfil a slight formality. Your clear statement of the case has fully convinced me. Only as I perceive, from the statement itself, Monsieur Joseph de Rancogne is but very imperfectly acquainted with the document on which you base your claim, and that, too, only since a few days, will you permit me to read it to him again?"

"I have no objection," said Legigant, as he took the precious paper out of his pocket and handed it to the count.

The latter took it with the tips of his fingers, and, with a contemptuous gesture he could not altogether suppress, opened the sheet and began to read.

Strangely enough, he now suddenly raised his voice, which he had kept in that low key peculiar to educated people, and in ringing tones read the will which was worth so many millions.

It was as if he read not only for the visible witnesses present, but also for the concealed listeners in the adjoining room.

This paper, which was nothing else than Biasson's will, contained the following:

"Joseph, my son, the work which I gave you to do is accomplished, the evil-doers are punished, and Rancogne is saved, for you are reading to-day these lines which I wrote, and which I bequeath to you as the most precious recompense, while they are to be, at the same time, my rehabilitation.

"The curse is lifted from me. The deep grief I caused Count Juan, my father and your grandfather, you, my son, have atoned for by your courage and self-denial.

"To-day you can take the place at the family hearth made vacant by my banishment, for, through you, the family has been restored again.

"I am a nobleman by birth. My father's will made me a peasant. You were born a peasant, but your self-denial makes you a nobleman again.

"And you, who were born in anxiety and mourning, you, who were surrounded by snares, even before your birth, open your arms to the heir of a disinherited race, wipe out, with a word, a glance, a clasp of the hand, a filial kiss, the brand which my criminal disobedience imprinted on his brow. Acknowledge in the humble servant who reared and saved you, a worthy offspring of the old count. GUILLAUME DE RANCOGNE."

As the count read these last words in an impressive tone, he half turned his head toward the slightly-open hangings.

When he concluded, he gazed keenly at the motionless face of the former student, Marie Joseph Tarantas, and added:

"You may be proud, count, of the coat of arms which you are now entitled to wear, for I know none that can equal it in rank. You, all alone, have, under the most difficult circumstances, restored the work of your great ancestors. They had created our nobility, you have reawakened yours from the dead. With joy I place into your hands this fortune to which you, alone, are entitled."

Strangely enough, Legigant and Toinon arose to rush to the table, while Marie Joseph Tarantas, to whom the count had addressed his words, did not move from his chair.

The count placed both his hands on the securities.

"A word more," he said, with a diplomatic smile.

He then turned again to Marie Joseph, and continued:

"What I most admire in you is your modesty. These sincere friends"—here he bowed low toward the two other gentlemen—"these two friends, who assisted you in all your labors, and who shared your trials and hardships, are, nevertheless, unaware of a certain phase of your work, a phase which I regard as the most admirable, and—if I may be permitted to so express myself without hurting your modesty—the most heroic.''

Count de Puysaie was silent for a moment and then continued:

''These worthy friends do not know that your coming here to-day to claim a fortune, to which, I hasten to admit, you have the most undoubted right, is, after all, only to fulfil a duty of common justice—a duty of which your personal interest does not at all come into question.''

Legigant and Toinon pricked up their ears.

The count, however, without seeming to pay any attention to this, continued:

''These gentlemen do not know that your personal fortune, Count de Rancogne, since you are, from this day on, the only and legitimate heir, amounts to a sum in comparison to which these securities are mere nothings. They have no knowledge of your wonderful undertaking, of that subterranean trip in the grewsome caves of Rancogne, of the discovery of the treasure which you made in spite of the terrors of darkness, solitude, and hunger.''

Toinon and Legigant did not know what this meant.

They looked at each other with frightened, questioning glances.

Tarantas lowered his head at this flood of praise, of which he very well knew he was entirely unworthy.

''I however,'' enthusiastically continued the count—''I know the labors which would have done honor to a modern Jason, and I also know with what an unselfish motive they were undertaken. I have done more. I have hunted up an unknown witness of that gigantic undertaking—a hero, like you, who faithfully assisted you; who, for a long time, has lost sight of you, and who is looking for you—a friend, a Pylades, more than all this, a brother. This is the surprise I had in store for you, and that is why I wished your presence here. In giving back your fortune to you, I wanted at the same time to restore to your arms the other half of your being. You will pardon this, won't you? The sight of this reunion is the only recompense that I ask for a restitution which is such a matter of course that it really does not deserve any recompense at all."

He then turned again toward the hangings, and exclaimed:

"You need not conceal yourself any longer, Clement. Come quickly."

"I think things are growing crooked," whispered Toinon in his accomplice's ear.

The latter replied only by secretly giving Toinon a poke in the ribs.

CHAPTER LXII

PLAYING THE TRUMP CARD

CLEMENT actually entered and, to the doctor's great surprise, and Legigant's dismay, fairly to the horror of the former student, who had sprung up from his seat, threw his arms around the latter's neck, exclaiming:

"Joseph, my brave Joseph, at last I find you again!"

Marie Joseph Tarantas, who was not a little frightened at this unexpected recognition, with difficulty stammered a few unintelligible words.

"He is too deeply moved for utterance," said Count de Puysaie to the two dumfounded confederates. "In fact, gentlemen, such an emotional spectacle is grand; but we must not be egotistical, and, if it is all the same to you, we will leave these two friends, who have not seen each other for so long a time, alone together."

Legigant nodded assent, but he repeated, in a whisper, the words which Toinon, a little while before, had uttered:

"I think things are going crooked."

With the distinguished politeness of a nobleman, the count conducted Legigant and Toinon into an adjoining room. He, however, kept them company only a few moments, for he almost immediately returned to his library through another door.

Clement and Tarantas had made use of the short time in which they were alone to relinquish their embrace, and stood silent, at some distance from each other.

"Now we will speak with each other," began the count coldly. "The two outcasts with whom you, sir, whom I do not know, came here, deserve no pity. Even you, I tell you plainly, only deserve it in a very moderate degree. You are, however, young, and perhaps you may not yet be dead to every good impulse. I, for my part, would not have forgiven you; but others, the very ones from whom you wished to steal this fortune, desire that the chance of redemption be not cut off from you. Now have you anything to say?—speak!"

The hangings of the adjoining room had been entirely raised and on the threshold stood the Countess of Monte-Cristo, holding with one hand Don Jose, and with the other Cyprienne—her two children.

Tarantas held his hands before his eyes as if dazed, then sank on his knees and, stretching out his hands, exclaimed:

"Pardon! Kill me if you wish, but do not dishonor me! Have pity for the sake of my poor mother!"

The Countess of Monte-Cristo let go of Don Jose's and Cyprienne's hands, slowly approached Tarantas, touched his forehead with a gesture of gentle authority, and said:

"This young man belongs to me."

Then addressing him she continued:

"Unhappy son, you knew that your mother, were she

to discover this, would grieve herself to death, and yet you acted thus?"

These words, spoken without anger but only with infinite pity, deeply moved Marie Joseph.

"I did it all for my mother's sake," he stammered. "Oh, if you only knew!"

"I know all," replied the Countess of Monte-Cristo.

"We know all, do we not, Joseph? While you, unhappy man, harbored the idea of robbing him of his inheritance, he was striving to discover excuses for your act.

"Legigant was the clew which must unavoidably lead us to you. Yes, we know your pitiful story. We know the stain on your originally pure character. We know that, in the beautiful region which is also our home, you have a mother; and for her sake—understand well, for her sake—we forgive you. To-day the difficult problem is to make you an honest man again. We will not assist you in solving it, for any aid from us would disparage the merit of your penitence. Your mother, however, shall pass her last days in peace and comfort, and what was to be the price of crime shall now be the price of confession and repentance."

Marie Joseph was not able longer to control the sobbing which threatened to burst his heart. He, who had not shed a tear for so long a time, wept like a child. He seized hold of the countess's proffered hands, but could only say:

"Oh, madame, Heaven bless you! Heaven bless you!"

"Depart," she said, kindly raising him up. She gently pointed to the door, and added, "Depart, and sin no more!"

As soon as he had left the room, Count de Puysaie opened wide the door of the adjoining room, in which were the two confederates.

"Come, gentlemen," he said to Legigant, with such an amiable smile that the latter felt relieved of all his anxiety; "come, we are waiting for you."

Then he approached the table and said to Don Jose, whose face Legigant could not plainly see:

"Well, count, five millions in securities of different kinds, the same sum in bank-notes or ringing coin, and then the castle, estimated to be worth fifteen hundred thousand francs, that is all, isn't it?"

"Yes, that is all," replied Joseph.

The sound of this voice made Legigant start.

The Countess of Monte-Cristo and Cyprienne, by the way, were no longer present.

Legigant's suspicions awoke again stronger than before, but it was necessary for him to preserve his self-control. He, therefore, did not move from the spot or change a feature.

"Then," continued the count, "you have nothing further to do than to sign this receipt."

"In my name," asked Don Jose, "or in that of the widowed Countess of Rancogne?"

From behind the hangings arose a voice, at the sound of which an icy shudder passed through Legigant's form.

"In your name, my dear son," said the voice. "In this world nothing belongs to me any more."

As Don Jose still hesitated, Countess Helene de Rancogne herself entered the room, approached the desk, and handed Don Jose the pen.

All this was done simply and quietly, as if Legigant

and Toinon were not at all present. Their presence seemed to be fairly forgotten.

"Ha! there she is again," exclaimed Legigant, as he beheld the pale face of the woman he thought had forever disappeared from the world of the living. "There she is again. Has she a compact with the infernal regions?"

He saw that he was lost, and when they finally took the trouble of bothering themselves about him, he answered only with a gesture of helplessness and despair.

When, however, the first fright was over, this man, who seemed to be fairly the incarnation of evil, raised his head with a gesture of fierce pride.

"It is well," he said, "you have conquered and I am defeated. Take me to court, send me to prison; what more will you do? You will not push the matter so far that it will cost me my head, for, in that case, you would also have to dishonor Matifay's memory, and two criminal trials in one family would, after all, be too many. I don't care for the galleys. I will some day get out of that."

He then caught hold of good Dr. Toinon's arm, and added the not very consoling words:

"We went into a trap, old friend. Complaining about it won't help us any. Come, the police are already at the door; we must not let these gentlemen wait long."

With these words, he took his accomplice by the arm and drew him toward the exit, which, in fact, was guarded by officers of the law.

Joseph and the Countess of Monte-Cristo had not spoken a word, but with a gesture had kept back Count de Puysaie and Clement, who wished to spring upon the wretches. Their mission was not to punish, but to save.

As soon as this domestic drama was ended. Count de

Puysaie, who, until now, had been sustained only by an artificial and fictitious strength, sank exhausted and swooning in a chair.

Cyprienne rushed toward him, knelt before him, and rubbed his hand; but when she let it go, it sank back limp and helpless.

In a few moments this man, whom, at the beginning of this incident, we saw so strong, so skilful, so young and wise, had become, with the exception of his hair, which still remained black, almost a decrepit old man.

His under lip hung down limp, his face, distorted by internal contractions, formed long, horrible wrinkles around his eyes and mouth, and when he tried to reply to the passionate caresses of his daughter, only a childish babbling escaped from his lips.

His eyes, however, had remained vivid and eloquent; so eloquent that his glances assumed an almost commanding expression, while they incessantly wandered to and fro between Don Jose and Cyprienne.

They did not grow calm until the latter, obeying this mute request, took Don Jose's hand and clasped it in hers.

"Poor father," she sighed, "shall he remain alone?"

At this instant the Countess of Monte-Cristo, who had a few moments ago disappeared, returned.

She led in her hand little Lila, and approached with her to the easy-chair in which the count sat.

"No, he shall not remain alone," she said; "has not this child to atone for the sin of her unhappy father?"

EPILOGUE

THE SISTERS OF THE RETREAT

THERE is no new development in life.

The events which either make a child's life happy or unhappy, are the immediate and fateful result of those which made the father's life either happy or unhappy.

For each generation life begins anew and moves through the same periods and alternations.

The man who could write the history of only one century in its reality and entirety, would at the same time have written the history of all humanity.

In the same way we feel—we, who have torn a page out of the gigantic book of life—at this moment, when we should write the long-looked-for words "The End," greatly embarrassed.

Is not this word "End" at the same time the commencement of another book, which is a thousand times more interesting, because it is the one we have dreamed of?

On one and the same day, and in one and the same church, three marriages were celebrated at different altars.

The first was that of Joseph de Rancogne with Cyprienne de Puysaie, the widow of Baron Matifay.

The second was that of Clement with Rosa or Madame Rozel.

The third was that of Louis Jacquemin with Ursula.

Each one of the three brides had received a letter that morning which was signed by a different name.

The one addressed to Cyprienne was signed: "The Countess of Monte-Cristo."

The one which Madame Rozel received was signed: "The Widow Lamouroux."

The one to Ursula was signed: "Aurelie."

The contents of the letters were the same, for they were all asked to go to a certain spot, after the weddings had been solemnized.

Three carriages awaited the newly married couples in front of the church, and all three then rode off in the direction of the heights of Passy.

They stopped in front of the iron gate of a large park, in the centre of which were many small houses and pavilions.

The park gate was noiselessly opened, and the carriages rolled through and up to the terrace of a large house.

On the topmost step of the terrace stairs a woman stood awaiting the newcomers.

It was Madame Jacquemin.

Cyprienne asked after the Countess of Monte-Cristo.

Ursula after Aurelie.

Madame Rozel for the Widow Lamouroux.

Madame Jacquemin answered the three questions with a low bow, and asked the young ladies to follow her.

The room they entered was bare of furniture. It looked like a chapel, and in the rear was a headstone of white marble, the masterpiece of some great sculptor.

The monument was in the form of a bed, and on the stone pillows lay the slim form of a young girl.

The statue bore the features of Blanche.

In the centre of the chapel, on the bare floor, two women dressed in mourning were on their knees praying.

At the noise made by the four women entering, they raised up their heads.

Ursula recognized Nini Moustache, her elder sister.

Cyprienne recognized her mother.

The kneeling women arose and, stretching out their arms, clasped the two young women to their bosoms.

This double embrace did not last long.

A new-comer had entered the room.

The Countess of Monte-Cristo, Madame Lamouroux, Aurelie—these three different persons, who were embodied in a single being, which from now on had only one name—Helene.

"You are," she said, "my beloved daughters, the chosen souls, in whom I see myself live again, and whom I have selected to continue my work of charity. That is why I said: 'Come to me!'"

She made a short pause, and then continued:

"My mission is accomplished. The Divine Father, in taking this angel"—(here she pointed to the headstone)—"from me, took my courage away at the same time. That is why I to-day authorize you, my daughters, to continue my work. Go into the world and spread the light of faith, the blessings of love, and the treasures of hope! Society has made us, to judge from appearances, very weak; but the woman who is a daughter, wife, and mother possesses a strength which is almost all powerful. *Our* strength is love. Through love and devotion we succeed in transforming the world. The work which I tried to accomplish alone I now divide between you. You, Cyprienne, Countess de Rancogne, are the successor of the Countess of Monte-Cristo. You will occupy yourself with the misery of the rich and the happy, with the tears which are silently wept at night on silken pillows, and with the sobs which lie beneath a smile. To you, Ursula, and you, Rosa, I recommend the sufferers who were formerly consoled by Madame Lamouroux. The poor have lost their mysterious protectress; I know your hearts, though, and know that the poor will lose nothing."

Thereupon Helene turned to Nini Moustache.

"I now speak to you, Celine, who have sinned most, but who are, nevertheless, none the less dear to me. You will replace the handsome, brilliant, eccentric Aurelie in her coquettish house in the Chaussee d'Antin!"

"Mercy, mercy!" sobbed Nini. "Do not condemn me to this martyrdom; let me stay with you!"

"It must be," replied Helene. "You will now play the comedy of what was your shame. I know very well that the work I give you is the most painful of all. Your colleagues will only have to struggle with pride, vanity and poverty. You, however, I give the most dangerous enemy—vice."

She then turned to all the missionaries, whom she was about to send into the world, and said:

"If, among those whom you have saved, there are inconsolable ones, send them here to the Retreat, which will never be locked to them. In our eyes none is unworthy. Every woman is capable of becoming an apostle of love—and now, my daughters, go and pray for me as I shall pray for you."

The Order of the "Sisters of the Retreat," which the Countess of Monte-Cristo founded, still exists.

"In our eyes none is unworthy!" Helene had said.

And, in fact, no woman is refused admittance to this secret order. Every drawing-room has its Madame de Miramion, every house its Magdalen.

A few words more and this long story is finished.

On a beautiful summer evening, a young married couple on their wedding tour made an excursion to the harbor of Toulon.

The boat, as is usually the case, was manned by galley-slaves.

The newly married couple—they were both young and handsome—seemed to be entirely absorbed in their mutual love.

Sitting hand in hand, they enjoyed, so to speak, with all their senses the magic of the beautiful summer evening.

Suddenly the young man's gaze fell upon the two chained galley-slaves who sat nearest to him.

He unconsciously trembled, bent over to his young companion and whispered a few words in her ear.

The two galley-slaves, to whom he pointed with his eyes while he spoke, were the most repulsive-looking wretches one can imagine.

One of them was big and strong, like an athlete, with broad shoulders, thick lips, and broad face.

The other one was lean and bent, with pale face, tricky look, and, even in the green cap and the red jacket, still somewhat of a dandy.

The young wife involuntarily made a gesture of disgust. At her husband's command the boat was turned around and headed for the shore.

When Cyprienne de Rancogne stepped on to the dock she slipped a purse into Hercules Champion's hand.

About this time the promenaders in the garden of the Tuileries saw a curious couple every night at the same hour.

An old man, whose back was slightly bent, and whose face still showed traces of youth, was led by a young girl, who was still almost a child, but whose face already sparkled with a divine beauty.

They walked slowly, this young girl and this prematurely old man. He leaned on her arm, and she led him with childish caution, smiled at him, and spoke caressing words to him.

It was not a pagan Antigone, but a Christian one, out of whose blue eyes the gentleness of the divine Shepherd shone—the Shepherd who was the first to speak the word which gave the world another form, the word:

"Love one—another!"

The prematurely old man was Count Loredan de Puysaie, and the young girl Lila.

"THE COUNTESS OF MONTE-CRISTO"

(PART TWO)